A CASE FULL OF CATS

CURLY BAY ANIMAL RESCUE COZY MYSTERY BOOK 3

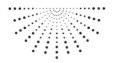

DONNA DOYLE

CONTENTS

CHAPTER ONE

I t was a dark and stormy night, but Courtney Cain was sleeping soundly through it. She heard a few rumbles of thunder as they shook her apartment, but they simply soothed her back to dreamland.

"Good morning!" she chirped to Dora several hours later when she arrived at the Curly Bay Pet Hotel and Rescue for work. Courtney had been hired on as the manager after she'd lost her bigtime marketing job in the city, fired by her very own fiancé. It'd been a devastating blow at the time, but moving off to a small town and taking up a job she'd never have envisioned herself doing had been exceedingly good for her. "I just love sleeping during a storm, don't you?"

They were still in the front parking lot, but Dora wasn't paying any attention to Courtney. As the groomer who took care of all the purebred pets that came to visit the hotel and spa side of the business, she was a very serious woman. This morning, she fisted her hands on her hips as she marched over to the corner of the building. "Look at that!"

"What?" Courtney jogged over, shocked to find that the roof was entirely covered with greenery. Giant branches stuck out at all angles. "The storm knocked over a tree!"

"Let's get inside and make sure everyone is okay!" Dora ushered her toward the front door.

"I'm trying." Courtney's hands shook as she fiddled with her key ring to find the right one, horrible visions of the poor cats and dogs trapped inside running through her mind. Finally, she twisted the right key in the lock and flung the door open.

The two women immediately turned left into the rescue side. Courtney's foot shot out from under her as she stepped in a large puddle, and she grabbed Dora's arm for support. "Aah!"

"Careful." Dora's strong grip closed over Courtney's arm until she was sure her manager was safely on her feet again. "Looks like everything in the cat room is okay. Let's check out the dogs." They moved further on and opened the door to the room that housed the canines.

"Oh, you poor babies!" The ceiling had cracked open, a dark branch coming straight through it. Insulation hung down around the branch like a raggedy skirt, and Courtney could see daylight through the hole. "That certainly explains all the water. We got a lot of rain with that storm. We're lucky, though. All the damage is over the supply area and not the kennels."

Even so, the dogs were terrified. Dora opened the cage of the one closest to the damage, squatting down to comfort the lab mix. "It's okay, Francine. You're all right, sugar."

"Do you think we have room for them over on the hotel side?" Courtney opened the next cage, where a little terrier mix named Edgar was cowering in the corner. As soon as he saw her, he came bolting forward and jumped in her lap.

"We'll just have to make room, and the hotel clients who were supposed to come today will have to find something else to do," Dora said firmly, stroking Francine's head and clipping a leash to her collar. "I think the kennels furthest away from the damage are all right, though, so we can get away with leaving some of the bigger dogs in here."

Courtney smiled. That was exactly how she felt about the situation, but she knew Dora usually preferred the pampered purebreds over the strays. Courtney was the manager, and when it came down to brass tacks, she was the one who called the shots. Still, she liked to give her employees a chance to feel as though they had a say as well. "Perfect. We'll get these guys moved, and then I'll start calling the customers."

"They're not going to like it," Dora said with a slight roll of her eyes as they brought the first two dogs to the other side of the building completely untouched by the storm. A Yorkshire terrier with its topknot in a little pink bow gazed at them sleepily from her kennel. "Most of these folks take their dogs with them as many places as they can go, but they've gotten into a habit of never leaving them home alone."

"I'm sure they'll understand." But Courtney quickly found that Dora was right. While the customers were horrified to hear the news of the storm damage, they were equally horrified to find that they didn't have a trusted place to drop off their precious babies for the day.

"But you said the damage was on the shelter side," Mrs. Atkinson argued over the phone. "Can't Peaches still come and spend the day while we're out on the water?"

Courtney rolled her eyes up to the ceiling, having had far too many conversations like this just in the last few minutes. "I'm afraid not. We've had to move all the rescue dogs over to the hotel side, and there simply isn't enough room. I'll be glad to give you a call as soon as we're fully open again, and I really appreciate your patience with us. Perhaps you could just put a little bikini on Peaches and take her with you?"

The long pause on the other end of the line made Courtney cringe. She knew they needed the spa and hotel patrons to help fund the shelter, and that was the whole reason the business had been split in two in the first place. If she irritated too many of their regular clients, the animals could really lose out.

"You know, that's not a bad idea!" Mrs. Atkinson exclaimed. "She does like the warm weather, and she could sit with me out on the deck. We are just going for a day trip, after all."

"You two have a wonderful time!" Courtney hung up, smiling to herself. People were so funny, and she wouldn't be surprised if Mrs. Atkinson really did put a bikini on her dog. Peaches had already been in the spa for a nail trim and polish, a mud mask, and a massage last week.

When she'd finally hung up and was about to call someone to get the tree off the roof, Mrs. Throgmorton strolled in. She was dressed in a leopard print wrap dress that looked like it belonged on someone half her age, but her recent divorce from her husband was probably the reason for that. He'd arranged for their dog to be stolen, and Mrs. Throgmorton wasn't about to forgive him for that. Fortunately, Sir Glitter had been recovered and was happily tucked under his owner's arm.

Courtney couldn't find it in herself to be happy to see them, though, considering the condition of the hotel. "Mrs. Throgmorton! It's nice to see you this morning, but I didn't think we were expecting Sir Glitter today. Otherwise, I'd have called you. You see, that storm brought a tree down right on top of the building, and we've had to move all the rescues to the hotel side."

"Oh, dear!" Mrs. Throgmorton fanned her fingers over her chest, just under a thick strand of pearls. "That's terrible news! But I might be able to help with it, actually. I didn't come to drop my baby off. I came to talk to you about organizing a fundraiser. I told you before I was going to do that, and I admit I got a little busy with some other projects I had going on, but I don't want you to think I forgot about you."

Courtney's shoulders sagged with relief. "That would be great. I have no idea how much it's going to cost to get everything fixed, but I highly doubt we have the money for it. Just tell me what you need from me."

Mrs. Throgmorton grinned and snuggled her dog close to her face. "Oh, this'll be so much fun! I love doing events like these. There's nothing better than throwing a big party for a good cause. We just need some time to sit down and figure it all out together. I'd love for you to be involved, since this is really just a big thank-you from me to you for everything you did for Sir Glitter."

Courtney affectionately reached across the counter to scratch the Pomeranian's ears. "I'm happy to help. I used to be in the marketing sector, so I might have some input. It definitely can't be today, though. I've got too much to take care of here. I still have to call someone to get this tree off the building, and then I need a contractor."

Mrs. Throgmorton nodded wisely. "There's a young man who brings us wood for the fireplace. I'll give him a call for you. He'd probably be more than happy to come take it down, and charge next to nothing as long as he gets to keep the wood."

"That would be wonderful! I can't thank you enough!"

"Of course, darling! I owe you big time, after all. How does Wednesday look for you? Could we get some planning done then?"

Courtney didn't even bother looking at the calendar. The repairs to the shelter were likely to be incredibly expensive, and the sooner they could get this fundraiser rolling, the better. "Sounds great."

"Perfect. I'll pick you up here. See you Wednesday!" Mrs. Throgmorton used Sir Glitter's paw to wave goodbye as they backed out of the building.

A uniformed officer opened the door for her and let her out before coming in. Courtney recognized him as Brian Jacobs from Animal Control, and he carried a battered plastic carrier in one hand. "Good morning, Courtney. Looks like you've had an eventful day already." He pointed to the roof to indicate the fallen tree outside.

"Unfortunately, yes. Who do you have there?" She bent her head to peer through the front of the carrier, expecting to see a pitiful creature shivering in the back corner. Instead, a tuxedo cat purred loudly as he rubbed his cheek on the bars of the door.

"This is Ritz, or at least that's what we decided to call him since he looks like he's wearing a little tux. Animal Control is full right now, so I thought I'd see if you have any room for him."

"You're in luck. Our dog room is the one that's damaged, but we do have a free cage for a kitty. What's his story?"

Brian set the carrier on the counter and opened the door. Ritz marched out, taking in his surroundings while still purring like a boat motor. "It's kind of strange, actually. I'm sure you've heard about the break-ins that've been happening all over town?"

"Yes, but I've been trying to ignore it. I know nobody has any reason to break into my little place, but news like that isn't very comforting when you live alone." She shuddered. Courtney thought of Curly Bay as a pretty safe little town, and she'd worried far less here than when she'd lived in the city. That is, until those reports started coming in on the news.

"Well, an incident that we believe was tied to the perpetrator of all these burglaries was called in over in the Majestic Oak district. The lights and sirens scared away the crook, but this cat was found outside by one of the officers. He was wearing a harness and leash, and the handle was caught in a bush."

"Poor little guy. And nobody claimed him?" Courtney stroked Ritz's head. The cat rewarded her for the attention by headbutting her gently in the stomach. "He's certainly tame enough."

"I thought he must belong to someone in the neighborhood, but nobody's claimed him yet. This would be a good place for him to stay until someone comes forward."

"Not a problem. I'll go put him up and we'll get the paperwork started." Courtney scooped up Ritz, who didn't seem to mind at all, and carried him into the cat room. She scratched his chin and let him nuzzle her neck, glad for some distraction from the rest of the morning chaos.

CHAPTER TWO

Courtney didn't sleep well that night. She was too worried about the shelter, and she'd made the mistake of turning on the news just before she went to bed. The only thing anyone wanted to talk about was the break-ins. Some of them happened in nice neighborhoods like Majestic Oaks, where the targets were jewelry and cash, but others happened in typical suburban areas like where she lived. Courtney knew she didn't have much that would be worth a prison sentence to someone, but she still didn't like the idea of anyone prowling around her apartment.

She had a few minutes before it was time to leave for work, so she did a quick online search and made a call.

It rang so long that Courtney nearly hung up before someone finally answered. "Hinkle's Security Systems. How may I help you?"

"Hi, I was thinking about getting a security system for my apartment." She brushed a strand of hair behind her ear nervously. Somehow, actually getting an alarm made the burglaries seem that much more real.

"Certainly. I'm afraid we're a little shorthanded right now considering the high demand, but I can take your name and number and give you a call back."

"Yeah, that'd be fine." She frowned, wishing they'd given her a different answer. Now that she was thinking about an alarm, she wanted one right away.

She was still thinking about it when she headed to work and unlocked the door, but she soon had her mind pulled away from the safety of her own home. As soon as Courtney walked in the foyer, she saw a familiar tuxedo cat watching her from the counter. Courtney turned around and looked out into the parking lot. Nobody else had gotten to work yet.

"How did you get out , you little rascal?" Courtney picked up Ritz, who nuzzled his head happily against her cheek and purred loudly. "I see. You're very proud of yourself, aren't you? Got a little freedom, and now you're going to tease everyone else with it."

But as soon as she stepped behind the counter and into the office, Courtney realized that Ritz wasn't the only one out. A fat marmalade cat sat square in the center of Courtney's desk, loudly licking himself clean for the moment. A gray tail disappeared down the hall. Opening the door to the shelter side, Courtney found that every single cat had been let out of its cage.

"Holy smoke!" Jessi said from behind her, having just arrived for work herself. "What happened?"

"I'm trying to figure that out, myself." Courtney put Ritz in his cage before turning around and scooping up a little white kitten. "I just got here, and they're all over the place. I saw some in the office, too. There's no telling where they've all gotten to."

"I just hope we can find them all. At least Madeleine is easy." She pointed to an older tortoiseshell, who was curled up asleep in her cage even though the door was wide open. Jessi closed and latched it.

"It's going to be an interesting day." Courtney and Jessi moved throughout the shelter, glad to see that at least the door to the hotel side had been shut, so they wouldn't need to look for any of the cats in there.

Courtney retrieved the marmalade, who was now curled up on her desk and trying to nap. He let out a disgruntled trill as she picked him up, clearly pleased with his new bed. She found a calico in the supply room, batting at the duster. Jessi rounded up two kittens who'd ventured into the office and were chasing around the electrical cords as though they were snakes. She picked up one in each hand and scolded them in a sweet sing-song voice as she carried them back to their cage.

When the phone rang, Courtney went to answer it begrudgingly. She already had enough to worry about with the roof issues, and now she had to worry about the cats as well. They had work to do no matter what was going on, though. "Good morning, Curly Bay Pet Hotel and Rescue. This is Courtney. How can I help you?"

The other end of the line was silent.

"Hello?" When she still didn't get an answer, she hung up and lifted a solid black cat down from the top of the filing cabinet.

"I clearly missed something," Dora commented when she came in to work and saw their faces.

Courtney explained it as best she could. "They were just all out. I've checked the latches on their cages, and everything seems to be in working order. It makes me wonder if someone came in and let them out."

Jessi shrugged. "I already checked the outside security cameras, and there wasn't anything on them. I suppose someone might've snuck past it and I didn't see it."

"I can call Detective Fletcher and ask him if he can take a look at the footage, just in case there's something we're missing. In the meanwhile, it looks like we're missing a kitten still." Courtney pointed to the cage where four kittens were supposed to be housed, and yet only three little faces were peeking out at them.

Dora, Courtney, and Jessi all began the search, checking behind furniture, under the desks, and even inside drawers. Courtney pulled out all the cleaning supplies to check for a little furball behind the spray bottles, but she found nothing. Dora headed into the hotel side to look around, just in case. Jessi began worrying that the missing baby had somehow slipped out the door when they'd come in.

The phone rang again, and Courtney was the closest to the office. Silence greeted her on the other end of the line, and she hung up with more force than was necessary. "I don't have time for this," she grumbled.

That's when she noticed the door to the dog room was open a crack. Her heart jumped up in her throat, knowing there was still a big hole in the roof. They'd been fortunate enough that it hadn't rained again since the big storm, and it wasn't likely that a small kitten could get all the way up to the ceiling, but things had been strange enough for the day that there was no telling what else might happen.

Courtney glanced up at the bright sunshine coming through the roof. She looked all around, waiting to see a tiny paw or tail, but there was nothing. "Kitty, kitty, kitty!" she called softly.

"Mew?" came a tiny response.

Her heartbeat quickened. "Where are you, kitty?" she called again, keeping her voice light and sweet. Cats had a certain way they liked to be talked to. The kitten was probably frightened, and she didn't want to do anything other than coax it to come out. "I'm here to help you, sweetie. I might have a treat in it for you, if you come out."

"Mew? Mew?"

Courtney followed the sound back along the row of kennels. They were fronted in chain-link, making it easy to see inside. The walls between them were solid, so that they didn't have to worry about the dogs snapping at each other if they didn't get along. Every single cage was empty until she got down to the last ones, which still held the bigger dogs. A big lab stood at the front of his kennel and wagged her tail eagerly. A shaggy mutt named Charlotte lapped from her water bowl. A big Australian shepherd mix named Beau slept soundly with a little ball of gray fluff between his paws. A boxer danced happily in hopes of getting to go for a walk soon.

"Hold on." Courtney backed up the to the Australian shepherd mix's cage. She lifted the latch on his door and walked slowly inside, seeing a tiny face peeking out at her from between the dog's legs. "What do you think you're doing in here?"

"Mew?" the kitten asked again innocently, blinking up at her, but not moving from its cozy spot.

"Beau, did you find yourself a little friend?" Courtney bent down and picked up the kitten. It was warm from having snuggled with the large dog.

Beau's ears drooped as he looked up at Courtney with sad eyes and sniffed the air toward the kitten.

"Aw, is this your little buddy now?" Courtney scratched the top of his head. Poor Beau looked so upset that she was taking the kitten away. "I'm sorry, honey. She's got to go back in her cage with her siblings, but maybe I can arrange for the two of you to have some playtime together later."

Finally putting the last cat away, Courtney rounded up the other two women and slumped into her chair in the office. "I hope that never happens again."

"The key is figuring out how to prevent it," Dora commented.

"Yeah, I've been thinking about that. With all the break-ins happening lately, I put in a call to Hinkle's Security Systems earlier today. I was thinking about my apartment, but I wonder if they'd be able put up something in here."

Jessi nodded as she started up the coffee pot. "I've heard of several other shelters that have live video feeds that can be monitored remotely, so the animals can be checked on any time of day."

"If you want to get real fancy, we could put a camera in each cage of the hotel, and patrons could pay extra to log in from their phones and see what their babies are up to," Dora added.

"That all sounds wonderful, but I'm concerned about affording any of it. We didn't even have the funds to get the outside security cameras fixed right away. But this incident with the cats has really made me think. We're going to have to do something." She glanced at the door to the shelter side, hoping they could get everything fixed with the fundraiser money from Mrs. Throgmorton. "We could just put locks on all the cages. Then nobody could let them out unless they had the keys or a bolt cutter."

Jessi shook her head. "That's a no-go. We talked about that once, but Ms. O'Donnell is concerned it would be a fire hazard. You need to be able to get the animals out quickly in case there's an emergency."

"That makes sense," Courtney agreed.

The phone rang, and Dora answered. She hung up a moment later. "There's nobody there."

Courtney was beginning to wonder if there was.

CHAPTER THREE

"**A**ll right, dear. The first thing we have to do is make sure there's a reason for people to come." Mrs. Throgmorton was driving, speeding along behind the wheel of her Cadillac as though she were the only woman on the road. "The wealthy are willing to pay steep prices to attend a fundraising event like this because they want the bragging rights. It's not just bragging about supporting a good cause, though, it's also about the event itself."

Courtney was trying not to leave nail marks in Mrs. Throgmorton's leather interior. "How much do you think we should charge to get in?"

"Well, let's see. I was thinking we should do this really big. It'll be short notice, since you need the money so badly, so we have to find the perfect balance on the price. If we can pull it all together well enough, and I assure you we can with my connections, then we can have dinner, music, a silent auction, and a fashion show. We can charge a good price for all that, but we need to make sure we're not investing more than what you're getting out of it." Mrs. Throgmorton took a hard right that left another car hitting the brakes and honking their horn.

"I should let you know that the shelter really doesn't have any money to invest," Courtney said through gritted teeth, not wanting to upset the woman who was offering to help them out by insulting her driving.

"Don't you worry! I've set up so many of these fundraisers for various causes around town. Everyone will work with you and expect payment once the event is over. I'll be taking care of part of the bill myself, which will help as well." Not bothering with her turn signal, Mrs. Throgmorton swung into a parking lot in front of the caterer's.

"Mrs. Throgmorton!" enthused the man behind the counter when he saw her enter, coming around the counter to give her a hug. "It's so nice to see you today. And here you are with your lovely niece?" He held out his hand to take Courtney's and brush his lips against the back of it.

She didn't know if she should be flattered or embarrassed, but she was a little bit of both.

"This is Courtney Cain, the manager of the pet hotel where Sir Glitter stays," Mrs. Throgmorton explained.

"And where is your lovely little dog today? I have a special treat for him if he's waiting in the car."

"Oh, no! He's staying at my sister's for the day. You see, I'm putting together a fundraiser. The pet hotel is also a shelter, and they've had significant damage from the storm. What can you put together for us by next Friday night?"

"Oh, my!" Federico clucked his tongue as he moved back behind the counter to look at his calendar. "You're in luck! We have a wedding on a Saturday, but we're free on Friday. For anyone else, I'd say there simply isn't enough time to put it all together. For you, I'll be more than happy to make the arrangements. What would you like?" Federico produced a menu.

Mrs. Throgmorton waved it away. "You know I trust you with the selections!"

"Ah, perfecto! Let's start with a mushroom crostini appetizer, followed by clam risotto, grilled polenta with spinach, and beef braciola. With a vegetarian option available, of course." He rolled his hand in the air with a flourish.

"That sounds wonderful, Federico! Add some wine and a salad and we've got it made," Mrs. Throgmorton trilled.

"I have you in the most permanent of ink on my calendar, my lovely. It was so nice to meet you, Miss Cain." The caterer didn't kiss her hand this time, much to Courtney's relief.

What she wasn't relieved about was the dishes themselves, and she told Mrs. Throgmorton so as they walked back out the car. "All of this sounds incredibly delicious, but I'm still really worried about the cost," she admitted. "I don't want the catering to cost so much that we don't have any money to fix the roof."

Mrs. Throgmorton waved her finger in the air as she got behind the wheel. "It's not just the catering you have to think about! There's going to be a fee for the venue, and of course the band won't work for free."

"Which is exactly why I'm worried," Courtney replied.

Turning up the air conditioning, Mrs. Throgmorton shook her head, making her diamond earrings dance in the sunlight. "My dear, you have absolutely nothing to fear. I'll do all the math. When Ken and I were still married, he always thought I wasn't good at anything but spending money. I am very good at that, I assure you, but I do know how budget when I want to. You just leave it to me, and I'll make sure you have plenty of funds."

"Okay." It was hard for Courtney to completely let go of this, but Mrs. Throgmorton did seem to know what she was doing.

"Speaking of funds, does the pet hotel have some sort of safe? You're going to want a secure place to put all the money as it comes in." Mrs. Throgmorton zipped off to the other side of town.

"No. I'll look into getting one, though. Do I have a reason to be concerned?" Courtney thought once again about the burglaries happening in Curly Bay. Her stomach did a flip that had nothing to do with Mrs. Throgmorton's driving.

"It's simply one of those things you learn from being rich for so long. You can't trust most people, even if they're rich as well. Once you find someone good, though, someone you really can trust, you keep them

24

close." Her mouth turned to a hard line as she drove, for once without the gas pedal all the way to the floorboard.

Courtney wondered if she was thinking of her ex, but she wasn't going to ask. "You really do seem to know a lot about putting these fundraisers together," she said cheerily. "I'm so glad I have you to help me."

Mrs. Throgmorton's smile returned. "I do pride myself on event coordination! All those dinner parties paid off, and now I can use my skills for a good cause. It wouldn't be proper of me to say exactly how much, but you'd be surprised what I was able to help raise for the children's home! Ah, here we are!" She swung into the Old Train Depot.

"This is interesting." Courtney took in the tall brick walls, stained glass windows, and tiled roof. "What a pretty place."

"Isn't it, though? I've held quite a few events here. It used to actually be the train station for Curly Bay, but it was shut down for decades when passenger trains went out of style. Eventually it was purchased by the Larsons and fixed up, and this larger building on the back was added, so there's plenty of room." Mrs. Throgmorton jangled her keys, finding the right one and unlocking the door. She smiled at

Courtney over her shoulder. "I call and ask for the key so often that eventually they just gave me one of my own."

"Wow." The high beamed ceilings stretched up overhead, leading off to the ticket booth in the back corner that was now used as a concession window. Courtney was impressed by all the original hardwood, including the floors. "This is quite a piece of history."

"You and the pet hotel will be the absolute talk of the town, dear. I've gotten in good with the Larsons, so I get this place for next to nothing. It makes all the other wealthy women incredibly jealous, but that's something I'm willing to live with." Her heels clacked against the hard floor as she sauntered through the main room.

Courtney smiled. Mrs. Throgmorton was a character, and she hadn't been certain she liked her when she'd first come to Curly Bay. That was quickly changing. "Have you already talked to the Larsons to make sure the depot is available?"

"Oh, yes! Everything is settled. The band can play right over here, where the acoustics are the best. Federico can set up his catering tables here. There's plenty of floor space for dinner and dancing. I thought we'd use the new building for the silent auction." Mrs. Throgmorton led the way through a door into the next room. It wasn't nearly as fancy as the original part of the depot but had plenty of space.

"Silent auction?" Courtney asked.

"There's no better way to pry money out of the hands of those who have it! Local businesses and families donate items, which are all tax deductible for them. They come to us at no cost, and everyone wins! Oh, speaking of." Mrs. Throgmorton began rummaging around in her purse. "Now, where did I put that thing? Ah, here."

Courtney gaped at the diamond-encrusted dog collar the older woman put in here hand. "This isn't real, is it?"

"Of course, it is! Nobody will bid on it, otherwise! You keep that, and as we get other items donated for the auction, we'll gather them up at the pet hotel and then bring them all here on the night of the event."

Gripping the collar tightly in her hand to make sure she didn't drop it, Courtney bit her lip. "I had an idea for the fundraiser I'd like to run by you."

Mrs. Throgmorton lifted one perfectly tweezed brow. "Go ahead."

"What about an adoption event? We bring several animals in and set them up with handlers, maybe here in this part of the building where things will be quieter. Guests can interact with the animals, see if there's one that suits them, and adopt them on the spot." She watched the other woman's face, expecting to see a bit of a sneer at the idea of bringing strays and rescues into such an elite event.

But Mrs. Throgmorton's face split into a wide grin. "That's perfect! There's actually a room right back here that might work the best." She led the way into a side room, where things would be even more peaceful for the potential adoptees. "We can have a table set up with all the paperwork and information, and we'll announce several times during the event that folks can come back her and visit with the animals. I love it. I just love it!"

Courtney was beginning to love it, too. "This will be wonderful. We'll get the money for the roof as well as new homes for the rescues." Her heart soared as they walked back through the building and locked it up.

"Now on to meet with the band, my dear," Mrs. Throgmorton announced. "I'll leave you in charge of the bid sheets for the silent auction items and any social media stuff you want to do. I have many talents, but a computer simply isn't one of them."

"Not a problem." Courtney put on her seatbelt and hardly noticed Mrs. Throgmorton's terrible driving this time. Everything was going to be okay.

CHAPTER FOUR

Courtney left home and headed for the shelter early the next day. She had a lot of work to do. There was always the work of the shelter itself, managing the hotel and spa appointments that mostly had to be postponed for now, making sure the current tenants got all the care they needed, and generally keeping things clean and presentable. There was also a contractor coming that day to take a look at the storm damage, not to mention getting a start on work for the fundraiser. She hoped she'd have at least a little bit of time to take the diamond collar from Mrs. Throgmorton out of her bottom desk drawer in the office, figure out how much it was worth, and create a bid sheet for it.

As soon as she pulled in the parking lot in front of the Curly Bay Pet Hotel and Rescue, a black car whipped out of a parking spot near the door. It screeched across the asphalt, nearly swiping the side of Courtney's car as it zoomed out onto the street without even a turn signal. Courtney yanked her wheel to the side to keep it from hitting her and slammed on the brakes. By the time she turned around to look at it, the car was nothing but a dark blob in the distance.

Automatically, Courtney looked to the front door of the building. It didn't look to be open or damaged, but there was definitely something suspicious about a car leaving like that. Courtney pulled her car into a slot and dove out. She had visions of all the cats and dogs running around loose inside the building. It'd only been the cats out the other day, but what if someone was trying to wreak havoc on the business? What would give someone the motivation to do such a thing? Courtney gripped her keys tightly to keep her fingers from shaking as she unlocked the door.

The office was quiet. Not even Ritz was lurking through the building. Courtney moved through the shelter side, seeing that all the cats and dogs were in their respective cages. The most excitement came from some of the dogs that were ready for a morning walk outside. Just to be sure, Courtney peeked into the hotel side as well. Yorkies and Shih Tzus slept soundly next to Persians and Bengals. Everything was okay.

Taking a deep breath of relief, Courtney immediately began her typical work for the day. She fired up her computer to do payroll for the week and then opened a different program to make sure the schedules were filled out for the next month. She picked up a pencil cup that'd somehow been knocked to the floor and scribbled out a few notes. Then she took to the shelter's social media pages to start making posts about the upcoming fundraiser when someone hollered from the office.

"Anyone in here?"

Courtney trotted to the front to find a big man standing at the counter. He wore a denim shirt that he'd left unbuttoned at the top, giving a rather unsavory peek at his hairy chest. His hat and his toolbelt told her who he was. "You must be from Cooper's Construction. I really appreciate you coming by to take a look at things. I'm Courtney Cain."

He tugged the front of his cap in greeting. "Yes, ma'am. The name's Mark Cooper, and it's nice to meet you. I'm sorry I wasn't able to come by earlier. A situation that involves a damaged roof is something I take very seriously, and I usually try to come the same day."

Courtney opened the gate and waved him behind the counter. "I understand completely. I'm sure you've had a lot of calls after that big storm. I've seen several trees down through town."

Mark nodded soberly. "I wish I could say it was just the storm."

"Oh?" Courtney paused with her hand on the doorknob to the shelter.

"I'm sure you've heard about the burglaries here in Curly Bay. Unfortunately, that also means a lot of broken doors and windows. I like it when business is good, but not when it's for reasons like that." Mark shook his head and rubbed the stubble on his jaw.

"I see. That makes sense. I called Hinkle's about a security system, and they were so busy they didn't even have time to talk to me." She still hadn't gotten a call back, either. Courtney opened the door and led him past the cat room.

Mark paused and put a heavy hand on her shoulder. He leaned in close and whispered, "I like the guys at

Hinkle's, and I wouldn't want to do anything to take away from their business, but there is another option."

"What's that?"

"You can buy a security system yourself. They sell them all the time online and in the electronics stores. Might set you back a couple hundred bucks, and you have to monitor it yourself, but it's a heck of a lot better than nothing." He gave a short but firm nod.

"That's an interesting idea. I'll be sure to look into that." It certainly fell in line with the conversation she'd had with Jessi and Dora about finding a way to monitor the inside of the building. "The damage is right through here."

Mark let out a low whistle. "Oh, yeah. That storm got you good. I guess there was a tree right through this hole?" He stepped over to the damage and stood underneath it, squinting up at the sunshine that came pouring through the roof.

"That's right. I was lucky enough that a friend of mine had a connection to a firewood guy, and he took the tree down. Unfortunately, it left quite a gap." Courtney frowned up at the hole in the roof.

"And that's just the damage you can see from down here," Mark commented.

"Oh. I hadn't thought about that." Courtney gulped, afraid of what the bid sheet was going to say. "How much do you think this is going to cost?"

"I won't even venture to say at the moment. I want to look at everything thoroughly, both inside and out. You might have some external damage you can't see from down here, and it won't do you any good not to get it fixed properly. Then another good storm comes along and whoosh!" He swept his big hands through the air to mimic the damage that would ensue.

Courtney nodded, not liking the idea. "I'll let you do what you need to do, then. I'll either be in my office or at the counter if you need me."

"I'm not going to risk letting any animals out if I come in and out of here, am I?" Mark's dark eyebrows knotted in concern as he held the back of his hand in front of Charlotte's cage. The shaggy dog poked her nose through the chain link and wagged her tail.

"No. I'll make sure everyone stays put up unless we have someone out on a leash."

"What about that one?" Mark pointed toward Courtney's feet.

She looked down to see Ritz looking up at her. He blinked his big golden eyes before giving her a light meow of greeting and rubbing his cheek on her pant leg.

"You naughty boy!" Courtney scooped him up. "How did you get out again?"

Ritz responded with a gentle headbutt to her chin.

"Uh huh. Let's get you put back up where you won't cause any trouble for Mr. Cooper, shall we?" Courtney left the contractor to do his job. She put Ritz back in his cage, jiggling the latch to make sure it was working properly.

As she sat down at her desk, Courtney's cell rang from her back pocket. It was Lisa. "Hey!" Courtney answered, glad to hear from her. Lisa, just like Courtney, was also a recent import to Curly Bay. The two of them had met a month ago as they joined the search party for a missing girl, and they'd quickly become friends.

"Good morning! I'm really in the mood for pizza from Russo's today, so I thought I'd see if you wanted to get together for lunch."

Courtney started to answer yes without even thinking about it. She loved Russo's, especially their garlic bread sticks. It was quickly becoming one of her favorite places to eat, even if her waistline didn't always agree. Reality stepped in and stopped her from accepting. "I can't. I've got a contractor here to look at the storm damage, plus I've got to work on some things for the fundraiser. I'm not even sure if I'll take a real lunch today. Maybe we can get together tomorrow."

"I hope you're still planning to eat something," Lisa chided.

"Yeah, I'll find something." Courtney peeked in the top drawer of her desk, where she sometimes stashed a few snacks. A pack of cheese crackers was the only thing that greeted her.

"Let me at least bring you a takeout meal," Lisa offered. "I've got a full hour for lunch over here at the library, so I've got time to kill."

"You know, I just don't think I can turn that down," Courtney replied, shutting the drawer and leaving the cheese crackers in the dark. "Pepperoni and olive pizza, garlic breadsticks, and a big Coke."

"I'll see you around noon!"

They hung up and Courtney smiled. When the life she'd built in the city had shattered into a million pieces, she thought she'd never recover. She'd worked so hard to get through school and make the slow climb up the corporate ladder to her position with a prominent marketing firm. The icing on the cake had been her handsome and successful fiancé, Sam Smythe. Just a short time ago, it seemed impossible to leave all that and her great apartment behind, but she'd done it. Now, Courtney couldn't imagine living anywhere but Curly Bay.

After rattling away at her computer for a bit, Courtney checked the clock and headed to the kennels. The dogs needed their walk, and they couldn't wait just because she was busy with all the pencil pushing that came with running the shelter. She opened the door and found Mark Cooper crouched on the floor in front of Charlotte's cage.

"Hey there, sweet thing," he cooed, oblivious to being watched. "You're a big girl, aren't you? A big sweet girl! How could anyone not want you? How could you not have a home?"

Courtney cleared her throat.

The big man practically leapt to his feet, his cheeks ruddy with embarrassment. "Um, sorry. I didn't hear you come in."

"There's nothing to be sorry about," Courtney assured him. "The animals here need as much loving and attention as they can get."

"I, um, I was just about to come find you." Mark picked up his clipboard. "I have some figures to go over with you."

"Charlotte here is due for a walk. We can take her out and discuss everything." Courtney took a leash down from the rack on the wall.

Mark nodded. "That'll work. I've got some things I want to show you on the outside of the building, anyway. Um…" He glanced down at the dog and then up at Courtney.

"What is it?" she urged.

"Could I be the one to walk her? She seems really sweet. My dog passed away about a year ago, and I kind of miss having one around." He ruffled Charlotte's ears affectionately.

"Absolutely," Courtney said with a smile. She handed over the leash and grabbed a second one. "That means I can walk Beau, and we can get them both done at the same time. We'll just go out the back door." They walked around the outside of the building with the two dogs, who seemed more than content to have some outdoor time.

"The hole in the roof is obviously a big problem," Mark began. "We're very fortunate we haven't had any more rain, or the water would've created even bigger issues for you."

"That's true, but it's hard to take solace in the sunny weather when it keeps shining down on my head through that big hole," Courtney groused.

"The hole isn't any fun, but it's not your only issue." They came around the back corner of the building and over to the side, where the damage was. "I'm not sure if you can see it, but I got up on the roof to get a good look at things. You're missing a few shingles here and there, but the bigger problem is all the structural damage underneath. That tree was a heavy one, and it smashed a lot of the supports underneath the roof. Essentially, we'll have to tear this whole section off and rebuild it."

Courtney's jaw dropped, literally. "You've got to be kidding me."

"I'm afraid I'm not. You could just patch it up, but then it's only a matter of time before some other storm comes along and everything caves in."

"We can't have that, especially not when we're talking about the safety of the animals inside. Is everything okay for the moment?"

Mark nodded. "Okay enough that we can get it tarped over to keep the building protected until we can come out and do the actual work. With everything booking up so quickly, I wouldn't be able to promise you a crew out here for at least another two weeks."

"And how much are we talking?" Courtney let out Beau's leash so he could explore the grassy area behind the building.

"Here." Mark handed her the clipboard.

Courtney skimmed past the itemized list to the grand total at the bottom. The number she saw there made her want to pass out. "This is a lot."

"I know," he replied with a nod, "and I'm sure it's not easy with you being a rescue and all. I can assure you I have the best prices in town, but I won't be offended in the least if you'd like to get some other opinions."

"We're having a fundraiser in just over a week, and I'm hoping we'll have the funds to cover this by then. How much would you charge to tarp it?" Courtney glanced up at the roof, not interested in climbing up there herself.

Mark shook his head. "You folks do great work here, so I'll do that at no charge."

"Really?" Courtney thought she could hug him. "Would you really?"

"I will, but I do wonder if you might do me a favor."

Uh oh. There was no such thing as a free puppy, as the old saying went. "What's that?"

"I really like this dog, but I'd like to see what my wife thinks of her, too. I don't suppose you do any sort of trial where she can stay with me for a day or two to see how she fits in before we officially adopt her?" The contractor had that embarrassed look on his face again. Charlotte was far less self-conscious about the bond the two of them had formed, considering the way she leaned heavily on the man's leg.

Courtney beamed at him. "We have paperwork that covers exactly that. Let's go back in, and you can take her home with you right now."

CHAPTER FIVE

J essi poked her head in the office. "There's someone at the front counter to see you. Her name's Lisa, and she's got food!"

"Oh! Is it noon already?" Courtney glanced at the clock. The contractor had taken up a significant part of the day. He'd brought in a crew to stretch a tarp over the bad part of the roof, and then he and Charlotte had left. She was just settling down to do some paperwork again and had completely lost track of time.

Lisa was waiting for her at the counter with a cardboard box and a big soda. "Here you are!"

"What do I owe you?" Courtney fished in her pocket for some cash.

"Don't worry about it. You can get me back another time." Lisa waved off the money.

"Have you eaten yours yet?"

Lisa shook her head. "I was just going to bring it back to the office. I hate sitting in a restaurant by myself."

"I know the feeling. Why don't you just join me at my desk? I can't spare a lot of time, but we could chat for a few." Courtney had fully planned to work straight through lunch, but she'd already done so much in just the morning that she was ready for a real break.

The two women settled down on either side of Courtney's desk, spreading out their pizza and breadsticks. "So, tell me more about this fundraiser," Lisa prompted.

Courtney swallowed a big bite of breadstick and leaned back in her chair. "Well, I can tell you we're definitely going to need it. Check out this bid from Cooper's Construction."

"Yikes." Lisa shook her head. "That's exactly why the library hasn't done a big remodel. As soon as I started working there, I noticed all the things that could use some updating. It turns out the board had gotten the bid and simply couldn't afford it."

"I know. The one advantage I have is that Mrs. Throgmorton is behind this. Do you know her at all?"

Lisa shook her head again as she took a bite of mushroom pizza.

"She's wealthy, has a lot of connections, and loves doing fundraisers. Her dog comes here all the time, so she's more than willing to help. I could use my marketing skills to put a few things together, but I don't know Curly Bay like she does." Courtney had been impressed with what Mrs. Throgmorton had already done, and she couldn't wait to see how it all turned out.

"How will this work?" Lisa asked after washing her pizza down with her soda.

"Everyone will pay a fee to get in," Courtney explained. "That will cover the cost of the venue, the music, and the food, plus a little extra. There will be a pet fashion show, where both hotel patrons and rescues can show off. Pets will be available for adoption, and there's a silent auction."

"Sounds interesting."

"Yeah, check out our first items for the auction." Courtney wiped her hands and reached down into her bottom drawer. "Mrs. Throgmorton gave me this diamond collar that - Wait a second. Where is it?"

Lisa came around the desk. "Is it under something else?"

"It shouldn't be." Courtney was down on the floor now, all thoughts of lunch forgotten. She pulled every item out of the bottom drawer, just to be sure. "I put it in a little pouch and set it in here, because we don't have a safe yet. It can't have just gone missing."

"Let's check the other drawers, just to be sure."

The two women pulled apart Courtney's desk. They even took out the drawers to make sure nothing had fallen behind them. Courtney was beginning to break out in a cold sweat. "This isn't good. This isn't good at all. I've got to find it! I know it was worth a ton of money."

Lisa glanced around. "Is there any chance someone stole it?"

"No, of course—" But then Courtney stopped. There was that vehicle that went screeching out of the parking lot that morning, and someone had let all the cats out of their cages the other day. "I don't know. Maybe. I'll call the police, just in case."

She left a message with Detective Fletcher down at the precinct before they continued looking. When the phone rang again, Courtney eagerly snatched it up.

"Hi, this is Samantha Larson from the Old Train Depot. Is this Courtney Cain?"

Courtney had been hoping it was Detective Fletcher calling her back, and she didn't have time for anything else. "Yes, it is," she replied politely.

"I'm so sorry to bother you. I tried to get a-hold of Mrs. Throgmorton, but she wasn't available. She had you listed as the next available contact."

Samantha was being very polite, but Courtney wished she'd get to the point. "Yes, the event she's holding there is for the benefit of the shelter I manage."

"I see. I wanted to call as soon as possible because we have some plumbing issues and the Old Train Depot will no longer be available for the fundraiser."

The whole world stopped. Courtney pressed her free hand to her head and closed her eyes, hoping that when she opened them again, she'd find out that this whole thing had been a nightmare. The storm damage, the missing collar, all of it. "Plumbing issues?"

"I'm afraid so. I went in and found that several pipes had burst. We have a very reliable plumber that we use, but I'm afraid he's out of town at the moment. We're doing what we can to find someone else, but-"

"Yes, I understand." Nope, not a nightmare. Real life, unfortunately. "I'll get with Mrs. Throgmorton and see if we can find a different place. I really appreciate the call."

Lisa gently touched Courtney's arm. "I'm sorry, but my lunch break is just about over, and I've got to get back to the library. Call me later, okay?"

"Okay. Thanks." Courtney walked Lisa to the front lobby, where a man was just walking in. She didn't want to deal with anyone else right now, but Jessi and Dora were both busy taking care of the animals. "Can I help you?"

His dark curly hair fell down over his brows, and he kept his hands shoved in his pockets. "Show me the cats. I'd like to adopt one. Today."

Any other time, Courtney would be more than happy to let him see the available cats and talk to him about adoption. Right now, the only thing she could think about was the missing diamond collar and the money they'd be losing out on if she couldn't find it. Besides, she needed to be available in case the police showed up. "We're a little busy at the moment, actually."

He lifted one hand out of his jeans pocket and gestured sharply at the room. "You don't look busy to me."

"We are. Trust me. If you'd like, I could get you an application to fill out and get you started while you wait." She reached for the binder on the counter.

"Application? It's not like I'm here for a job, lady. I just want to adopt a cat. For my daughter."

She gritted her teeth together, trying to remind herself that customer service was important. "I understand, and I'm glad that you're so interested in getting a cat from us. However, there is a process. First, you have to fill out an application. Then we have to call your references, and—"

"References? What's the matter with you people? It's not like taking care of a cat requires any special skills." His dark brows furrowed together, and he paced anxiously in place.

"We have to talk to your veterinarian. And at any rate, there are some things happening here that are going to prevent me from really being able to help you today. My advice for the moment is to take an application and check out the available cats on our social media pages."

The man stepped closer to the counter, leaning over it in an attempt to get in her face. "How can you expect anyone to give these animals a home if you won't even let someone in to see them? You want to whine and complain about them being in the shelter, and then you won't let anyone adopt them! You're sick!"

Courtney had already put up with too much from this man. "Take an application or not, but either way I suggest you leave."

Before the man had a chance to answer, Detective Fletcher and a uniformed officer strode through the door. The man glared at her. "Fine. I'll be back later."

"Detective Fletcher, I'm so glad you could come." Courtney was grateful for more than just checking into the collar, since that man had been getting so irate. She quickly explained the situation to him, and he and the officer looked all around. They checked the footage from the outside security cameras and looked for any evidence of a break-in, but when they returned to her at her desk Detective Fletcher just shook his head.

"There's no real evidence to go on, I'm afraid," he said in his typical gloomy voice. "The best I can do is make an official report about the collar, just in case it shows up somewhere. We can check to see if any of the other nearby businesses have cameras up and might've caught anything suspicious. You do have some gaps, you know."

"What do you mean?"

Fletcher shrugged. "Your security cameras really only cover the doors. If there was anything else that happened, like a window opening, then you wouldn't know."

"I see. That's something else I'll need to take care of," Courtney sighed. Between the missing collar and the plumbing problems at the depot, it felt like someone was trying to sabotage the fundraiser.

CHAPTER SIX

When Courtney went to work the next day, she'd hardly slept at all. The short burst of sleep she did get was filled with images of the missing diamond collar. Her stomach was constantly in knots over it. How could she tell Mrs. Throgmorton, who was putting so much time and effort into helping the shelter? Granted, the woman had tons of money, and if she could simply throw it in her purse and hand it over so casually, then it must not mean a lot to her. But Courtney didn't want to risk letting her down, or worse, making Mrs. Throgmorton pull out of the fundraiser completely.

She was doing her best to just get through the day when the phone rang. "Good morning. Curly Bay Pet Hotel and Rescue. This is Courtney. How can I help you?" She prided herself on the way they answered the phone these days. When she'd first taken up the position as manager, the greeting was usually a simple hello.

"Hi." The voice on the other end was distant and crackly. "I know this is a long shot, but I'm looking for my cat. He's a black and white tuxedo."

"We do have a cat that fits that description. He just came in a few days ago," Courtney replied as she tucked the phone against her shoulder and headed toward the cat room on the shelter side. She knew there were plenty of male tuxedos in the world, so she didn't want to get anyone's hopes up. "Does he have any other defining characteristics?"

A crackle came through the line, obscuring anything the woman was saying. "I'm sorry. What was that?"

"He has a little-"

The static was bad enough that Courtney held the phone away from her ear. "You might want to call me back. I can't hear anything you're saying."

More static. "-take a few days-"

"If you can hear me, we're open until six." The line went dead, and Courtney hung up. She pushed her fingers through the bars of Ritz's cage. "I'm sorry, buddy. If there's someone out there looking for you, then I hope she calls back."

Ritz, seemingly oblivious, rubbed his chin vigorously against her knuckle.

"At least you don't seem to mind the shelter life too much. And even if that wasn't your owner on the phone, I have no doubt you'll find someone who wants to be." She gave him one last ear scratch before she headed back toward the office.

"There's someone at the front desk you might want to talk to," Dora said, stopping her from sitting down. "He says he's from the city."

"Hmm," Courtney frowned. "Maybe they've heard about the fundraiser and they have something to donate for the silent auction."

But the slim man who frowned at her from the other side of the front counter didn't exactly look enthusiastic about being there. He held a clipboard clamped underneath one arm.

"Hi, I'm Courtney. Is there something I can do for you?"

"You the manager?" His frown deepened a little.

"Yes. Courtney Cain." She held out her hand.

He ignored it, instead handing over a business card between two fingers. "Stewart Bircham, code enforcement. I see you still have some damage from last weekend's storm."

There was something about the way he talked that Courtney simply didn't like. Part of it was that he made it sound as though the storm had happened weeks ago, when it was really only a few days. Still, there was no denying the giant blue tarp stretching over one end of the roof. "Yes?"

"I need to take a look at it, please."

She blew a breath through her lips, thinking about putting him off. She could always say she needed the owner's permission. Ms. O'Donnell was taking care of a sick relative, and there was no telling when she'd get around to coming in. The deepening lines around Mr. Bircham's mouth made her decide it was easier and quicker to just get this over with so she could move on to more important things, like figuring out where the diamond collar had gone.

She opened the gate. "You can come on back and I'll show you. There's a little bit on the outside, but you can't see it without taking the tarp off. Mark Cooper helped us out with that." She smiled in an effort to be friendly.

It had zero effect on Mr. Bircham. "That's nice of him, but I just may have to do that."

"Why?" Courtney opened the door. The dogs immediately trotted to the fronts of their cages, looking for love and a chance at a home. Courtney was pretty sure they weren't going to have any luck with the code enforcement officer.

Completely ignoring the dogs, Mr. Bircham strode to the other end of the room. He braced his fists on his hips as he squinted up at the hole in the ceiling and let out a low whistle. "That's not good. Not good at all."

Courtney was well aware of this, and in fact was so aware that she was tired of talking about it. "I know. That's why I had Cooper's Construction come out here and give us a bid. The price is pretty steep, though."

Mr. Bircham took his clipboard from under his arm and began taking notes. His pen moved like lightning across the paper. "Tree?"

"Hmm? Oh, yes. It was a tree." Courtney distracted herself by rubbing Beau's nose through the chain link.

"And you have customers come in here?" He gestured around the room with his pencil.

Courtney realized this was far more than a simple survey of local natural disasters. "Well, normally we do. Coming back to meet the cats and dogs is the only way people will know if a pet is the right one for them. Ever since this happened, we've had to drastically reduce everything that happens around here. Most of the animals had to be moved to the other side, which is the hotel. No customers have been over here."

He shook his head as he started scribbling again. "What about that room over there? Can I see if there's any damage?"

"Sure." Courtney knew the cat room was fine, and so she brought him there. "It's fine, but we haven't had anyone in here, either. In fact, I turned away a gentleman just recently who wanted to adopt a cat." She had only turned him away because she was freaking out over the missing collar, but still.

Mr. Bircham had nothing for her but head shakes and frowns as he tapped his pen on the side of the clipboard. "I'm afraid it just won't do. There's a chance this whole end of the building could collapse if we got another good storm, or if it's more damaged than I can see. We can't let you endanger people's lives by letting them in here."

Courtney nodded. "I understand. I'll just tell potential adopters to look at the animals on our website, and I'll bring them out to the lobby."

"No, no." More shakes of the head from Mr. Bircham. "You can't be in here, either. Neither should the dogs, if the animal welfare folks have anything to do with it. The whole place has to be shut down. Find some other place for these animals and lock the doors until you get that roof fixed. Curly Bay is cracking down on anything that might be unsafe for its citizens."

"You can't be serious! What would we do with all of them?" She gestured helplessly at the dogs. "People don't just take them in, or else they wouldn't be here in the first place."

Courtney pressed her hands to her cheeks. Why was all this happening? "Please, Mr. Bircham. We're a rescue. We're trying to keep pets out of the pound and off the streets. We're having a fundraiser in a week so that we can get the repairs done. What if I just get these few dogs out of this room and then lock only this door? That way we don't have to displace every single pet, and I still won't allow any customers past the front counter."

He squinted at her, looking like he was about to list off a series of ordinances she was violating by even suggesting such a thing. "Most people would claim they were trying to fix a problem and never get around to it, which is why I wouldn't normally allow such a thing. But I know you folks are trying to do a good thing here. I'll allow it, but I'll only give you twenty-four hours to get these dogs out and the door completely locked. Clear?"

"Yes. Absolutely. Understood." A bead of sweat trickled down her temple as she walked with him back to the front. The hotel would be packed to the gills, and she might have to find a few volunteers to foster any pups that wouldn't fit. "I really appreciate it."

"Well, just don't tell anyone or else they'll all expect the same treatment. You'll be getting a letter from the city to explain everything officially." Without another word, he turned around and left.

Courtney jumped when the phone rang. It'd been a crazy day already. She answered quickly, wondering if it would be the woman looking for the tuxedo again. It wasn't.

"Hi, this is Melissa from Retro Resurgence. Mrs. Throgmorton had left your number with me."

Courtney frowned, confused at first. "Oh, the band! Right. What can I do for you?" She was afraid of the answers, as nothing seemed to be going her way lately.

"I'm sorry to say that our singer has come down with laryngitis."

Was it unprofessional to bang her head on the desk? Courtney looked around for her favorite pen so she could take notes, but it was nowhere to be seen. "I understand. So, you won't be able to do the fundraiser?"

"I'm afraid not."

"You wouldn't happen to know of another band that's available, would you?" Courtney made a mental note to check in with Mrs. Throgmorton soon. She'd been avoiding it ever since she'd found out the collar was missing. Thinking of that reminded her that she hadn't had a chance to look for it again that day, and she let out a frustrated sigh.

"I do, but they're a metal band. I don't think that's quite what you're looking for."

"No, not really. Thanks for letting me know." The phone rang again as soon as she hung up and Courtney was beginning to wish the phone had never been invented. She could hear the curtness in her voice as she rattled off her greeting.

"Hey, it's Lisa."

"Oh, hey!" At least it wasn't another cancellation. "Was I supposed to meet you today?"

"We didn't have any definite plans. I just thought I'd check in with you after the way things had gone the other day."

She was referring to the collar, Courtney knew. "Nothing's changed on that front, and everything else has only gotten worse."

"Anything I can do?"

Courtney started to shake her head, but then she changed her mind. It'd always been her habit to have an I'll-take-care-of-it-myself attitude, but she really did need help. "You don't know anyone who'd be willing to foster a dog, do you? I've got five I have to get out of here, or else the city is going to shut me down."

"I'll do it," Lisa answered immediately.

"Really?"

"Sure. I mean, I can only take one of them. I'd be happy to spread the word at the library and help you find a spot for the rest of them."

For the first time that day, or maybe even in a few days, Courtney's heart felt light. "That's so great! Thank you so much! Come by when you get off work and you can pick out your foster baby!"

"I don't get off until six," Lisa replied.

"I'll happily stay open late." She hung up, hoping this was a sign that everything would soon balance out.

CHAPTER SEVEN

Struggling to get in the door with the box in her hands, Courtney decided another upgrade they couldn't afford for the Curly Bay Pet Hotel and Rescue was an automatic door. She was eager enough to get inside and open the box that she quickly forgot her troubles with the door.

Jessi was already there, leaning against the counter and staring at her phone with wide eyes.

"Is everything okay?" Courtney asked.

"Sshh! Listen!" Jessi tipped the phone so that her boss could see the screen.

It was the local news report. "Burglaries continue to surge throughout Curly Bay," the anchor drone. "Police say there doesn't seem to be a particular pattern, which is going to make the perpetrator even harder to catch. One report suggests that this may be the same burglar who shook up Ruby Cove with a massive string of burglaries just last summer. The police say they are getting closer to finding the culprit, but they won't release any details of the investigation just yet. Now on to the weather."

Jessi turned off the screen and shook her head. "This is scary! There never used to be anything like this in Curly Bay. It's the sort of town where people don't lock their doors or cars at night because they know it's safe."

Courtney pressed her lips together to keep from smiling. When she lived in the city, she wouldn't have dared to do such a thing. "Locks are just there to keep honest people honest. Those who want to get in badly enough are going to do it anyway, which is exactly why I bought these." She fished a pair of scissors out of the drawer and opened the top of the box.

"What are these little gadgets?" Jessi reached inside and pulled one out, turning it over in her hands. "Oh, security cameras! They certainly don't look like the ones on the outside of the building."

"No, those are far more expensive. I still hadn't gotten a call back from Hinkle's yet, so I took Mark Cooper's advice and just bought some online. There's no professional monitoring, but I can check them from my phone, and we can all review the footage on the computers here in the office. It's better than nothing."

"I thought we had to wait until the fundraiser to do any big purchases like this. Did you finally get a hold of Ms. O'Donnell?" Jessi unpacked a few more cameras, along with an instruction booklet.

Courtney pulled a face, hoping that once she did inform the owner she wouldn't be in too much trouble. "No. I bought these with my own money. I've had several more instances of animals getting out of their cages when we're not here, and I saw a car speeding away one morning. You put the missing collar on top of that, and I'm not willing to wait any longer."

"Looks like they're pretty easy to put up." Jessi skimmed through the instruction booklet. "They're so small that we can just stick them up with adhesive or use a small screw. I think we can handle that."

"I take it that means you'll help?" Courtney asked hopefully. "I've got several people coming in to pick up foster dogs today, thanks to Lisa, so it's going to be another busy one."

"That's all they ever are around here," Jessi commented as she pulled a step ladder out of the supply closet. "Don't get me wrong. There's a lot I like about my work. But it just infuriates me that people will leave these animals on the streets or in abandoned homes, not caring what happens to them. Even the ones who at least make the effort to bring them to a shelter make me angry, since so many times it's that they're moving, or they just don't want a cat anymore, or they didn't bother to train their dog, and now they're mad that it chews the furniture." She snapped the ladder open with a bang.

"I know it's rough, but at least we know we're making a difference." Courtney stepped up on the ladder and held a camera to the wall, pointing at the door to the cat room. "What do you think?"

"I think we should put it at the other end of the hall, and that way it'll cover both doors. We might not be able to use the dog room right now, but eventually we will." Jessi held the ladder steady as Courtney climbed down. "And you're right. We're making a difference, but is it enough? It's not as though the world is running out of strays."

"That's true," Courtney agreed. "I think part of the problem is that it takes so much money to get them all cared for. We not only have the cost of veterinary care, but the building itself. I guess I'll have to put a bug in Mrs. Throgmorton's ear about hosting a fundraiser more often if this one is successful." She held the camera up on the wall and checked the positioning before fixing it into place.

"That's another thing that really gets my goat," Jessi groused. "We've got all these people like the Throgmortons who will come to this fundraiser just so they can brag about how they helped all the poor animals, when the real reason they're coming is to rub elbows and be seen by the other socially elite. They've got the money. They know there's a problem here. Why should we have to bribe them into donating?"

Courtney climbed back down the ladder and frowned. "That's a good point. I'm not sure people really do know. I mean, they know, but it's not something that's put right in front of their faces every day. Maybe we need to do more to get out in the community."

Jessi opened her mouth as though she was going to argue, but then she closed it again. "Yeah, maybe you're right. We're sitting here on the edge of town, and it's mostly the hotel and spa guests who know about us. A few of them will take in a rescue, but most of the time they're looking for purebreds. Maybe that's something we can work on."

"As soon as we get past this fundraiser, absolutely," Courtney promised. "I'm going to download the app for this security system really quick and see if we can get the camera to link up to it. That way we can make sure it's in the right position before we put up the rest."

"And speaking of security, I take it we still don't have any leads on the diamond collar?" Jessi asked.

Courtney shook her head. "I checked in with Detective Fletcher, but I don't think the police will be able to do much about it. They don't have enough leads. They're focusing more on that string of burglaries that was just on the news, although I personally think this could be part of the same thing."

Jessi sighed. "I guess I can't blame them, there. Oh, by the way, let me know if you find an earring anywhere around here. I lost one the other day, and I haven't seen it since."

"What did it look like?" Courtney was able to see the feed from the first camera, so they took the ladder to the other side of the building and started again.

"It was a dangle earring with little wire twists. It's not the kind of thing I'd normally wear to work, but I wanted to try them out. Of course, I had to end up losing one." She rolled her eyes at herself.

"We'll keep an eye out for it," Courtney promised.

By the time they were done, they had one security camera pointing down the hall of the shelter side, one that overlooked the hotel side, and one that watched the lobby area. Courtney had them all linked in with the app, and it would record plenty of hours of footage for them to review if anything else strange happened.

The day flew by as Courtney arranged for homes for the rest of the dogs who could no longer stay in the kennel. Lisa had taken Beau, and she'd contacted enough friends and coworkers that the other big dogs were all playing in someone's back yard by the end of the day.

This made her heart feel light as she turned onto her street. The dogs may not be in permanent homes, but those who'd come in to serve as foster parents had seemed genuinely interested in preparing these dogs for the time when they'd be permanently adopted. It would be so much better for them to live in a home instead of a shelter, and Courtney was once again reminded that a true foster program was a great idea.

As with any other happy thoughts she'd had lately, it quickly ran away when she noticed a dirty black car sitting on the side of the street in front of her apartment, just past her driveway. As she crept closer, it fired up its engine and zoomed away. She could swear it was the same one that'd left the Curly Bay Pet Hotel and Rescue in such a hurry, a notion that didn't sit well with her.

Courtney parked inside the garage and locked the car even once she'd closed the garage door. She then locked the door that led into the house behind her and retrieved the package she'd set on the kitchen table the previous evening. It had an identical security system to the one they'd just installed at the shelter. Her savings account had been hit rather hard by the two purchases, but she felt much better by the end of the evening when she'd gone through an installation all over again.

CHAPTER EIGHT

There was something about sleeping with cameras pointing out each of her doors that was just so comforting, and Courtney was grateful for a good night's sleep. News bits didn't normally keep her up at night when they were national stories that didn't directly affect her, but hearing the burglary reports creep closer and closer to home had been unnerving, to say the least.

She called Lisa on her way in to work. "It's been a couple days, so I just thought I'd see how Beau is doing."

"Oh, he's great! Aren't you, Beau? Aren't you the handsomest man? You ready for your breakfast?" The dog's gentle woof could be heard in the background.

71

"I can tell the two of you are getting along swimmingly," Courtney said with a smile.

"We really are," Lisa admitted. "I knew I wanted to do this because the shelter and Beau needed my help, but now that he's here I realize I'm doing it just as much for myself. I haven't gotten to know a whole lot of people since I moved to Curly Bay, and Beau is great company. Last night while I was sitting on the couch watching TV, he lay right down on top of my feet and went to sleep."

"That's wonderful. We really did need your help, and in finding foster homes for the other dogs, you've been more help than you could possibly imagine. The code enforcement officer showed up promptly yesterday afternoon to make sure that end of the building was blocked off." She still couldn't believe what bad luck she was having.

"I'm honestly surprised it worked out so well," Lisa replied. "I just started asking everyone I could think of, figuring they'd mostly say no. Maybe there's something appealing for some folks in knowing that they're only keeping the dog temporarily. In my experience, though, temporary usually turns to permanent."

"You think so?" Courtney couldn't wait to get the building fixed so they could start moving on with new programs for the shelter, and this foster thing was so exciting!

"Oh, yeah. I remember finding a kitten on the side of the road when I was a kid. I brought it home and cleaned it up. It had a few little wounds from being out on its own. I knew my dad would never let me keep it, so I asked if I could keep her in a box in my room just until it was healthy enough to find a new home. Well, the kitten started curling up to sleep on my dad's chest, and it never left our house again," Lisa chuckled.

"That's a good one! Listen, we're thinking about starting up a foster program at the shelter. Do you think you'd be interested? I'd love to have people who can help get these pets acclimated to life in a real home and increase their chances of being rescued. I'd do it myself if Mrs. Peabody wouldn't get so up-in-arms about it." Courtney had already tried once to bring home a shelter dog who was pitifully grieving the loss of his owner. Gunner had been a good boy, and Courtney had never intended to keep him, but she didn't need to risk another run-in with her landlady.

"Keep me on the list, for sure. I might not always be able to do it, especially if I'm planning a vacation or something, but I'd love to help again."

"Have I told you how awesome you are?" Courtney loved to know there were other people in the world who cared about the animals, and if they did do this foster thing, Jessi might come to see it as well.

"Don't give me a big head, now! I've got to get ready for work, but I'll talk to you later."

Courtney smiled as she drove to work, but it was wiped off her face when she walked in. "What's going on here?"

Dora and Jessi were already there, as it was Courtney's scheduled day to arrive late. Dora was chasing a Bichon Frisé with a pink bow in her hair through the lobby, while Jessi stood on the stepladder to lift a calico from the top shelf.

"They got out again," Dora explained. "This time, it was the whole building. Cats and dogs from all over. It's been a fun morning already."

Courtney took a leash from the wall and clipped it onto a schnauzer who was snoozing in one of the lobby chairs. "Did anyone check the security cameras yet?"

"Haven't exactly had time," Jessi said, straining to reach the cat. Every time she reached for the calico, it inched away down the shelf before sitting down to casually lick its paws.

"Right." Courtney escorted the schnauzer down the hall to the hotel. She couldn't put it back in its cage because someone else happened to be sleeping in it. "Ritz, what do you think you're doing here? You might be dressed fancy, but this isn't where you belong." She scooped out the cat, who purred happily against her shoulder.

As she brought Ritz back to the cat room, she noticed a small ball of gray fluff sitting near the thoroughly locked door to the dog room. Sighing, she put Ritz away and went to retrieve the kitten. "I'm sorry, but Beau isn't staying here right now. You'll have to be content to cuddle with your siblings." She returned the kitten to its cage, found that fat marmalade bathing himself on her desk again, and pulled a Brussels Griffon from the trash can it'd knocked over.

When the three women reconvened in the office, Courtney pulled the security software up on her computer so they could all see more easily. "Okay. We'll start here, which is right as we left the building. We know everything was fine at that point.

I'll just fast-forward while we're here on this screen, where we can see all the cameras at once. Let me know if you see anything we need to slow down for." She and the others practically held their breath as they reviewed the footage, waiting to see someone walk in the front doors or climb through a window.

Instead, they saw Ritz waltz out of the cat room, several other cats behind him. They watched him roam to the other side of the building, where he nudged past the door to the hotel side. Courtney leaned forward, keeping her eyes on the black-and-white figure. Due to the angle of the camera here, she could see Ritz walk up to the cages of the guests. With a few flicks of his paw, he opened the latch and let out an Abyssinian!

"I can't believe this!" She rewound the video just to be sure. "It's Ritz! I mean, I had my suspicions, but still."

"And look, you can see him let out several of the others," Dora said, pointing out that Ritz had moved past the Abyssinian's cage to free a Persian.

Courtney sat back and rubbed her hand over her face, laughing. "What a little brat! I know we're not supposed to have locks on the cages, but we'll have to figure out something."

Jessi nodded. "That's true. We've been lucky enough that the animals who have gotten out haven't gotten into any spats. The last thing we need is one of our patrons to get upset because her pooch got a scratch on the cheek from a feisty feline. The way things have been going for us, I wouldn't be surprised."

"You're right. Hmm." Courtney slowly stood up, thinking.

"What is it?" Dora asked.

"Well, if Ritz is the one who's letting all the animals out, then we know we don't have to worry about a person somehow getting in to do it, right?"

"Right," they both said with a nod.

"And you saw on that video how easily the cat was able to manipulate the latches. It was no problem for him, and he clearly is a very curious cat who doesn't just stop with letting out one animal."

"What's your point?" Jessi asked.

"I'm going to see if Ritz will make it for me." Courtney led the way from the office and into the shelter with the other two women following close behind. She opened Ritz's cage and took him out, handing him over to Jessi. The tuxedo cat didn't mind any of the attention, settling easily into Jessi's arms.

Courtney's hand was shaking as she pulled back the folded blanket that served as Ritz's bed. Something glimmered at her from underneath the corner, and she pulled out an earring. It was a dangly one made of long, twisted wires of silver. "Jessi, I believe this is yours."

"My earring! Awesome!" She took it from Courtney. Ritz reached out and grabbed her hand with his paw, bringing the earring close to his mouth where he tried to bite it. "I don't think so," Jessi scolded him.

"And here's my missing pen." Courtney held up the pen she'd been looking for the other day. She'd stopped thinking about it once she couldn't find it, but there was only one way it could've ended up in Ritz's cage. "Now cross your fingers," she said as she lifted the bedding back the rest of the way.

The diamond collar from Mrs. Throgmorton glimmered from the recesses of the cage. Courtney eagerly snatched it up and laughed out loud. "All this time, it's been right here!"

"Someone has an eye for shiny things," Dora commented as she scratched Ritz beneath the chin. "What do we do with the little thief?"

"What do you think, Ritz? Should we call Detective Fletcher and have him book you?" Courtney teased. "For now, we'll have to find a different latch to put on his cage. We may have to risk some sort of lock, because we really can't have him or anyone else wandering around. In fact, I think that's more dangerous than a lock."

"Agreed. I'll see if I can get a hold of Ms. O'Donnell and get her approval for something," Dora offered as she headed back into the office.

"Thanks." Courtney and Jessi made sure Ritz wasn't hiding any other contraband in his cage before putting him back in and using a twist tie to keep him —at least temporarily—confined.

Courtney walked into the lobby just as Mrs. Throgmorton strolled in with Sir Glitter under one arm. She sported a deep tan, and the dog wore a tiny pair of designer sunglasses perched on top of his head. "Courtney, dear! I'm so sorry! I took some time off to go to the beach house, and I completely forgot that I get terrible reception there! As soon as I got back into town, I saw all the missed calls and voicemails. Please tell me you didn't do anything to fix the issues with the fundraiser?"

She hadn't exactly had the time. "I haven't, I'm afraid."

"Good, because I did. I wasn't about to come over here and talk to you without doing something about it myself. I have a good connection with a plumber, and I sent him straight over to the Old Train Depot. He assures me he'll have everything fixed in time for the event. Then I called my cousin, because I know her daughter sings with a band in the city. Long story short, she's coming out to sub in for the fundraiser, and everything is back on track." She waved her arms as though she'd pulled it all together with magic.

Courtney pressed a hand to her chest. "That's so wonderful to hear! The repairs only seem to be causing me more trouble at every turn, and I'm eager to get them done. I also need to be honest with you."

Mrs. Throgmorton tipped her head to the side. "What is it, dear?"

"The diamond collar you donated went missing for a few days. I was afraid of telling you, because I didn't want you to be upset, but it turns out one of our cats swiped it." She could feel heat blooming in her cheeks, embarrassed at not having taken better care of such an expensive item.

But Mrs. Throgmorton let out a loud laugh. "A real cat burglar! How about that? You should put something about it on the bid sheet. A dog collar that even the cats can't keep their paws off of!" She laughed again, obviously not bothered in the least by the fact that the collar had been missing in the first place.

"I'll do that! Is there anything you need me to do as far as the event goes? I've been posting about it like crazy online, and Jessi put some flyers up around town." Courtney had been starting to wonder if they'd ever be able to hold the fundraiser with the bad luck they were having. Now, with everything straightened out, she realized it'd been just that, bad luck.

"Oh! I have tons of silent auction items. We'll get them brought in so you can do the bid sheets."

By the time they'd brought it all in, the front lobby held a signed guitar, a vintage lamp, a pair of tickets for a cruise, several gift cards, vintage wine, several pieces of jewelry, and even an antique chair. There were numerous experiences and opportunities that could be won as well, and Courtney paged through them with surprise. "Become a named character in Connie Gilbert's next novel. Gourmet dinner for two made in your home. Backstage passes, autographed pictures, vacations, wow! You really went all out, Mrs. Throgmorton!"

She waved off the praise. "You might as well get something out of schmoozing with the wealthy, right?" she said with a little laugh.

Courtney grinned. With these items, they would make more than enough money to fix the roof.

CHAPTER NINE

"What do you think of this one, Mom?" Courtney stood back so that the camera on her phone could pick up a full-length image. She tipped her head from side to side to see how her faux diamond earrings looked with her ensemble. "I need something that's formal enough to wear to this event, but still lets me work with the animals. I told Mrs. Throgmorton I'd be working with the animals most of the night, but she still insists I get up in front of everyone and say a few words."

"And so you should! You've worked very hard to make all this happen, dear. You deserve a little recognition. Personally, I wouldn't go with the velvet. You'll be covered in fur as soon as you walk in the door. Maybe a suit in a lighter color?"

"Oh, I didn't think about that! I've got that gray Calvin Klein sheath dress with the matching blazer. That should work." She turned around to dig it out of the closet. "I put most of my business attire all the way at the back, since I don't really need it here."

"You seem to be settling in nicely," Mrs. Cain commented. "I'm glad to see you looking so happy."

Courtney laid the dress and blazer on the end of her bed and picked up her phone so she could see her mother more clearly. "Do I?"

"Yes, you really do. I was worried about you after all the stuff with Sam. It's not easy for any woman to get her heart broken, and in such a cruel way. I always did think you were too good for him, though, and I can see you've very much moved on." She smiled at her daughter.

"Thanks, Mom. I have. I mean, I've had times when I've still been really angry with him. The funny thing about Curly Bay, though, is that it just makes the rest of the world go away. I don't worry about what I'm missing in the city or where I could've been with my career if I'd stayed in marketing. I really like it here."

"And I much prefer to hear stories about smart cats who know how to get out of their cages than corporate lackeys causing drama," Mrs. Cain joked.

Courtney laughed. "I know! The work doesn't weigh me down the way marketing did. The shelter has had its challenges, for sure. This fundraiser has certainly been one of them. As of tomorrow night, though, it'll be all over and I can get the roof repaired."

"Do you have any last-minute preparations?"

"I need to check my notebook." She'd wanted to keep all her ideas in one place, and the little binder she was using also had a pocket where she'd put all the printed bid sheets. Courtney walked into the living room and opened her purse, but the notebook wasn't there. She checked the kitchen table, the counter, and her car, but still no luck. "I think I left it at work. I'll have to go get it."

"You could just get it in the morning," her mother suggested.

"Yeah, but it's a short drive and I'd rather not feel like I'm forgetting to do something." She fetched her purse and keys.

"I'll let you go then, honey. Good luck tomorrow night, and let me know how it goes!"

"Will do! Love you!" After changing back into jeans and a t-shirt, Courtney headed back across town on a short drive that she was getting to know like the back of her hand. The traffic was much lighter than usual as she went through the downtown area, since it was already past the dinner hour. She'd be back at home and ready to try on that gray dress in no time, as well as look over all her notes and make sure there wasn't a single thing missed.

Courtney didn't think a thing about showing up at work so late at night. Nobody was supposed to be there, and other than potentially waking up a few of the animals, it shouldn't be a problem. But as she put her key in the lock and opened the door, she noticed the light on in the office. Her mouth went dry. She'd thought about putting alarms on the doors, but had settled for only the cameras. They wouldn't help her now.

Courtney slowly moved further into the building, pushing her keys through her fingers as a makeshift weapon and hoping her phone didn't ring from her pocket, announcing her presence. She was tempted to call out, hoping it would either let her know one of the other ladies had come in or that it might chase away whoever was here, but she couldn't do it. She was simply too scared, and things had been too strange in Curly Bay lately.

"Come on," grunted a gruff voice from the office. "I don't have all night!"

Peeking in the office door, Courtney spied a man with dark curly hair standing in front of her desk. He was facing away from the door, watching Ritz. The cat was up on top of a cabinet, watching the man with a feisty look in his eyes.

"Seriously, cat. We've got work to do." The man reached up at him, but Ritz easily danced out of his reach.

The stranger's position allowed Courtney to see the side of his face, and she immediately recognized him. They'd had almost no customers in the building over the past week, but even so it was easy to recognize the man who'd come in to adopt a cat. He'd gotten so belligerent over not being able to take a cat home that day that Courtney hadn't even gotten his name, and he'd left when Detective Fletcher arrived.

Suppressing a gasp of shock, Courtney dodged out of the doorframe before the man saw her. She could slip out the front door and call the police, but that would leave this creep in the building with Ritz and the other animals, not to mention the silent auction items that were stored there. Pressing one hand to the side of her face to help her think, she realized her shiny crystal earrings she'd been trying on with her velvet dress were still in her ears. Courtney took one out. Silently, she took a leash down from a hook on the wall. Her breath and her heartbeat were so loud she thought the man might hear her, but he was too distracted with the cat.

"Come on, you stupid cat! You've caused me enough trouble already, getting yourself locked up in here." He swiped a hand up at the cat again, but Ritz hissed at him.

Courtney raised a brow. The tuxedo had been the sweetest cat ever since he'd shown up, but he definitely didn't like this guy. Hoping her plan would work, and hoping it was worth the risk, Courtney hooked the clip end of the leash over the door hinge. She watched the man carefully, hoping he wouldn't turn around as she stretched it across the doorway and held the loop firmly in her hand. Then she took her cell phone out of her pocket. She shielded the light from the screen with her hand as she turned her call volume all the way down, and then dialed a number that was quickly becoming familiar to her. She then turned off the screen and put it back in her pocket.

Stepping just to the edge of the doorway, Courtney reached out and dangled her earring in the air. It immediately caught Ritz's attention, but because of the angle the man thought the cat was looking at him.

"That's a good kitty. Come on down, now. I've got a new harness waiting for you, and just think of all the goodies we're going to get." He dangled a blue harness and leash in the air.

Ritz's pupils thinned down to tiny slits as he focused on the earring. He dug his claws into the wood of the cabinet as he wiggled his rear end and prepared to pounce.

"That's it! Just jump right down into my arms, buddy. I'll buy you a big old bag of cat treats!"

Courtney tossed the earring under the lobby counter. It landed silently on the carpet, but Ritz still knew it was there. He leapt off the cabinet and bounced off the man's shoulder. Courtney dodged to the side of the doorway as Ritz hurtled out of the office, and she pulled hard on the leash.

It was only a few inches off the floor, but the man was too focused on Ritz to see it as he chased the cat. First one foot twanged against it and then the other. Courtney held tight, and it yanked hard at her shoulder, but she was determined to make this work. The man toppled forward, his hairy arms flailing uselessly before he hit the floor.

Courtney sprang up. The leash's hook had come off the hinge, but it was still underneath the man's legs. She quickly wrapped it around him before snagging another one off the wall and binding his wrists behind his back.

"Hey! Hey, what's going on here? What is this?"

She didn't want to. She didn't want to have anything to do with this man, and she certainly didn't want to touch him any more than she had to. He'd been rude to her, and he obviously wasn't interested in Ritz's welfare. Even so, Courtney knelt down hard, digging her knees into his back.

He rolled to the side, like a whale trying to avoid a harpoon. "Get off me! You have sharp knees!"

She twisted the leash that was wrapped around his wrists as she pulled her cell out with the other hand. It was difficult to get the volume turned back up, but she was grateful to see the time still running on the call. "Detective Fletcher? Are you still there?"

"I'm on my way. Are you at the shelter? What's going on?"

"I am, and I hope you've got your handcuffs with you. Someone was breaking in and trying to steal a cat." She struggled as the man tried to get away once more, grateful for having spent the last few months dealing with big dogs on leashes who sometimes thought they should be able to run off and chase a squirrel. "I've got him."

"I'll be there right away, Courtney. Just hang tight."

Courtney could hear the sound of sirens in the distance, and she knew he was close. She looked up the cat, who was watching the whole show from the safety of the counter. He dipped his head as he tried to comprehend what was happening.

"You did a good job, Ritz. You caught the bad guy."

Ritz responded by walking just a little further down the counter, pausing near a plastic cup of pens. He casually knocked it down with his paw, aiming perfectly so that it fell on the man's head.

CHAPTER TEN

"Courtney, you did a wonderful job up there! You should be in public speaking!" Mrs. Throgmorton cooed over a glass of white wine. She wore a sparkling black dress with blindingly brilliant diamonds in her ears and at her throat. "Everyone loved you, I could tell. And did you see the current bids on the silent auction? This fundraiser is an absolute hit!"

"Don't give me all the credit, you're the one who pulled it all together." Courtney gave the older woman a gentle nudge and winked. She'd been so worried about this event, and even once they'd gotten past the problems with the venue and the band, she'd still been concerned that something might go wrong. Courtney was surprised not only at how well it was going, but how comfortable she was. Mrs. Throgmorton's friends were all so nice.

"No, I just pulled a few strings I had access to. Courtney, you've got such charisma! People like you, and you know how to make them really care about these animals." Mrs. Throgmorton leaned closed and looked around the room before saying in a conspiratorial whisper, "Now, don't tell anyone I told you, but I just so happened to see Mrs. Wingate actually get down on the floor to pet a dog! I've never seen the woman stoop for anything before, and you managed to get to her!"

"That's wonderful! We've had several adoption applications put in already tonight, and I'm so excited. We'll get the roof fixed, and then we'll move on to the next project. I don't suppose you know anyone who wants to foster a cat or a dog, do you?"

Mrs. Throgmorton laughed. "You know, I'll pass the word around, my dear, but don't count on me. Sir Glitter wouldn't tolerate sharing me with anyone! Say, isn't that your detective friend?" She pointed across the room, where the older gentleman had just come in the door.

"It is. I'd better go save him from having to buy a ticket." Courtney trotted over. "Detective Fletcher. What brings you here?"

He smiled, a look she didn't often see on his face. "What, I can't support my favorite shelter? I can't tell you how much we love our Artemis." Detective Fletcher had adopted a fluffy tuxedo cat just the previous month.

"I'm so glad to hear it. He's a wonderful cat."

"And so is that Ritz who helped you out last night," Fletcher commented. "Tell me, did you find it interesting that the cat who was a crook also helped you catch a burglar?"

"Well, yeah, actually," Courtney admitted. "In the moment, I was just focused on saving the animals. After I got home and had more time to think about it, I was desperate to know what the connection between the two of them was. Why was he trying to get Ritz? That cat didn't seem to want to have anything to do with him, yet he's friendly with everyone else. He's actually part of the adoption event tonight, and he's loved on everyone who comes near him."

The detective nodded wisely. "Those tuxedo cats are pretty smart, and Ritz is no exception. The man we arrested at your shelter last night was Darryl Skaggs, and he's the one who's been breaking into homes all over Curly Bay."

Somehow, hearing that out loud made it all the more terrifying. Courtney could feel her heart thundering underneath her gray dress. "Seriously?"

"Yes, ma'am. It turns out he was just trying to get his partner back. He'd found Ritz, whom he just called Cat, and knew he was smart. He trained him to steal for him, and he used him to get into homes undetected or crawl in through cracked windows."

"That explains why he stole the diamond collar and Jessi's earring and my fountain pen. I thought he just liked shiny things, which is why I used my own earring to lure him into the lobby last night." The roar of the crowded depot behind her turned to a roar in her ears as anger bubbled up in her blood. "I can't believe he'd use an innocent cat that way!"

"Oh, but he did. That explains why he was found near one of the crime scenes with a harness on, too. Darryl wasn't expecting us to respond as quickly as we did to the tripped alarm, and he was more concerned about getting away himself."

"I suppose this means Ritz is still looking for a new owner. He very well may find one here tonight."

Courtney glanced around the room at the supporters who'd gathered in their finest attire. Some of them danced on the cleared area in front of the band, and others chatted and clinked their wine glasses. It was beautiful, really, but it also made Courtney think of the conversation she'd had with Jessi. Was this just a thinly veiled excuse to show off? Or did any of these people actually care about what happened with the animals?

"Courtney, I need you," Jessi said at her elbow.

Blinking back to reality, Courtney nodded at Fletcher. "I've got to go, but thanks for the update. Please, feel free to stay and enjoy some food."

Jessi took her by the crook of the elbow and pulled her toward the back of the building. Her steps were urgent, but her eyes were alight. "You know how we were worried about finding enough room for all the cats and dogs between the hotel and what we could use of the shelter?"

"Yes?"

"I don't think you'll have to worry about it after tonight! These people are going absolutely nuts for the animals! I'm so ashamed of myself. I thought for sure they didn't care, but they do. Not only are they shelling out all their money, but they actually want to take these pets home!" Jessi was practically giggling with excitement.

"Really?" Courtney glanced at the current bid on the diamond collar as they walked by. Her eyes widened, knowing there'd be plenty of money for the roof and more. "Oh!"

"Wait until you look in here!"

Courtney peeked in the door of the side room where they'd decided to hold the adoption portion of the event. The sound of the band and the party was nearly drowned out in here anyway, but it was completely obliterated by the coos, laughs, and baby talk of the patrons. The dogs were out on leashes so they could interact, and even though Courtney had worried about having enough volunteers, most of the dogs had been taken over by the socialites. Just as Mrs. Throgmorton had described, they were completely ignoring the care directions for their designer suits as they petted, scratched, and played. The cats were just as big of a hit, and the fat marmalade who liked to bathe on Courtney's desk was currently being held like a baby in the arms of an older woman with a pouf of curly gray hair.

She noticed one dog who didn't seem interested in visiting, and she walked over to Beau and Dora. "What's the matter? Do you think he's scared?"

Dora shook her head and smiled. "No. I think he's in love." She pointed to the opposite corner of the room, where Lisa was helping someone with paperwork.

Courtney looked down at Beau, who was watching Lisa intently from around Dora's legs. "Interesting."

Fortunately, Lisa spotted her, and Courtney waved for her to come over. "Courtney, this is just going so well! Everyone's going nuts over these sweet babies!"

"Yes, but someone here isn't having a good time." Courtney looked down at Beau. The dog had completely changed now that Lisa was nearby. Instead of quivering behind Dora, he stood up and wagged his tail happily as he watched his foster mom.

"Actually, I was going to ask you about him," Lisa said shyly. "I really fell in love with him while he stayed at my place. I already knew I liked him, but when I had to bring him back for this event, the idea of him going home with someone else just broke my heart."

Courtney gave her sidelong glance. "Are you saying what I think you're saying?"

"Yes!" she squealed with a vigorous nod of her heard. "I want to adopt him."

"Then welcome to the family," Courtney said as she gave her friend a big hug. "There's just one thing I have to ask you about," she said as she pulled back.

"Sure. Anything."

"Beau has built up a special bond with someone at the shelter. Come with me." She brought Lisa and Beau over to the cats, where she pulled the little gray kitten out of its cage. "This little guy was curled up with Beau when he escaped from his cage, and I was pretty sure that neither the dog nor the cat wanted to be separated. I knew for sure when the kitten got out a second time and was curled up pitifully against the kennel door. Would you consider taking them both?"

"Oh. I hadn't thought about a cat." Lisa took the kitten from Courtney's arms and stooped down, holding it out where Beau could see. "Is this your buddy?"

Beau responded with a fierce whisk of his brushy tail that whacked nearby patrons in the knees. He sniffed the kitten and then licked Lisa's face, whining slightly.

"I can't possibly say no to that!"

Courtney took out her cell to take pictures, but before they could finish celebrating, Detective Fletcher tapped her on the shoulder. "I'm sorry to bother you, but there's a woman here you need to talk to. I think you'd find it urgent." He stepped aside to reveal a woman in her late twenties whom Courtney didn't recognize.

"Hi, I'm Courtney. What can I do for you?" She held out her hand.

"I'm Sable, and—" The woman clapped her own hand to her mouth as tears sprang to her eyes. "Can it really be? Is that my sweet Ritz? It just can't be!"

Courtney followed her to Ritz's cage and took the cat out. "This is your cat?"

Ritz nudged his head up under her chin, but of course that only meant Sable was a good person. He treated everyone but Darryl Skaggs that way.

"I sure think so, but I'm too scared to look. Tell me, does he have a perfect little row of three black buttons on his belly? Like he's actually wearing a tuxedo?" Sable picked up the cat's front end so Courtney could see his underside.

"You know, he does!" Courtney exclaimed.

Sable practically screamed as she hugged the cat to her chest. "I can't believe this! I've been looking all over for you!"

"How long has he been missing?"

"Two years!" Sable exclaimed. "I'm a circus performer, and when I adopted him, he always wanted to help me practice my acts. I started working with him and training him, and I even got him his own segment in the show. But the crowd scared him, and he ran away. I haven't stopped looking for him, because I just knew he had to be out there somewhere. Oh, Ritz! I'll bet you've had a very interesting life, haven't you?"

"You have no idea," Courtney said. "And is his name really Ritz? That's the name animal control gave him, too."

"I guess it's just common for cats like him," Sable said with a shrug. "I just always thought of that old song when I saw him in his little tuxedo."

Mrs. Throgmorton had meandered in and overheard the conversation. "He's a circus cat? What can he do?"

"I don't know if he still can. I don't know if he remembers, but we can try. Let's start with a simple one." Sable set Ritz down on the floor and walked about ten feet away from him. The cat kept his eyes glued on her. When she snapped her fingers above her right shoulder, he instantly ran right toward her and leapt up, landing on her without any assistance.

"Is there more?" Mrs. Throgmorton pressed. "I've got a whole crowd of people down there looking to spend money. We could raise even more money for the shelter if we charge the guests+ a few bucks a piece to come be part of the show."

"Oh, Mrs. Throgmorton, I don't know if she wants to do all that," Courtney hedged, not wanting to push the reunited pair.

"We'd be thrilled!" Ritz balanced perfectly on Sable's shoulders as she followed Mrs. Throgmorton to the other room. He purred happily.

Courtney watched them go. There were so many animals who were getting homes. Charlotte had gone home with Mark Cooper. Beau and the gray kitten would have tons of fun adventures with Lisa. Ritz, after a long journey and even a little law-breaking, was finally with his person once again. As she looked around the room, she knew that wasn't the end of it. The woman holding the marmalade was filling out paperwork, as were several others. This was by far the best thing Mrs. Throgmorton ever could've done for the Curly Bay Pet Hotel and Rescue, and Courtney would have to find a way to truly thank her.

"So," Detective Fletcher said as he came up beside her, "are you going to tell that young lady that she better watch her jewelry around that cat?"

Courtney slid him a smile as she shrugged. "I'll let them get acquainted, and of course she'll still have paperwork to fill out. Then I'll let the cat out of the bag."

THANK YOU FOR CHOOSING A PUREREAD BOOK!

We hope you enjoyed the story, and as a way to thank you for choosing PureRead we'd like to send

you this free Special Edition Cozy, and other fun
reader rewards…

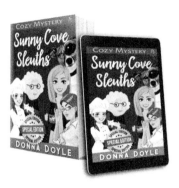

Click Here to download your free Cozy Mystery
PureRead.com/cozy

Thanks again for reading.
See you soon!

Also, be sure to get your free copy of Sunny Cove Sleuths

PureRead.com/cozy

OUR GIFT TO YOU

AS A WAY TO SAY THANK YOU WE WOULD
LOVE TO SEND YOU THIS SPECIAL EDITION
COZY MYSTERY FREE OF CHARGE.

Our Reader List is 100% FREE

Click Here to download your free Cozy Mystery
PureRead.com/cozy

At PureRead we publish books you can trust. Great tales without smut or swearing, but with all of the mystery and romance you expect from a great story.

Be the first to know when we release new books, take part in our fun competitions, and get surprise free books in your inbox by signing up to our Reader list.

As a thank you you'll receive this exclusive Special Edition Cozy available only to our subscribers...

Click Here to download your free Cozy Mystery
PureRead.com/cozy

Thanks again for reading.
See you soon!

Printed in Great Britain
by Amazon

NEW YORK

Lipstick City Guides

Debbie Lindsay

CONTENTS ➤

CONTENTS

Lipstick Building

LIPSTICK CITY GUIDES

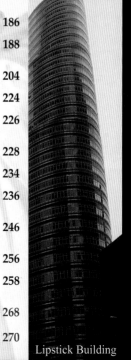

Lipstick Building

lipstickcityguides.blogspot.com

ISBN number 978-0-9570774-0-9

First Edition 2011. Published by Lipstick Publishing Limited, Somerset
LIPSTICK CITY GUIDES - NEW YORK © Deborah Lindsay Newman
A catalogue record for this book is available from the British Library.

Cover, Layout, Maps, Artwork - 21stBookDesign.blogspot.com

Printed in the UK by Gomer Press Ltd of Llandysul, Wales.

Front cover: Stilletos by Marc Jacobs, Loubinette Handbag by Christian Louboutin

A Love Affair. That's the only way I can truly describe it.

My Love Affair. With New York City.

It began in the Autumn of '91 and has kept me dangling for almost two decades. From my first glimpse I was smitten. It seduced me shamelessly and I'm now a slave to its Streets. I have visited many times since and the passion remains. The time spent writing this book both in and out of the City has taught me it's forever. So you have to know it will always leave you wanting. It may spoil you for anywhere else and you may never, ever, have enough.

Let's start with the shopping. Sheer bliss! From designer to denim. Department store to discount. Diamonds to diamonds and even more diamonds. The "Big Juicy Apple" has it all.

There are Uptown Ladies from upscale condos. Midtown Moguls from magnificent mansions. Downtown Dreamers from bohemian lofts. Styles merge. Trends mix. In a City forever changing.

Skyscrapers and brownstones sit side by side. Townhouses and lofts vie for attention. Smart meets shabby. Shiny meets sombre. And so far out meets so far in. With everything in between.

Sleek stretch limos edge shimmering stretch hummers. Throbbing their way through night after night.

Parks are many. Yellow cabs too. Weaving their way through Streets and Avenues.

Museums excel. Landmarks abound. With something for every taste.

Bars beckon. Restaurants tempt.

There is no escape….So Ladies.

Just give in. Sit back. Relax. And enjoy the ride.

For this, is New York City!

Central Park, Uptown

Times Square, Midtown

NEW YORK CENTRAL Nº31
31

South Street Seaport, Downtown

INTRODUCTION

INDEX

NEW YORK CITY (MANHATTAN)

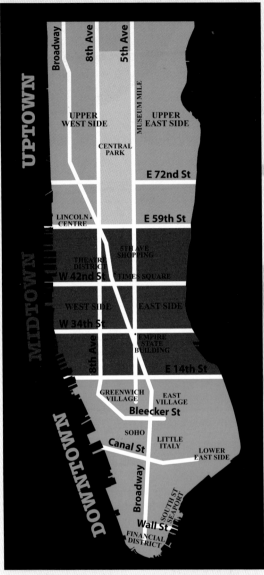

See main maps on pages 160 - 167

INTRODUCTION TO NEW YORK

In order to get you started, the next few pages will give
a brief and easy guide to New York City, its three very
distinct areas plus places of interest within each. You can
then move to the individual chapters depending on what
you hope to achieve.

There are five main Boroughs within "New York" these
being Manhattan Island, the Bronx, Brooklyn, Queens
and Staten Island. Manhattan is what most people
perceive as being "New York City" and for the purpose
of this book, is the only Borough covered in detail.

NEW YORK CITY (MANHATTAN)

UPTOWN, MIDTOWN, DOWNTOWN

Manhattan is approximately 13 miles long by 2.3 miles
wide, with a population of around 8.4 million, and is the
financial, cultural and shopping hub of New York City.

The three main areas of UPTOWN (Green),
MIDTOWN (Pink) and DOWNTOWN (Blue), are
colour coded within each chapter, and where possible,
this guide is arranged alphabetically, for ease of use.
Each of these areas is detailed on the following pages. →

UPTOWN
60th Street up to 119th Street
approximately 3.5miles long by 2 miles wide

Think "Green" for the leafy UPTOWN area of the City which includes
Central Park, the Upper West Side (UWS), Upper East Side (UES) and
Harlem (North of Central Park).

PLACES OF INTEREST

American Folk Art Museum (UWS), American Museum of Natural
History (UWS), Brownstone houses (UWS), Central Park, Cooper
Hewitt Design Museum (UES), Dakota Building (UWS), Green
Farmers Market (UWS), Guggenheim Museum (UES), Harlem (North),
Hayden Planetarium (UWS), historic townhouses (UES), Lincoln
Centre (UWS), Madison Avenue Wedding Dress Shops and Designer
Stores (UES), Museum Mile (UES) and Riverside Park (UWS).

DISTRICTS AND NEIGHBOURHOODS

Central Park, from 59th to 110th Streets and 5th to 8th Avenues
UPTOWN

Flanked by the Upper West and
Upper East Sides, Central Park is
843 acres of beautiful parkland with
around 30 statues. These include
Alice in Wonderland, Hans Christian
Andersen, Romeo and Juliet, William
Shakespeare and Thomas Moore. It
also boasts a Literary Walk, castle,
ice rink (Winter), meadow, waterfall
and zoo as well as Strawberry Fields
(with the Imagine Memorial to John
Lennon), a Wildlife Conservation
Centre and the Loeb Boathouse Restaurant. See www.centralpark.com
for more details.

Upper East Side/Museum Mile (East of Central Park), UPTOWN

Home to "Museum Mile", the Upper East Side is where you have the Cooper Hewitt National Design Museum, Frick Collection, Guggenheim, Metropolitan Museum of Art (see left), Museum for African Art, El Museo del Barrio, Museum of the City of New York and the Jewish Museum. It is also a moneyed, upmarket, residential area with swanky hotels, luxury condominiums, mansions, Madison Avenue designer shops (Oscar de La Renta, Ungaro, Prada and Valentino) and wedding dress retailers (Vera Wang, Reem Accra and Clea Colett). The Upper East Side is one of the most expensive real estate areas in the World.

Upper West Side (West of Central Park), UPTOWN

Here you will find a leafy residential area with a mix of Brownstone houses, historic, ornate apartment buildings and modern condominiums. In this neighbourhood you have the American Folk Art Museum, American Museum of Natural History, the Dakota Building (where John Lennon lost his life), Green Farmers Market, Hayden Planetarium, Lincoln Centre for the Performing Arts, Metropolitan Opera House, New York Ballet, New York Philharmonic and Riverside Park.

Harlem (North of Central Park), UPTOWN

This part of New York is often referred to as the "Black Capital of the World" and is renowned for its rich culture, jazz music, Duke Ellington Statue, the Cotton Club, Black Fashion Museum and the National Black Theatre. There are several tours on offer that you may like to take including the Historic Harlem Tour, Harlem Gospel Tour, Soul Food Tour or Hip Hop Tour (see Tours and Excursions).

MIDTOWN

59th Street down to 14th Street
approximately 2 miles long by 2.3 miles at its widest

Think **"Pink"** for the **MIDTOWN** "heart" of the City with its high rise skyscrapers, wide Avenues that stretch for miles and endless Streets that run from river to river. Here you will find Bryant Park, Chelsea, Columbus Circle, Diamond District, Fashion (Garment) Manufacturing District, 5th Avenue Shopping, 6th Avenue Entertainment, Flatiron District, Flower District, Gramercy Park, Herald Square, Music Row, Theatre District, Times Square and Union Square.

PLACES OF INTEREST

Carnegie Hall, Chelsea Art Galleries and Nightclubs, Chelsea Piers Sports Centre, Chrysler Building, CNN TV Studios, Discount Designer Stores, Empire State Building, Fashion Institute of Technology Museum, Fashion Walk of Fame, Flatiron Building, 5th Avenue Department Stores, Designer Shops and High Street Chains, Grand Central Terminal, Intrepid Sea, Air and Space Museum, Lipstick Building, Lladro Museum, Library Way, Macy's, Madison Square Garden, Madison Square Park, Museum of Art and Design (MAD), Museum of Modern Art (MOMA), NBC TV Studios, New York Public Library, Penn Street Station, Post Office, Radio City Music Hall, Rockefeller Centre, St. Patrick's Cathedral, Time Warner Shopping Centre, Trump Tower and Union Square Green Market.

DISTRICTS AND NEIGHBOURHOODS

5th Avenue, Madison Avenue, Park Avenue, Lexington Avenue and 3rd Avenue, from East 59th to East 39th Streets, MIDTOWN

This is the hub of New York's mainstream clothes shopping with Department Stores (Bergdorf Goodman [see left], Bloomingdale's and Henri Bendel), Designer Boutiques (Versace, Chanel and Dior) and well known Jewellers (Tiffany, Bulgari and Harry Winston). High Street Chains such as H & M, Zara and Quicksilver complete the picture. Look for the Lipstick Building, MOMA, St Patrick's Cathedral and Trump Tower.

6th to 8th Avenues and Broadway, from West 48th to West 59th Streets, MIDTOWN

These Avenues are where you will see Bad Boy Entertainment, Carnegie Hall, CNN TV Studios, the David Letterman Show, Love Sculpture, Museum of Art and Design (MAD), NBC TV Studios, Radio City Music Hall, Roc-A-Fella Records, Rockefeller Centre and the Time Warner Shopping Centre. Broadway Theatres also abound in and around this area.

Bryant Park area, (including Chrysler Building and Grand Central)
5th, 6th and Lexington Aves, West/East 40th to 42nd Streets, MIDTOWN

The International Photography Centre is to the North West of Bryant Park and the New York Public Library is on the Eastern edge at 5th Avenue. Head East on Library Way (East 41st Street) to see a host of pavement plaques bearing literary quotations. East 42nd Street at Park Avenue will bring you to Grand Central Terminal, whilst the Chrysler Building is on Lexington Avenue.

Chelsea, above West 14th Street to West 30th Street and between 8th and 11th Avenues, MIDTOWN

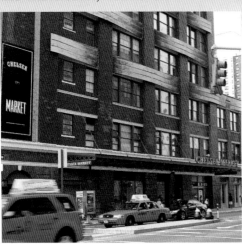

This flamboyant part of New York hugs the Hudson River (West Side) and is home to numerous art galleries, auction rooms and artists studios plus renovated townhouses and historic buildings like Cushman Row. This is also a buzzing nightlife area with restaurants, bars and the Chelsea Nightclub scene.

Columbus Circle, Central Park South, (West 59th Street) at Broadway and 8th Avenue, MIDTOWN

The South West entrance to Central Park is where you will find a monument dedicated to the explorer Christopher Columbus. You will also see the World Globe Sculpture, Trump International Hotel and the USS Maine Monument. This is the point where all distances from New York are measured.

Diamond District, along West 47th Street between 5th and 6th Avenues, MIDTOWN

Hub of the New York diamond industry, this is bling, bling, bling all the way. Many of the jewellery shops are owned by Hasidic Jews so look out for them in their dark suits, knee length coats, distinctive beards and top hats. Drag your loved ones here when you need some serious spoiling!

Fashion (Garment) Manufacturing District, 6th to 9th Avenues from West 34th to West 42nd Streets, MIDTOWN

Once the textile manufacturing capital of America, this is now filled with fashion wholesalers, designers, and showrooms. There are often "sample sales" here plus lots of shops bursting with embroidery cottons, ribbons, buttons, threads and embellishments. Keep an eye open for the 26 white bronze plaques embedded in the pavements celebrating people who have contributed to American fashion. www.fashioncenter.com

Flatiron District around Madison Square Park, 5th Avenue and Broadway, MIDTOWN

This is a relatively small neighbourhood by New York standards named after the Flatiron Building which dominates the vista down 5th Avenue. It was formerly called the Toy District because it once housed a concentration of toy manufacturers and is still today where they hold the American International Toy Fair. Other places of interest are Madison Square Park and the Museum of Sex.

Flower District, West 28th Street between 6th and 7th Avenues, MIDTOWN

Around for more than a hundred years, the "Flower District" is now confined to just a small area filled with flower wholesalers selling real and artificial blooms, plus indoor and outdoor tropical plants. This is where hotels come for their verdant foliage and is worthy of a wander for the smell alone.

Herald/Greeley Square areas, (including Empire State Building) around West 34th Street, Broadway and 6th Avenue, MIDTOWN

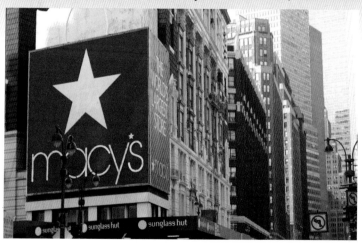

Originally named after the New York Herald newspaper (which no longer exists), Herald Square is where you will find Macy's, the Manhattan Mall, the Empire State Building, Madison Square Garden, Penn Street Station, Port Authority Bus Station and the main Post Office.

Music Row, West 48th Street between 5th and 6th Avenues, MIDTOWN

Music Row hosts a concentration of shops selling guitars, saxophones, pianos and drums, with most under the "Sam Ash" umbrella. Around for more than 80 years they are still passionate about music today and actively encourage you to spend time trying out the instruments.

Theatre District, West 42nd to West 53rd Streets from 6th to 8th Avenues around Broadway, MIDTOWN

With more than 36 theatres showing a diverse range of shows like the Lion King, Jersey Boys, Phantom of the Opera, Priscilla Queen of the Desert, Mamma Mia and Wicked, the Theatre District is always filled with life, glitz and throngs of people. Taking in a "Broadway" show is one of New York's highlights and there is a discount ticket booth right in the middle of Times Square where you can queue on the day to see what is available. Alternatively have a look at www.broadway.com for details of show times and full price tickets to purchase in advance. This site also lists "off Broadway" shows.

Times Square, West 42nd to West 47th Streets between Broadway and 7th Avenue, MIDTOWN

A busy place day and night, packed with people, dazzling neon advertisements, restaurants, clubs and shops. The buzz is literally electric as you are bombarded with flashing signs, theatre posters and fast food chains. Named after the New York "Times" building, this is where they "drop" the magnificent Waterford Crystal ball at midnight on New Years Eve. If you crave peace and quiet then look elsewhere as this is a magnet for tourists and locals alike. That said, it is definitely a "must see" area at night for the sheer "wow" factor.

Union Square/Gramercy Park Area, at Broadway and Park Avenue between East 14th and East 16th Streets, MIDTOWN

Go here for discount designer shopping where you will find Filenes Basement and T.J. Maxx. This area also hosts a Green Market each week on a Monday, Wednesday, Friday and Saturday. Walk three blocks North to Gramercy Park which is surrounded by attractive red brick townhouses built in the 1840s. If you then head to West 18th Street there is a large concentration of home and interior shops.

DOWNTOWN

13th Street down to Battery Park
approximately 3 miles long by 2.3 miles at its widest

Think "Blue" for the bohemian DOWNTOWN area of the City with water on three sides, characterised by its attractive Brownstone houses, red brick terraces, cast iron facades, converted warehouses, loft apartments, cobbled streets and leafy suburbs. Look for Battery Park, Chinatown, East Village, Financial District, Greenwich Village, Little Italy, Lower East Side, Lower Manhattan, Meatpacking District, Soho, South Street Seaport and Tribeca.

PLACES OF INTEREST

Beekman "Twisted" Tower, Brooklyn Bridge, City Hall, Ellis Island Immigration Museum, Federal Reserve, Freedom Tower, Lower East Side Tenement Museum, 9/11 Memorial and Museum, New York Stock Exchange, Skyscraper Museum, Staten Island Ferry Terminal, Statue of Liberty, St. Paul's Chapel, Titanic Memorial, Trinity Church and Wall Street.

DISTRICTS AND NEIGHBOURHOODS

Battery Park (Statue of Liberty, Staten Island Ferry, Ellis Island), Battery Place at State and Whitehall Streets, DOWNTOWN

Next to the Staten Island Ferry terminal, this riverside park has panoramic views to the Statue of Liberty and the Ellis Island Immigration Museum. Battery Park is where the history of modern day New York began with the first Dutch trading post and where today you will see the mangled Sphere sculpture which once stood in the plaza between the World Trade Centre Towers.

Chinatown, Canal Street and below, around Lafayette and Allen Streets, DOWNTOWN

This represents one of the largest Chinatowns in America and is a tangle of narrow streets offering Chinese everything. There are restaurants and bars selling all types of Asian food with shops and markets selling fake goods. Enjoy this bustling area and look out for the Dumpling Festival and Food Eating Contest.

East Village, around St. Mark's Place, Tompkins Square and the Bowery, DOWNTOWN

Famous for its punk rock, dive bars, tattoo parlours and body piercing establishments, the East Village is colourful in culture with a gritty feel to the neighbourhood reflecting its past immigrant history. Check out Tower Records and also St. Mark's Comics which featured in Sex and the City.

Financial District, around Church, Liberty, Vesey, Wall, Water and Whitehall Streets, DOWNTOWN

Filled with skyscrapers and "Suits", this is where the "money men" of the financial world do their stuff. See the Federal Reserve, New York Stock Exchange, St. Paul's Chapel (above), Trinity Church, Wall Street Bull, 9/11 Museum, Memorial and Freedom Tower, plus Century 21 discount designer store.

Greenwich Village (in and around Bleecker Street), from West 11ᵗʰ Street go East, DOWNTOWN

Tree lined streets, quaint Brownstone houses, redbrick terraces, quirky shops, popular cafes, designer stores plus music and dive bars are the mix you will find in the "Village". If Celebrity spotting is something you love to do then be on the lookout. I like this area for strolling about, having lunch and people watching.

Little Italy, above Canal Street around Mulberry and Mott Streets, DOWNTOWN

Narrow cobblestone streets and terracotta red brick buildings are the signature architecture here, once home to the many Italian immigrants who came to New York. Today it is for food lovers, bursting with Italian restaurants serving dishes of every kind. The Italian American Museum is also in this neighbourhood.

Lower East Side, around Allen, Orchard and Clinton Streets, DOWNTOWN

This is where the Lower East Side Tenement Museum resides, detailing the lives of immigrants who made their way to New York full of hopes and dreams, only to end up living in abject squalor. You will also find Katz Deli which is best known for its salt beef sandwiches and Meg Ryan's fake orgasm!

Lower Manhattan, around Brooklyn Bridge, Chambers Street, Park Row and South Street Seaport, DOWNTOWN

A walk across Brooklyn Bridge is a must for views out over the City which are breathtaking, and if you go to South Street Seaport (Pier 17), you will have equally spectacular views of the bridge itself. Here you will also find City Hall, the Beekman "Twisted" Tower, Government Offices and the New York County Court.

Meatpacking District, around West 13th Street at Gansevoort and Greenwich Streets, DOWNTOWN

The former centre of New York's meatpacking industry is now a regenerated district with converted warehouses, cobblestone streets and the Highline Elevated Park. Designer shops, graphic designers, top night clubs, swish hotels and high class restaurants make this trendy place a Celebrity favourite.

Soho (South of Houston), around Broome, Prince, Spring and Mulberry Streets, DOWNTOWN

Soho is where I head for fashionable boutiques, hip restaurants, artists' lofts and art galleries, housed in historic ornate buildings with protected cast ironwork. Restored facades and gentrification are the theme here, making it popular with Celebrities and where you will find the Dash Boutique owned by the Kardashian sisters.

Tribeca, (Triangle Below Canal), around North Moore and Franklyn Streets, DOWNTOWN

Filled with renovated lofts, updated industrial buildings and Millionaires Row, Tribeca is where the Greenwich Hotel and Tribeca Grill reside, co-owned by Robert De Niro. Just around the corner you will come across the Japanese restaurant Nobu as well as the Bubble Lounge and a range of Designer shops.

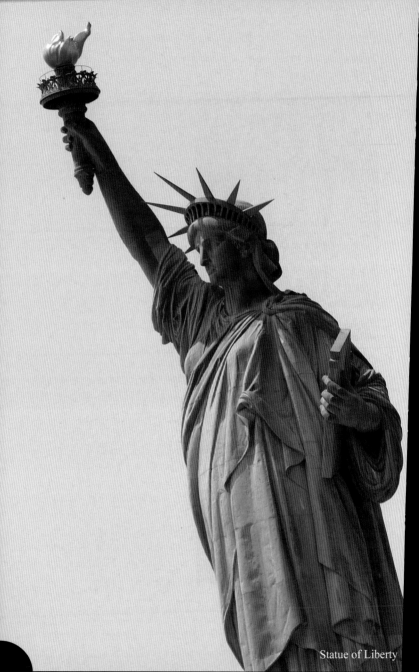

Statue of Liberty

OUTER BOROUGHS

The remaining boroughs of New York are the Bronx, Brooklyn, Queens and Staten Island which are briefly covered below, although more information can be obtained from their individual websites.

Bronx, www.ilovethebronxcom

Known for the Bartow-Pell Mansion, Bronx Zoo, New York Botanical Gardens, Pelham Bay Park, Van Cortlandt Park, Wave Hill Garden and Cultural Centre as well as the Woodlawn Cemetery. This is the Northernmost of all the boroughs and lies over the East River.

Brooklyn, www.visitbrooklyn.org

Across the East River from Manhattan on the Western side of Long Island, Brooklyn has the highest population of any borough. It is known for its Bridge, Brighton Beach, Botanic Gardens, Brooklyn Heights Promenade, Museum, Coney Island Amusement Park, Prospect Park and antique furniture.

Queens, www.queens.about.com

This borough sits on Long Island and is the largest in size. It is known for Flushing Meadow (U.S. Tennis Championships), the Hampton's, Rockaway Beach, Aqueduct Racetrack, Queens Museum and the Queens Giant, which is the tallest tree and oldest living thing in the Metropolitan area.

Staten Island, www.statenislandusa.com

With a more residential feel to it than the other Boroughs, Staten Island has leafy suburbs and is famous for its ferry that sails past the Statue of Liberty, its Zoo and the Verrazano-Narrows Bridge which you sail under when cruising into New York. Many films have also been made there over the years including The Godfather and Analyse This.

AFTERNOON TEA, COFFEE AND CHOCOLATE CAFES

AFTERNOON TEA, COFFEE AND CHOCOLATE CAFES

INDEX

If you are in need of refreshments whilst in New York you will pass many places to try on your travels, and just to whet your appetite, I have included below a few of my personal favourites. All are very different and each have their own quirky style. Throughout the City you will also find reliable options like Starbucks and Argo Cafes. It is worth remembering that most Department Stores, Museums, Hotels and Shopping Malls have either a restaurant or café on site with toilets nearby.

Alice's Tea Cup, East 64th Street between Lexington and 3rd Avenues, Upper East Side, UPTOWN

Telephone 212 486 9200 www.alicesteacup.com

With black, white, organic, green, red, decaf and tissane teas on offer, this little gem with its fantasy décor is based on Alice in Wonderland and serves a range of delicious cakes. Featured in Housewives of New York they have three locations in the City for you to try, the others being West 73rd Street and East 81st Street.

Serendipity, East 60th Street between 2nd and 3rd Avenues, Upper East Side, UPTOWN

Telephone 212 838 3531
www.serendipity.com/newyork

Opened in 1954 and technically a restaurant, it featured in "Serendipity" starring Kate Beckinsale and John Cusack. Many people go just for the desserts and the "Serendipitous" frozen hot chocolate. Be on the look out for famous faces.

City Bakery, West 18th Street between 5th and 6th Avenues, MIDTOWN

Telephone 212 366 1414 www.thecitybakery.com

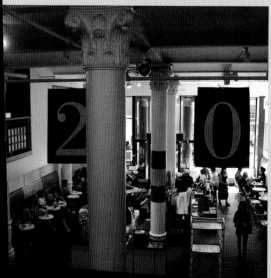

Each year City Bakery holds a "Hot Chocolate Festival" with many varieties rotating throughout the day, so for all those with a sweet tooth keep an eye on their website. Occasionally they also have a "Night of Knitting" which might just appeal to all you knitting fans.

31

L.A. Burdick Chocolate Café, East 20th Street between 5th Avenue and Broadway, MIDTOWN
Telephone 212 796 0143 www.burdickchocolate.com/newyork

Attention all chocolate lovers, head down to this café for a feast of goodies where not only can you buy delicious bars of the stuff, but you can sip it in their signature hot chocolate. Just to complete the picture why not add a little alcohol or munch on a yummy pastry.

Lady Mendyl's Tea Salon, The Inn at Irving Place between East 17th and East 18th Streets, Gramercy Park, MIDTOWN
Telephone 212 533 4466 www.innatirving.com

Clotted cream, caviar and strawberries await your taste buds in this famous Victorian tea salon. Step back in time with their five course afternoon tea in an elegant and romantic setting. Tucked away in Irving Place, this salon is delightful with its antique furniture, bone china and white table cloths.

Also try: Knit New York, Palm Court at the Fairmont Plaza Hotel and the Waldorf Astoria

Cacao Bar and Tea Salon at Marie Belle, Broome Street between Wooster Street and West Broadway, Soho, DOWNTOWN
Telephone 212 925 6999 www.mariebelle.com

Offering chocolates and pastries of varied shapes and flavours, this ornate tea salon nestles in the midst of a turquoise chocolate shop, in the fashionable district of Soho. What a way for chocolate lovers to spend an indulgent few hours whilst resting those weary feet after hitting the shops.

Magnolia Bakery, Bleecker Street at West 11th Street, Greenwich Village, DOWNTOWN
Telephone 212 462 2572 www.magnoliabakery.com

Frequent haunt of Carrie Bradshaw and friends in Sex and the City, this bakery has been here since 1996 and serves delicious cupcakes and coffee. Look out for their special events like Peanut Butter Month and Fashion's Night Out.

L.A. Burdick Chocolate Café

Magnolia Bakery

Cacao Bar and Tea Salon

Lady Mendyl's Tea Salon

33

34   Salon de Ning, Peninsula Hotel

BARS, CLUBS AND PUBS

INDEX

New York is filled with bars, pubs and clubs of every type, so included are a variety of styles and prices, from elegant and sophisticated to spit and sawdust with some just floating in between. There are those that entertain Celebrities, others with live music, cabaret or have spectacular views and some which are classic American hotel bars. As an alternative you could take a Nightlife Tour with included transportation between bars and clubs. Establishments which entertain Celebrities will generally have a strict door policy for entry but if you are dressed to the nines, blinged to the eyeballs and full of charm then who knows!

Useful Websites: www.clubplanet.com, www.clubzone.com

BAR WITH A VIEW

The Roof Garden, Metropolitan Art Museum, 5th Avenue between East 82nd and East 83rd Streets, Upper East Side, UPTOWN
Telephone 212 535 7710 www.metmuseum.org

The views across Central Park from this seasonal rooftop bar are stunning, as are the art exhibits dotted around, which change constantly. This is a relaxing place to unwind after a stroll around the Museum or to watch the distant sun set.

CABARET CLUB

Bemelman's Bar, Carlyle Hotel, East 76th Street between Madison and Park Avenues, Upper East Side, UPTOWN
Telephone 212 744 1600 www.thecarlyle.com

A legendary bar which has played host to socialites, politicians and movie stars, maintains its Art Deco theme, and still serves cocktails today which date back to the 1860s Prohibition era. Try the Jamaican Firefly, Gin-Gin Mule and Whisky Smash. You will also find the Café Carlyle within this Hotel.

CELEBRITY SPOTTING

Mark's Bar, The Mark Hotel, East 77th Street at Madison Avenue, Upper East Side, UPTOWN
Telephone 212 744 4300 www.themarkhotel.com

Situated within a trendy hotel and serving signature cocktails like the Lychee Raspberry Bellini, this bar has an exotic animal print décor, is open to non residents and would be perfect if you want to drink alone or with friends.

Also try: Mo Bar at the Mandarin Oriental

Photo Courtesy of The Mark Hotel

For a great way to see a different side to New York head for one of the many bars with spectacular skyline views. Whilst some are only open seasonally, others have outdoor heaters so you can enjoy them year round and although situated within hotels, non residents are normally welcome.

**Bookmarks Rooftop Lounge and Bar, Library Hotel,
Madison Avenue at East 41ˢᵗStreet,** MIDTOWN
Telephone 1-800 480 9545 or 212 983 4500 www.libraryhotel.com/newyork

A delightful rooftop bar and lounge with lovely views sits atop this charming hotel. Here you can relax with a cocktail in either the Writers Den or Poetry Garden. It is equally cosy on a cold winters day where you might find an open fire in the hearth or you can enjoy the outdoor terrace.

**Mad 46, The Roosevelt Hotel, East 45ᵗʰ Street between Park and
Madison Avenues,** MIDTOWN
Telephone 212 885 6095 or 866 530 9379 www.theroosevelthotel.com/newyork

On the 19ᵗʰ floor of the Roosevelt Hotel this open air bar is stylish and contemporary with music, cocktails and light bites to eat. Great for an early evening drink overlooking the City as the sun disappears into night.

R Lounge, Renaissance Hotel (Marriott), 7th Avenue at West 48th Street, Times Square, MIDTOWN

Telephone 212 765 7676 or 212 261 5200 www.rennaissancenewyork.com/marriott

A stylish first floor bar awaits with pink, orange and zebra print furnishings. Overlooking Times Square you can gaze out at neon signs and the hustle below whilst relaxing with a Sparkling Strawberry Cosmo or Red Stag Manhattan cocktail.

Salon de Ning Rooftop Bar, Peninsula Hotel, 5th Avenue at East 55th Street, MIDTOWN

Telephone 212 956 2888 www.peninsula.com/newyork

This smart rooftop bar is where I would always head to watch the night lights of New York start to glow. It has a black and red interior with far reaching views down 5th Avenue from its open terrace. Soft candlelight and rich Asian influences complete the mood.

The Terrace Bar, Novotel, West 52nd Street at Broadway,
MIDTOWN

Telephone 917 472 9662 or 212 315 0100 www.novotelnewyork.com/skydeck

The views from this open air terrace are striking as you look down 8th Avenue to Times Square and the Theatre District. The outdoor spaces glow with subtle mauve lighting whilst the stylish indoor area is cocooned behind ceiling to floor windows.

Also try: The View (revolving bar and restaurant) at the Marriott Marquis Hotel.

CELEBRITY SPOTTING BARS AND CLUBS

Look out for Celebrities at these establishments but try to be cool if you spot one, though nothing guaranteed of course. If you cannot be cool at least be classy and dress in your Sunday best as some of these bars have rigid door policies.

Jade and Rose Bars, Gramercy Park Hotel, Lexington Avenue at East 21st Street, Gramercy Park MIDTOWN

Telephone 212 920 3300 www.gramercyparkhotel.com/newyork

Both the Rose Bar with its soft hues of pink, and the Jade Bar in vibrant shades of green, blue and red, have been known to entertain Celebrities so you never know who you might see at the next table. Bookings are required to even get in the door after 9pm and smart dress is the norm.

Marquee, 10th Avenue between West 26th and West 27th Streets, Chelsea, MIDTOWN

Telephone 646 473 0202 www.marqueeny.com

A "star" gazers delight, this club lounge has always been popular with the jet set crowd and its stylish surroundings gives a hint as to why. Don't be disappointed if none come out to play though.

The Terrace Bar, Novotel

Jade Bar

Rose Bar

1 Oak, West 17ᵗʰ Street between 9ᵗʰ and 10ᵗʰ Avenues, Chelsea, MIDTOWN
Telephone 212 242 1111 www.1oaknyc.com

Inspired by the heyday of Manhattan's nightlife, this ultra exclusive
lounge in Chelsea from hospitality entrepreneurs Scott Sartiano, Richie
Akiva and Ronnie Madra features an elaborate interior design with
ostrich leather banquettes and a wall made of 10,000 wooden letters.
1 Oak regularly hosts events featuring an eclectic mix of Hollywood's
hottest stars like Rihanna, Katy Perry, Rachel Bilson and Chloe Sevigny.
Information courtesy of 1Oak.

Also try: 40/40 Bar, Pacha and the Stone Rose Lounge

CLASSIC AMERICAN HOTEL BARS

These bars are situated within quality hotels and are generally
sophisticated places to enjoy a quiet cocktail, whilst drinking in the
atmosphere and glimpsing moneyed New Yorkers at play.

**Bull & Bear Bar, Waldorf Astoria Hotel, Park Avenue between East
49ᵗʰ and East 50ᵗʰ Streets,** MIDTOWN
Telephone 212 872 1275 or 212 872 4900 www.waldorfastoria.com

Described by the New York Times as 'one of the three great classic bars
in the world', this is where slick "Suits" (Gordon Gecko look-a-like
businessmen) wind down on a Friday evening. Watch as they strut their
stuff keeping a close eye on the share price ticker tape.

King Cole Bar, St. Regis Hotel, East 55th Street at 5th Avenue, MIDTOWN

Telephone 212 753 4500 www.starwoodhotels.com/newyork

Featured in The Devil Wears Prada, this is a New York institution where Bloody Mary's are the signature drink. Admire the Maxfield Parrish mural of Old King Cole behind the sleek mahogany bar and relax as you enjoy a pre or post dinner cocktail in ambient surroundings.

JAZZ AND BLUES CLUB

For a class act in jazz, rhythm and blues try out this legendary club and slip into the groove.

BB King Blues Club and Grill, West 42nd Street between 7th and 8th Avenues, MIDTOWN

Telephone 212 997 4144

Artists such as Al Green, Dionne Warwick and Nils Lofgren have performed here making this Blues at its very best. Visit their in-house

restaurant Lucille's for Sunday brunch or they are open throughout the week for dinner but you will need to book in advance.

Chelsea Nightclub Tour or VIP Nightclub Entry, Chelsea, MIDTOWN
Telephone 888 491 9824 www.unclesamsnewyorktours.com

The Chelsea Nightclub Tour takes you into New York's nightlife with a tour guide and glass of bubbly. The VIP Nightclub Entry on the other hand lets you party like a Celebrity with queue jumping, a nightclub host and a reserved table at a top club. There is a strict dress code for both Tours with cocktail dresses and heels for Women plus jacket and tie for Men. Check the website for up to date prices and details.

Party Ride, MIDTOWN
Telephone 866 275 5466 www.thepartyride.com

This is a private coach hire company who will provide transportation for your Group whether celebrating a Bachelorette party, organising a bar and nightclub tour or just a birthday bash. Contact them to put together your tailor made arrangements.

Blue Bar, Algonquin Hotel, West 44th Street between 5th and 6th Avenues, MIDTOWN

Telephone 212 840 6800
www.algonquinhotel.com/bluebar

Look out for the "blue glow" as you walk down West 44th Street and enter this legendary bar for a cocktail. You might even end up with a $10,000 "Proposal Martini" complete with diamond ring! Drop those hints.

44 Bar, Royalton Hotel, West 44th Street between 5th and 6th Avenues, MIDTOWN

Telephone 212 869 4400
www.royaltonhotel.com/44bar

This sexy bar is filled with dark corners, dimly lit tables, brown leather sofas and chocolate coloured walls. A great place to take that special person for a quiet, romantic drink or something to eat.

Shoreham Bar, Shoreham Hotel, West 55th Street between 5th and 6th Avenues, MIDTOWN

Telephone 212 247 6700 www.shorehamhotel.com/bar

The turquoise and green colour scheme, peach lighting, clever use of glass and modern look, combine to make this a lovely space to enjoy a drink and as night falls it has a distinctly underwater feel.

Also try: Campbell Apartment at Grand Central Terminal

SPORTS BAR

Mickey Mantles Sports Bar, Central Park South (West 59th Street) between 5th and 6th Avenues, MIDTOWN

Telephone 212 688 7777 www.mickeymantles.com

This smart bar with live radio shows, screenings of baseball matches, sports memorabilia and occasional Celebrity sightings, was a haunt of Carrie Bradshaw in Sex and the City. Remember where there are sports bars there are generally lots of men!

Also try: Pete's Tavern

BAR WITH A VIEW

Beekman Beer Garden "Beach Club" (seasonal), Pier 17, South Street Seaport (Brooklyn Bridge side), Lower Manhattan, DOWNTOWN

Telephone 212 896 4600 www.beekmanbeergarden.com

With sand under your feet and staggering views out over the East River and Brooklyn Bridge, this outdoor bar tries hard to emulate a beach scene, with barbeques, bands playing blues and of course beer!

Also try: Harbour Lights and the Black Harp.

**Café Wha? MacDougal Street
between Bleecker and West
3rd Streets, Greenwich Village,
DOWNTOWN**

Telephone 212 254 3706
www.cafewha.com

Original sixties beat café where it is
said Bruce Springsteen, Bob Dylan
and Jimi Hendrix played in their
early years. The music is jazz, soul
or reggae and you may be surprised
at who pops in to join the party.

**Provocateur, Hotel Gansevoort, 9th Avenue at Hudson Street
between West 13th and Gansevoort Streets, Meatpacking District,
DOWNTOWN**

Telephone 212 929 9036 www.provocateurny.com

A luxury club elusive and expensive which could see you blow hundreds
or even thousands so be prepared. The lighting is soft and purple, the
door staff tough, the dance poles inviting and the DJ's up to the minute.

Also try: the Provocateur Café

**Tenjune, Little West 12th Street between 9th Avenue and
Washington Street, Meatpacking District, DOWNTOWN**
Telephone 646 624 2410 www.tenjunenyc.com

Featuring a DJ performance stage and favoured by the "in"
crowd, this club operates a tough entry policy which could
mean some serious grovelling. The décor is plush with velvet
seats, padded walls and marble fireplaces and the dress code
is classy to stand even a small chance of getting inside.

Also try: Gold Bar in Nolita

ELEGANT AND SOPHISTICATED

Bubble Lounge, West Broadway at North Moore and Franklyn Streets, Tribeca, DOWNTOWN
Telephone 212 431 3433 www.bubblelounge.com

Devoted to Champagne and nestled just steps from "Millionaires Row", this bar was never going to be cheap. There are around 300 varieties of bubbly plus a selection of cocktails, cognacs, oysters and caviar to tempt your palate.

Also try: Kiss and Fly in the Meatpacking District

ENGLISH STYLE PUBS

White Horse Tavern, Hudson Street at West 11th Street, Greenwich Village, DOWNTOWN
Telephone 212 989 3956 www.whitehorsetavern.com

Once frequented by the poet Dylan Thomas, this is one of the oldest bars in New York. Loved by tourists and locals alike, look out for his portrait on the wall and share in a piece of literary history when you drink or eat in this quaint pub.

Also try: Red Lion

JAZZ AND BLUES CLUB

Blue Note Jazz Club, West 3rd Street between 6th Avenue and MacDougal Street, Greenwich Village, DOWNTOWN
Telephone 212 475 8592
www.bluenote.net

Small and intimate, this famous Club opened in 1981 and is still today dedicated to all things Jazz! Try the Late Night Groove Series on Friday and Saturday nights or the Sunday Brunch, but book well in advance.

Also try: Arthur's Tavern and the Village Vanguard both in Greenwich Village

LATIN, R & B, AND HIP HOP CLUB

Sounds of Brazil, Varick Street at West Houston Street, Soho, DOWNTOWN
Telephone 212 243 4940 www.sobs.com

This Club is all about live music with Brazilian artists at the forefront. It is renowned for its influence on music trends and embraces a range of sounds including R & B, Hip Hop and Caribbean.

LESBIAN CLUBS

Cubby Hole, West 12th Street at West 4th Street, West Village, DOWNTOWN
Telephone 212 243 9041 www.cubbyholebar.com

Serving cocktails and weekly specials, this Lesbian bar holds a Cubby Girl Pageant on the first Wednesday of every month where the winner receives a $50 bar tab.

Also try: Henrietta Hudson and The Stonewall Inn

Useful Website: www.lesbianherstoryarchives.org

MUSIC AND DIVE BARS

Back Fence Bar, Bleecker and Thompson Streets, Greenwich Village, DOWNTOWN

Telephone 212 475 9221 www.thebackfenceonline.com

A tiny, relaxed, casual bar with a big atmosphere and live bands. Here since the Forties, it has hosted some iconic figures in the music industry even claiming that Bob Dylan once busked for pence outside its doors. Open until the wee hours, this has always been a personal favourite and I would like to say a special thank you to the barmaid Katherine Kaspar who helped with my research and poured a mean Cosmopolitan!

Kenny's Castaways Bar, Bleecker Street near Thompson Street, Greenwich Village, DOWNTOWN

Telephone 917 475 1323 www.kennyscastaways.com

Opened in 1967 by Patrick Kenny, this bar has a history which dates back to the 1820s when it was a brothel. Today it is aglow with purple, blue and red lights and has seen its share of famous musicians. Head to this easy going bar for fun and music.

Mulberry Street Bar, Mulberry Street between Broome and Grand Streets, Little Italy, DOWNTOWN

Telephone 212 226 9345 www.mulberrystreetbar.com

This famous bar has featured in many films and television programmes over the years like Law & Order, Donnie Brasco and The Soprano's. James Gandolfinho (Tony Soprano in the Soprano's) has made a guest appearance at this bar in the past so keep a look out for Celebrities.

Onieal's Bar, Grand Street at Baxter Street, Soho, DOWNTOWN

Telephone 212 941 9119 www.onieals.com

This is where Aidan and Steve had their bar (Scout) in Sex and the City and is one of the places you visit when you take the SATC Tour. Enjoy a Cosmopolitan, listen to the music and look out for the beautifully carved ceiling while you sit at the bar and watch New Yorkers relax.

Kenny's Castaways Bar

Mulberry Street Bar

Back Fence Bar

Onieal's Bar

bliss spa

BEAUTY SPAS, COSMETIC STORES, HAIRDRESSERS

INDEX

For all your pampering needs, these Beauty Spas and Cosmetic Stores offer manicures, pedicures, make up tuition, botox, massages and facials if you would like a treat when away.

You may also feel like getting your hair cut, styled or highlighted so a few hair salons are included to add that touch of glamour for a night out. However some are high end establishments who list Celebrities amongst their clients so prices will be steep, but then a girl deserves a treat every now and then!

COSMETIC STORE

The Body Shop, Lexington Avenue at East 61st Street, Upper East Side, UPTOWN

Telephone 212 755 7851 www.thebodyshop.com/newyork

If you prefer to buy your cosmetics from a familiar brand then the Body Shop stores (of which there are several in New York) offer everything you know and love.

BEAUTY SPAS

Bliss 49, Lexington Avenue at East 49th Street, MIDTOWN

Telephone 877 862 5477 www.blissworld.com

Bliss salons are much sought after with their in-house skincare products, ambient surroundings, serious pampering and spectacular prices. Try the "eyes have it", "lip service" and "the love handler" treatments.

J Sisters, West 57th Street between 5th and 6th Avenues, MIDTOWN

Telephone 212 750 2485 www.jsisters.com

These seven, slick, Brazilian wax divas are known throughout the City for their legendary skills with a wax pot. They will however leave very little to the imagination! Prepare for a wax like no other.

Also try: Bliss 57, Bliss Soho, Smooth Synergy Cosmedical Spa, Sothy's Institute and Susan Ciminelli

Body Shop

Susan Ciminelli Beauty Salon

COSMETIC STORE

Sephora, 5th Avenue between East 48th and East 49th Streets, MIDTOWN
Telephone 212 980 6534 www.sephora.com/newyork

Well known retailer of cosmetics with great in store events showcasing new products, promotions and trends. Daily beauty studios for make up lessons are available at the 5th Avenue and Times Square shops.

HAIRDRESSERS AND BLOW DRY SALONS

Sassoon Salon, West 18th Street between 5th and 6th Avenues, MIDTOWN
Telephone 212 229 2200 www.sassoon.com

Since he opened his first salon in the Sixties, the name Vidal Sassoon has been linked to all things creative when it comes to hair design, which started with his geometric bob. Go here for proven style and quality.

Also try: Blow Styling Salon and Sally Herschberger Hair Salon

COSMETIC STORES

Mac Cosmetics, 113 Spring Street between Greene and Mercer Streets, Soho, DOWNTOWN

Telephone 212 334 4641
www.maccosmetics.com

Loved by Celebrities and selling quality cosmetics, this stunning store in the heart of Soho offers makeovers and tips from helpful staff, in surroundings that are a vision to behold!

Also try: Kiehls in the West Village

HAIRDRESSERS

Bumble and Bumble, West 13th Street between 9th Avenue and Washington Street, Meatpacking District, DOWNTOWN
Telephone 917 606 5000 or 212 521 5000 www.bumbleandbumble.com

Celebrity stylists to the stars and featured on "Queer Eye for the Straight Guy", be prepared to pay handsomely for a cut in this top salon. Alternatively you may want to check out their in house hair Academy.

Also try: Serge Normant at John Frieda

TIFFANY & CO

There have been countless
books and songs written about
New York whether historical, factual,
fictional or romantic, and listed here are just a few to tempt you.
If you are looking for an out and out love story try "The Flower
Garden" by Margaret Pemberton to truly warm your heart. Although
it is more than 30 years old, it moves me to tears every time.

BOOKS ABOUT THE HISTORY OF NEW YORK

Gotham, A History of New York City to 1898
by Edwin G. Burrows and Mike Wallace

Inside the Apple, A Streetwise History of New York
by Michelle and James Nevius

The Historical Atlas of New York City by Eric Homburger

BOOKS SET IN NEW YORK

A Tree Grows in Brooklyn by Betty Smith

Bonfire of the Vanities by Tom Wolfe

← **Breakfast at Tiffany's** by Truman Capote

Catcher in the Rye by J. Salinger

Christmas at Tiffany's by Karen Swan

Cotton Comes to Harlem by Chester Himes

Fairytale of New York by Miranda Dickenson

New York by Edward Rutherford

The Complete Prose by Woody Allen

The Flower Garden by Margaret Pemberton

The Jewels of Manhattan by Carmen Reid

Washington Square by Henry James

NEW YORK MAGAZINES

New York has every magazine type imaginable and some you can even order before you go. They offer a real insight into the lifestyle, fashion and Celebrities of the Big Apple and make interesting reading whilst away. See www.magazinecity.com to order them in the UK, although you may pay a premium.

American Vogue - For over 100 years Vogue has set one of the highest standards in Women's magazines offering its readers articles on style, fashion, beauty, Celebrities and fitness.

Celebrity Hairstyles - As its title suggests this publication delves into the hairstyles of Celebrities offering style secrets, hints and tips for your own hair, while keeping you up to date with the current trends.

Cloth, Paper and Scissors - A respected American quilting magazine which can be bought in England.

House Magazine - This design magazine is for the New York metropolitan area and has features on interiors, architecture and social events from Long Island to Westchester.

More Magazine - Aimed mainly at women who are 40 and over, this covers fashion, health and beauty with articles on starting a business later in life, how to get through the loss of a loved one and many more relevant topics.

New York Magazine - A variety of subjects are debated here from news, features and beauty to fashion, health and weddings.

Quilting Arts - A contemporary quilting magazine offering something different for its readers.

Star Magazine - If Celebrities are your passion then look no further as this magazine gives all the insider gossip, photos, fashion and beauty secrets of your favourite stars.

The New Yorker - A weekly magazine which includes features on the arts, culture, humour, poetry and talk of the town.

Women's Wear Daily - www.wwd.com - An online daily publication about Celebrities, beauty and retail, plus all the gossip from New York fashion week and reviews from fashion shows around the world.

Also try: Allure Magazine

SONGS ABOUT NEW YORK

How many songs have you heard in your lifetime about New York? It has always been a popular choice amongst musicians and I guess a measure of just how much people love and are fascinated by the "Big Apple".

Across 110th Street - Bobby Womack

Angel of Harlem - U2

Arthur's Theme - Christopher Cross

Bleecker Street - Simon and Garfunkel

Breakfast at Tiffany's - Deep Blue Something

Brooklyn's Finest - Jay-Z feat. the Notorious B.I.G.

Cali to New York - Black Eyed Peas

Christmas in the City - Mary J. Blige

42nd Street - Written by Al Dubin

I Love New York - Madonna

Incident on 57th Street - Bruce Springsteen

Jenny from the Block - Jennifer Lopez

Kitty's Back - Bruce Springsteen

New York - Norah Jones

New York City - John Lennon and Yoko Ono

New York is a Woman - Suzanne Vega

New York Mining Disaster - Bee Gees

New York Moon - Louise Redknapp

New York, New York - Frank Sinatra

St. Patrick's Cathedral, East 51st Street at 5th Avenue, Midtown

BUILDINGS AND LANDMARKS

INDEX

This chapter features a selection of buildings and landmarks located throughout the City, noted for their outstanding architectural beauty, historical significance and stunning impact. Take time out to ponder each and every unique piece of New York's heritage.

Alice in Wonderland Statue, Central Park, 59th to 110th Streets from 5th to 8th Avenues, UPTOWN

Central Park has an abundance of landmarks all to commemorate various people and events including Shakespeare, Hans Christian Andersen, Christopher Columbus, Thomas Moore and the Alice in Wonderland Statue. Also look out for the Literary Walk, Bethesda Fountain and Belvedere Castle.

Dakota Building, Corner of West 72nd Street and Central Park West, Upper West Side, UPTOWN

The Dakota building has played host to many famous residents during its time including John Lennon, and where he lost his life in 1980. Yoko Ono still retains an apartment there overlooking Strawberry Fields and the Imagine Memorial in Central Park.

Chrysler Building, Lexington Avenue at East 42nd Street, MIDTOWN

A shimmering shrine of stainless steel, this is an imposing tribute to Art Deco in its purest form. It has red Moroccan marble walls and sienna coloured floors in the lobby, whilst its spire is adorned with gargoyles and Chrysler radiator caps. For great views and pictures of the Chrysler Building head to the top of the Rockefeller Centre at sunset.

Columbus Circle Monument, Broadway at 8th Avenue and West 59th Street, MIDTOWN

Dedicated to the explorer Christopher Columbus, this monument was erected in 1892 on the 400 year anniversary of his landing in America. It is also the point at which all distances from New York are measured.

Dakota Building

Alice

Columbus Circle

Chrysler Building

←Empire State Building, 5th Avenue between West 33rd and West 34th Streets, MIDTOWN

Telephone 212 736 3100 www.esbnyc.com

Completed in 1931, and more than a quarter of a mile high, this offers spectacular views day and night from its lofty observation decks. Check out the art deco lift doors and relive the "Sleepless in Seattle" moment when Tom Hanks and Meg Ryan finally meet on the 86th floor.

Grand Central Terminal, East 42nd Street at Park Avenue, MIDTOWN

Telephone 212 340 2583 www.grandcentralterminal.com

Built in 1871, Grand Central has a striking Beaux-art frontage, vaulted ceilings, Tiffany glass clock and signs of the Zodiac, which combine to make this station an architectural treasure. Visit at night and gaze skywards at the illustrated ceiling or try one of the many restaurants and cafes including Michael Jordan's Steakhouse.

Lipstick Building, 3rd Avenue between East 53rd and East 54th Streets, MIDTOWN

With smooth oval curves, red granite, steel and glass, this building is so called because it distinctly resembles a giant tube of lipstick with its telescopic form and red façade.

Louis Vuitton - Moet Hennessy Tower, East 57th Street between 5th and Madison Avenues, MIDTOWN

←A graceful, curving steel and translucent glass monument, with stylish lines which reach for the sky. Topped with a two storey high glass cube, it has hosted many a fashion party in its time.

Love Sculpture, 6th Avenue at West 55th Street, MIDTOWN

Sculpted by Robert Indiana, this symbolic piece of pop art is one of New York's most photographed landmarks. People sit, stand and even climb on top to achieve the best shot. Go as the sun is setting and the night lights of New York are starting to twinkle.

Mercedes Benz Manhattan, Park Avenue at East 56th Street, MIDTOWN
Telephone 1-800 798 4065 www.mb-manhattan.com

Designed by Frank Lloyd Wright in 1954, this building is now home to the iconic Mercedes Benz brand. Drool over dream cars in this historic space with its distinctive curved walls and mirrored interior.

Rockefeller Centre, 6th Avenue between West 48th and West 51st Streets, MIDTOWN

Telephone 212 332 6868 or 212 632 3975 (information line)
www.rockefellercenter.com

Travel 70 floors up to the "Top of the Rock" with its all glass observation deck for amazing views out over the City. When back on the ground find the various monuments in and around the Rockefeller Plaza such as Atlas carrying the heavens on his shoulders and the gold statue of Prometheus.

Trump Tower and Clock, 5th Avenue between East 56th and East 57th Streets, MIDTOWN

Telephone 212 832 2000
www.trumpintl.com

An orange marble monument to Donald Trump, this is a towering symbol of possibility. Trump became a billionaire, lost it all, then triumphed again. Don't forget to have your photo taken in front of the "Trump" clock outside.

Also look out for: St. Patrick's Cathedral - see the image at the beginning of this chapter.

BUILDINGS AND LANDMARKS

Beekman "Twisted" Tower, Beekman Street, Lower Manhattan, DOWNTOWN

With a distinct style and glimmering shell, this "Twisted" tower is an unusual addition to the New York skyline and a striking example of modern day architecture. Head to Brooklyn Bridge for a great picture as you look back towards the Financial District.

Brooklyn Bridge,➜ Chambers Street Station at Park Row, Lower Manhattan, DOWNTOWN

Opened in 1883 after ten years of construction, Brooklyn Bridge was considered to be one of the modern engineering achievements of its time. This vast gothic creation attracts many tourists and is the place to go for great views over the City, Lower Manhattan, the East River and Brooklyn.

Freedom Tower, 9/11 Memorial and Museum, Liberty Street at Vesey Street, Financial District, DOWNTOWN

www.national911memorial.org

As part of the 9/11 Memorial, the Freedom Tower will have an observation deck at the same height as World Trade Centre 2. There are also two pools (North and South) which are part of the Memorial Garden sitting in the exact footprint of the original Twin Towers, with a named entry for every person who died that day. The Museum itself will open in 2013. I took this photo from inside a building opposite the site and was struck by the eerie sweep of colour which appears to be emanating from the Freedom Tower itself.

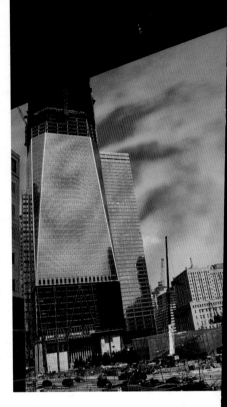

New York Stock Exchange, Wall Street, Financial District, DOWNTOWN
Telephone 212 656 3000 www.nyse.com

The New York Stock Exchange is the financial hub of the City and where the movers and shakers of the money markets strut their stuff. See the "Suits" who work at this powerful institution as you walk through Wall Street and visit nearby Trinity Church.

Statue of Liberty in New York Harbour (Southwest of DOWNTOWN)

A reminder of the American Declaration of Independence, the Statue of Liberty is modelled on the ancient Goddess "Libertas", whilst the seven rays on her crown represent the seven seas and continents of the World.

Titanic Memorial Lighthouse and Time Ball, at Pearl and Fulton Streets, South Street Seaport, DOWNTOWN

Erected one year after the sinking of the Titanic on 15th April 1912, this monument is in memory of all those who died that night and a poignant reminder of that dreadful tragedy.

Wall Street Bull (sometimes known as Charging Bull), Lower Broadway at Morris Street, Financial District, DOWNTOWN

This 7,000lb bronze bull designed by Arturo di Modeca in 1989 sits on Lower Broadway and legend has it that if you touch its "Jewels" you will be the next billionaire of New York. As you can imagine there is a constant stream of people willing to try!

Also look out for: St. Paul's Chapel

BUS LANE
🚌 BUS LANE
BUSES ONLY
7AM-6PM
↙ MON-FRI

401
Broadway

COOP

MOKA

Girl riding Segway Scooter on Broadway

For those of us who travel the World on business, there are certain criteria which are essential to make the trip a success. The hotels here have been carefully chosen to offer every comfort for your stay with a wide range of facilities and services allowing you to best utilise your time.

If you are a Soroptimist you might want to contact the New York branch prior to your stay - Email address - president@sinyc.org **or** www.siny.org **or** webmaster@sinyc.org

Trump International Hotel 5* - One Central Park West at West 61st Street, Upper West Side, UPTOWN
Telephone 212 299 1000 www.trumpintl.com

Situated at the South West corner of Central Park, this hotel caters well for the business traveller. There is a 665 square foot meeting room which allows teleconferencing plus high speed internet access, LCD projection monitor and a private kitchen. The 176 bedrooms and suites are also thoughtfully equipped with high speed wireless internet, in-room laptop computer (on request), iPod docking station, three dual line phones plus personalised stationery and business cards (on request). There is also a fully functional business centre. In-room dining is available 24 hours, with an overnight laundry and dry cleaning service completing the picture. As with all Trump Hotels you will find an array of leisure facilities on site from an indoor heated pool and spa to the world renowned Jean Georges restaurant.

THINGS TO DO AND SEE IN UPTOWN

Central Park, Dakota Building (UWS), Hayden Planetarium and American Museum of Natural History (UWS), Lincoln Centre (UWS), Madison Avenue Designer shops and Wedding Dress retailers (UES), Metropolitan Opera House (UWS) and Museum Mile (UES).

***

Library Hotel 4* - Madison Avenue at East 41st Street, MIDTOWN
Telephone 212 983 4500 www.thelibraryhotel.com

A charming, deluxe 60 roomed traditional hotel tucked away off Madison Avenue. The rooms are equipped with high speed internet access, data ports, speaker phones, bathrobes, hairdryers and in room safes. There is a meeting room for up to 12 people, a library with over 6000 books and a rooftop conservatory. A European style breakfast, wine reception and 24 hour tea/coffee is included for all guests and the New York Sports Club which is close by, offers complimentary privileges for people staying at this hotel.

New York Palace Hotel 4½* - Madison Avenue between East 50th and East 51st Streets, MIDTOWN
Telephone 212 888 7000 www.newyorkpalace.com

The 897 rooms of this smart hotel, are decorated in soft muted shades and offer guests a full sized desk, broadband internet access and high speed wireless plus three dual line telephones with voicemail. There is a spa and

fitness centre within the hotel plus an outdoor courtyard, an American brasserie and a Michelin starred restaurant. A full business centre and multilingual concierges are also available for guests.

THINGS TO DO AND SEE IN MIDTOWN

Bryant Park, Chrysler Building, Diamond District, Empire State Building, 5th Avenue Shopping, Grand Central Terminal, Macy's, New York Public Library, Rockefeller Centre, Times Square and the Theatre District.

***

Andaz Wall Street Hotel (Hyatt) 4 ½* - Wall Street at Water Street, Financial District, DOWNTOWN

Telephone 212 590 1234
www.newyork.wallstreet.andazhyatt.com/hyatthotels

This smart Wall Street hotel is in the heart of New York's financial hub, making it perfect for those who need to be near the Stock Market. It has a bar, business centre, currency exchange, high speed internet connection, hostess check-in (no queuing at reception),

in room dining and gym (both 24 hours), lounge, meeting rooms, restaurant and spa. The 345 rooms are modern in design and sharp in décor with a work desk, large safe for laptop storage, voicemail, data port, 24 hour concierge, hairdryer and robes.

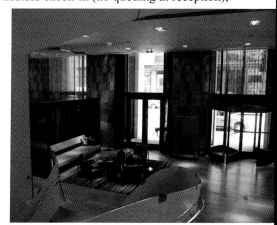

THINGS TO DO AND SEE IN DOWNTOWN

Battery Park, Brooklyn Bridge, Century 21 Discount Designer Clothes Store, Chinatown, Greenwich Village, Little Italy, 9/11 Memorial, Soho, South Street Seaport, Staten Island Ferry and Tribeca.

JANUARY

Chinese New Year (January/ February)
Sales in most shops and off season hotel savings
New York Restaurant Week (January/February)

FEBRUARY

New York Fashion Week
Valentines Day (14th)
Westminster Kennel Club Dog Show at Madison Square Garden

MARCH

Easter (March or April)
Macy's Flower Show (March/April)
Orchid Show, New York Botanical Gardens (March/April)
St. Patrick's Day Parade

APRIL

Cherry Blossom Festival at Brooklyn Botanical Gardens
TriBeCa Film Festival, Family Festival and Street Fair

MAY

Fleet Week - Ships from the Navy come to town!

JUNE

Bryant Park outdoor Summer Film Festival (free)
Lesbian/Gay Pride March and "Rapture on the River" dance
Museum Mile Festival, Upper East Side
New York Restaurant Week (June/July)
Shakespeare in the Park (free)
Taste of Time Square Food Festival

JULY

American Independence Day (4th)
Bryant Park outdoor Summer Film Festival (free)
Macy's 4th of July Fireworks display
New York Philharmonic concerts in Central Park (free)
Shakespeare in the Park (free)
Central Park Summer stage performances

CALENDAR OF EVENTS, FESTIVALS AND PARADES

AUGUST

Barneys Department Store Warehouse Sale
Bryant Park outdoor Summer Film Festival (free)
Summer in the City if you can stand the heat!
US Open Tennis Championships at Flushing Meadow
(continues into September)

SEPTEMBER

Barneys Warehouse Sale continues
Fashion's Night Out
Labour Day
Italian Food Festival of San Gennaro, Little Italy
West Indian Day Parade

OCTOBER

Columbus Day Parade
Greenwich Village Halloween Parade

NOVEMBER

New York City Marathon
Macy's Thanksgiving Day Parade
Black Friday - start of pre-Christmas sales in shops

DECEMBER

Christmas Window Displays in Department Stores and Shops
Rockefeller Christmas Tree Lighting Up Ceremony
Christmas
New Years Eve

Dylan's Candy Bar, 3rd Avenue at East 60th Street, Upper East Side, UPTOWN

Telephone 646 735 0078 www.dylanscandybar.com

Owned by Ralph Lauren's daughter Dylan, this candy store stocks an array of colourful sweets, striking iPod covers, laptop sleeves, pyjama bottoms and t-shirts, a favourite being the Barbie and Ken number in black and hot pink.

Godiva Chocolates, Rockefeller Centre, 6th Avenue at East 50th Street, MIDTOWN

Telephone 212 246 0346 www. godivachocolates.com/newyork

There are lots of Godiva shops in New York selling all your favourite chocolates with branches on Park, Lexington and Madison Avenues plus one on West 50th Street, so they are never out of reach.

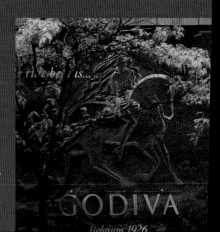

CHOCOLATE SHOPS AND CANDY STORES

Hershey Chocolate Land, West 48th Street at Broadway near Times Square MIDTOWN

Telephone 212 581 9100
www.hershey.com/newyork

If the smell does not grab you then the sight of all that chocolate will, for this is a chocoholics dream. Indulge your fantasy and step into the Universe that is Hershey Chocolates.

M & M Land, West 48th Street at Broadway, near Times Square, MIDTOWN

Telephone 212 295 3850 www.mmsworld.com

A colourful display of all things M & M awaits as you enter this sweet filled space, so be prepared for some serious temptation. Check out the eye-catching neon signage outside especially as the sun disappears.

We all love to try new drinks from time to time and below are a selection of fabulous Cocktails you may find on offer to give you that real "Sex and the City" feel. So don those killer heels, head out on the town and find yourself a seat at a stylish bar for a Cocktail or two "New York" style.

Buttery Nipple (right)

Vanilla Vodka, Butterscotch Snaps, Bailey's Irish Cream

Cosmopolitan

Lemon Vodka, Cointreau, Cranberry Juice, Lime Juice (see opposite)

Flirtini

Vodka, Pineapple Juice, Champagne

Harlem Nights

Tequila, Coconut Flavoured Rum, Coffee Liqueur, Pineapple Juice, Peach Schnapps, Maraschino Cherry, a slice of Orange

Manhattan

Whiskey, Sweet Vermouth, Angostura Bitters

COCKTAILS
NEW YORK
STYLE

New York Cocktail
Whisky, Lime Juice, Sugar Syrup, Grenadine Syrup

Prohibition Punch
Appleton Estate Rum, Grand Marnier, Passion Fruit, Cranberry Juice, Lemon Juice, Moet et Chandon Champagne

Tartini
Berry Vodka, Orange Liqueur, Pineapple Juice, Cranberry Juice, Juice of half a lime, Champagne

IN AN EMERGENCY DIAL 911

ALCOHOL

The legal age for drinking alcohol in New York is twenty one (21) and it will be enforced rigorously everywhere, so be prepared to provide identification at all times. It is illegal to drink alcohol on the Streets in any shape or form.

ARRESTED

DO NOT ARGUE IF YOU ARE ARRESTED - New York Police have a "zero" tolerance policy and will not put up with aggression of any type. If arrested you should be entitled to a phone call within one hour but always check your legal rights locally as laws can and do change.

AVOID AND BEWARE

New York is a big City so always be aware of the people around you, your surroundings, and where possible, avoid deserted areas day and night.

DISABLED TRAVELLERS

Access for All - For $5 you can buy a book called "Access for All" giving information on toilets, theatres, museums and major sights for the disabled plus audio services for people who are blind or partially sighted.

Visit **www.hospaud.org** (click on access guides)

New York Metro and Bus Service - Click "Access a Ride" on the following website for information if you have a disability and cannot use the metro or buses. **www.mta.infor/nyct/paratran/guide.htm**

DOCTORS, DENTISTS, HOSPITALS

If you require a Doctor, Dentist or Hospital and it is **not** an emergency contact your Hotel Reception or Concierge desk for advice.

In an Emergency dial 911.

EMBASSIES

**British Embassy in New York, 3rd Avenue
between East 51st and East 52nd Street, MIDTOWN**

Telephone 212 745 0200 (New York) or Fax 212 754 3062
www.ukinusa.fco.gov.uk/ny

**American Embassy in London
24 Grosvenor Square, London W1A 1AE**

Telephone: 0207 499 9000 (England)
www.london.usembassy.gov/www.usembassy.org

LEGAL AID SOCIETY

314 West 54th Street between 8th and 9th Avenue, MIDTOWN

Telephone 212 577 3300 Monday to Friday 9am to 5pm
www.legal-aid.org/ny
Contact them for general advice and remember to check how much
they charge.

TELEPHONE THE UK

Dial 01144 then the number (dropping the first 0) to phone home

THE SAMARITANS

Telephone 212 673 3000 www.samaritansnyc.org
24 hours a day 7 days a week counselling hotline

RADIO CITY

SALE
BEANIES
$5%
$12 99

6th Avenue, Midtown

Areas and Boroughs

The five main Boroughs of
New York are Manhattan Island,
the Bronx, Brooklyn, Queens and Staten Island.
Manhattan Island is the most visited and what people perceive to be
"New York City". This in turn is divided into the three main areas of
UPTOWN (North), MIDTOWN (Heart) and DOWNTOWN (South).

Currency

The US Dollar is used throughout North America including New
York and is around $1.50 to the pound. However, always check the
up to date rate of exchange before purchasing dollars as it can change
dramatically.

Electricity

You will need to take an adaptor suitable for North America as they use
120 volts with mostly two flat pin plugs although sometimes they do
use three pin plugs.

Flying Time

It takes approximately 7 ½ hours to fly from London to New York
(sometimes slightly less to fly back again) and around 6 hours to fly
from New York to Los Angeles.

History

Although once inhabited by native American Indians, it was the Italian explorer Giovanni da Verrazano who in 1524 was the first European to sight the island now known as Manhattan. However it was the Englishman Henry Hudson who first landed in 1609. His Dutch employers subsequently opened a trading post for furs and fruit in the area now known as Battery Park. Today New York still bears reminders of both men with the Verrazano-Narrows Bridge and the Hudson River.

After many Anglo/Dutch skirmishes it was ruled by the British from 1664 and named in honour of the Duke of York. It was lost again following the Revolutionary War of Independence and at that point it assumed brief Capital status of the newly formed United States. Despite the many subsequent battles fought over this sliver of land the name "New York" remains intact today. There are several tours you can take which will explore its history and culture in more depth and details of these are in the Tours and Excursions chapter.

Languages

Although English is the most common language spoken, you may hear more than 80 different ones during your stay including Chinese, French, Indian, Italian, Japanese and Ukrainian.

Location

Situated 3,174 miles West of Lands End across the Atlantic Ocean, New York is on the Eastern seaboard of America. Philadelphia and Washington DC lie to its South West, Boston to the North East, Pittsburgh to the West and Montreal to the North.

Population

There are around 20 million people living in the Metropolitan area at any one time while the City itself accounts for around 8.4 million. Here you will see every nationality, creed and religion imaginable living and working together in one very cosmopolitan place.

Size

As the financial, cultural and shopping hub of New York City, Manhattan is the 3rd most populated of the five boroughs yet the smallest in size. The area covered in this book is from 119th Street above Central Park in UPTOWN down through the Heart of the City in MIDTOWN to Battery Park in DOWNTOWN, a total of approximately 8.5 miles long by 2.3 miles wide.

Time Difference

New York varies between 4 hours behind the UK during Greenwich Meantime (end of October to the end of March) and 5 hours behind during British Summertime (end of March to end of October). The date the clocks change can vary each year so always check.

SEAN JOHN

only ★ macy's

NYC

THURSDAY
APRIL 28 8:00PM

Sean John for Macy's

FAMOUS NEW YORKERS

Many rich and famous people come from New York and love the City, as they can generally move around quite freely.
Check to see if your favourite Celebrities (past and present) are on the list.

Christina Aguillera, Singer
Ed Burns, Actor
Sean John Combs (Diddy) Record Producer, Actor, Entrepreneur
Robert De Niro, Actor
Vin Diesel, Actor
Bob Dylan, Songwriter, Singer, Musician
Tom Ford, Fashion Designer
Lady Gaga, Singer
James Gandolfinho, Actor
Sarah Michelle Gellar, Actress
Anne Hathaway, Actress
Billy Joel, Singer and Songwriter
Scarlett Johannsen, Actress
Michael Kors, Fashion Designer
Cyndi Lauper, Singer and Songwriter
Jennifer Lopez, Actress, Singer, Dancer and Designer
Sienna Miller, Actress
John Travolta, Actor, Singer and Dancer
Donald Trump, Businessman and TV Personality
Andy Warhol, Artist and Filmmaker
Christopher Wallace (Notorious Mr. BIG), Rapper
Denzel Washington, Actor and Director
USEFUL WEBSITE: www.who2.com

Rockport Fashion Shoot

When it comes to style New Yorkers have it all, from bohemian and outlandish to polished and clean cut.

The streets are a permanent fashion show with swirling models, twirling starlets and sashaying wannabes. My personal favourites are the everyday New York Women who have a unique take on fashion, always true to their own taste no matter how good the label!

Black is a New York staple worn for every occasion whether dressed down or up and comes in more shades, styles and sizes than you could ever imagine. New Yorkers also love labels from Manolo Blahnik, Jimmy Choo and Michael Kors to Kenneth Cole, Calvin Klein and Lanvin. There is nothing you cannot buy or indeed witness on the streets of Manhattan, so look out for inspiration.

Sharp tailoring and crisply cut clothes are synonymous with New York Women from the young to the not so young. For a real look at New York designer style watch "The Devil Wears Prada" starring Meryl Streep, Anne Hathaway and Emily Blunt and you will drool at all the beautiful people in their equally edgy clothes. The photographs here show a cross section of Uptown, Midtown, Downtown, West Side and East Side fashion as well as style on the streets so you can check out the competition.

FASHIONS AND STYLES THE NEW YORK WAY

Pages 92-97

USEFUL WEBSITES

www.jilllynne.com
For a "customized" fashion tour with World renowned Writer and Photographer Jill Lynne see "Tours and Excursions" for details or contact her directly on **jilllynne1@mac.com**

www.runway.blogs.nytimes.com
This blog gives details of forthcoming fashion shows, takes you behind the scenes of the fashion industry and gives you lots of relevant website links.

www.newyorkfashionweek.com
Check this out for information on New York Fashion week.

www.fashionsnightout.com
Fashion's Night Out is an extravaganza where shops stay open late with a street party atmosphere on 5th Avenue. You will often find special discounts and incentives to buy. To join in the fashion fun keep an eye on the website above.

www.fashionista.com
A New York based online fashion blog for up to the minute trends plus all your favourite Celebrity gossip.

Uptown Girls

ON 2

BLOOMINGDALE'S FASHION

Midtown Girls

Midtown Girls

ON 2

Downtown Girls

Westside Girls

ON 2

Eastside Girls

ON 2

Free People
on 2

95

FASHION
ON THE STREET

Film Set for "What Maisie Knew"

FILM AND TELEVISION LOCATION SITES

INDEX

New York is awash with film and television location sites and named below are just some you might want to visit during your stay. Alternatively you could take a tour, see pages 236-245.

AN AFFAIR TO REMEMBER
1957, Cary Grant and Deborah Kerr
←Empire State Building, 5th Avenue at West 34th Street, MIDTOWN

BAREFOOT IN THE PARK - 1967, Robert Redford and Barbra Streisand
Fairmont Plaza Hotel, West 59th Street (Central Park South) at 5th Avenue, MIDTOWN
←Washington Square Gardens, Greenwich Village, DOWNTOWN

BREAKFAST AT TIFFANY'S - 1961, Patricia Neal and George Peppard
New York Public Library, 5th Avenue at West 42nd Street, MIDTOWN
←Tiffany & Co. Jewellers, 5th Avenue at East 57th Street, MIDTOWN

Useful websites: www.screentours.com
www.overheardinnewyork.com
www.onthesetofnewyork.com
www.imdb.com
www.tribecafilmfestival.org,

BRIDE WARS - 2009, Kate Hudson and Anne Hathaway

Bloomingdale's, East 59th Street➔ between 3rd and Lexington Avenues, MIDTOWN
Fairmont Plaza Hotel, West 59th Street (Central Park South) at 5th Avenue, MIDTOWN

CONFESSIONS OF A SHOPAHOLIC 2009, Hugh Dancy and Isla Fisher

Dandelion Fountain on 6th Avenue➔ at East 56th Street, MIDTOWN
Henri Bendel Department Store, 5th Avenue at West 56th Street, MIDTOWN

FIRST WIVES CLUB - 1996, Goldie Hawn, Diane Keaton and Bette Midler

Barneys Department Store,➔ Madison Avenue at East 61st Street, Upper East Side, UPTOWN
Café des Artistes, West 67th Street at Central Park West, Upper West Side, UPTOWN

FRIENDS Television Series - Jennifer Aniston, David Schwimmer, Courteney Cox, Matthew Perry, Lisa Kudrow and Matt Le Blanc

Friends Apartment Building,➔ Corner of Bedford and Grove Streets, Greenwich Village, DOWNTOWN
Lucille Lortel Theatre, Christopher and Bedford Streets, Greenwich Village, DOWNTOWN

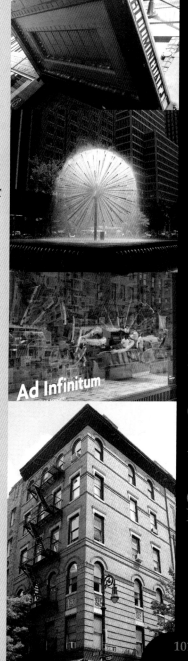

**GOSSIP GIRL Television Series
- Blake Lively, Leighton Meester,
Penn Badgley and Matthew Settle**

New York Palace Hotel, →
Madison Avenue at East 50th Street,
MIDTOWN

**HITCH - 2005, Will Smith, Eva
Mendes, Amber Valletta
and Kevin James**

Flatiron Building, Madison Square
Park at West 23rd Street, MIDTOWN
←Metropolitan Art Museum,
5th Avenue at East 82nd Street,
Upper East Side, UPTOWN

**IT HAD TO BE YOU - 2000,
Natasha Henstridge, Michael Vartan**

Bergdorf Goodman Department
Store, 5th Avenue at East 58th Street,
MIDTOWN
←Central Park, 59th Street up to 110th
Street between 5th and 8th Avenues,
UPTOWN

**LOOKING FOR KITTY - 2004,
Edward Burns, David Krumholtz**

Joe's Pizza, Bleecker Street between
6th and 7th Avenues, Greenwich
Village, DOWNTOWN
←Katz's Deli, East Houston Street
at Ludlow Street, Lower East Side,
DOWNTOWN

102

MAID IN MANHATTAN
2002, Jennifer Lopez and Ralph Fiennes

Central Park, 59th Street up to 110th Street between 5th and 8th Avenues, UPTOWN
Metropolitan Art Museum, 5th Avenue at East 82nd Street, Upper East Side, UPTOWN
Waldorf Astoria, East 49th Street at Park Avenue, MIDTOWN

NEW YORK, I LOVE YOU - 2009,
Natalie Portman, Bradley Cooper and Cloris Leachman

Diamond District, West 47th Street at 6th Avenue, MIDTOWN
Walkers Bar, N. Moore➔ and Varick Street, Tribeca, DOWNTOWN

SERENDIPITY
2001, Kate Beckinsale and John Cusack

Serendipity Restaurant, East 60th Street at 3rd Avenue, Upper East Side, UPTOWN
Trump Wolman Ice Skating Rink, Central Park 59th Street entrance, UPTOWN

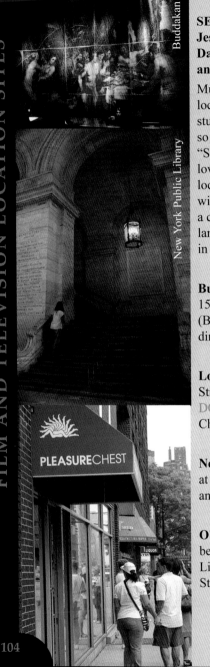

Buddakan

New York Public Library

SEX AND THE CITY - 2008, Sarah Jessica Parker, Kim Cattrall, Kristin Davis, Cynthia Nixon, Chris Noth and John Corbett

Much of Sex and the City was shot on location in New York rather than in a studio, which is why the list below is so big. You might like to take the "Sex and the City" Tour (which I loved) as it shows you all of these locations and many, many more. You will be led by a "Sexpert" and have a cupcake en route but be warned the language is explicit at times though in a fun and amusing way.

Buddakan, 9th Avenue between West 15th and West 16th Streets, MIDTOWN (Big and Carrie hold their pre-wedding dinner here)

Louis K. Meisel Gallery, Prince Street at West Broadway, Soho, DOWNTOWN (the gallery where Charlotte works)

New York Public Library, 5th Avenue at West 42nd Street, MIDTOWN (Big and Carrie should have married here)

O'Nieal's Speakeasy, Grand Street between Baxter and Mulberry Streets, Little Italy, DOWNTOWN (Aidan and Steve's bar - Scout)

Pastis, 9th Avenue at West 12th Street, Meatpacking District, DOWNTOWN (Carrie and Aleksandr Petrovsky go for dinner here)

Pleasure Chest, 7th Avenue at Perry and Charles Street, West Village, DOWNTOWN (where Charlotte buys her "rabbit")

SLEEPLESS IN SEATTLE - 1993, Meg Ryan and Tom Hanks

Empire State Building, West 34th Street at 5th Avenue, MIDTOWN
Tiffany & Co. Jewellers, 5th Avenue at East 57th Street, MIDTOWN

THE DEVIL WEARS PRADA - 2006, Emily Blunt, Anne Hathaway, Meryl Streep

Smith and Wollensky, 3rd Avenue at East 48th Street, MIDTOWN
←St. Regis Hotel (King Cole Bar), West 55th Street at 5th Avenue, MIDTOWN

THE WOMEN - 2008, Meg Ryan, Debra Messing, Eva Mendes, Annette Benning, Jada Pinkett Smith

Saks, 5th Avenue between East 49th and East 50th Streets, MIDTOWN

Other Television Programmes set in New York are: Criminal Intent, CSI New York, Damages, Kourtney and Kim Take New York, Law and Order, NCIS, NYPD Blue, The City, The Sopranos and Ugly Betty.

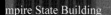

Empire State Building

Saks, 5th Avenue

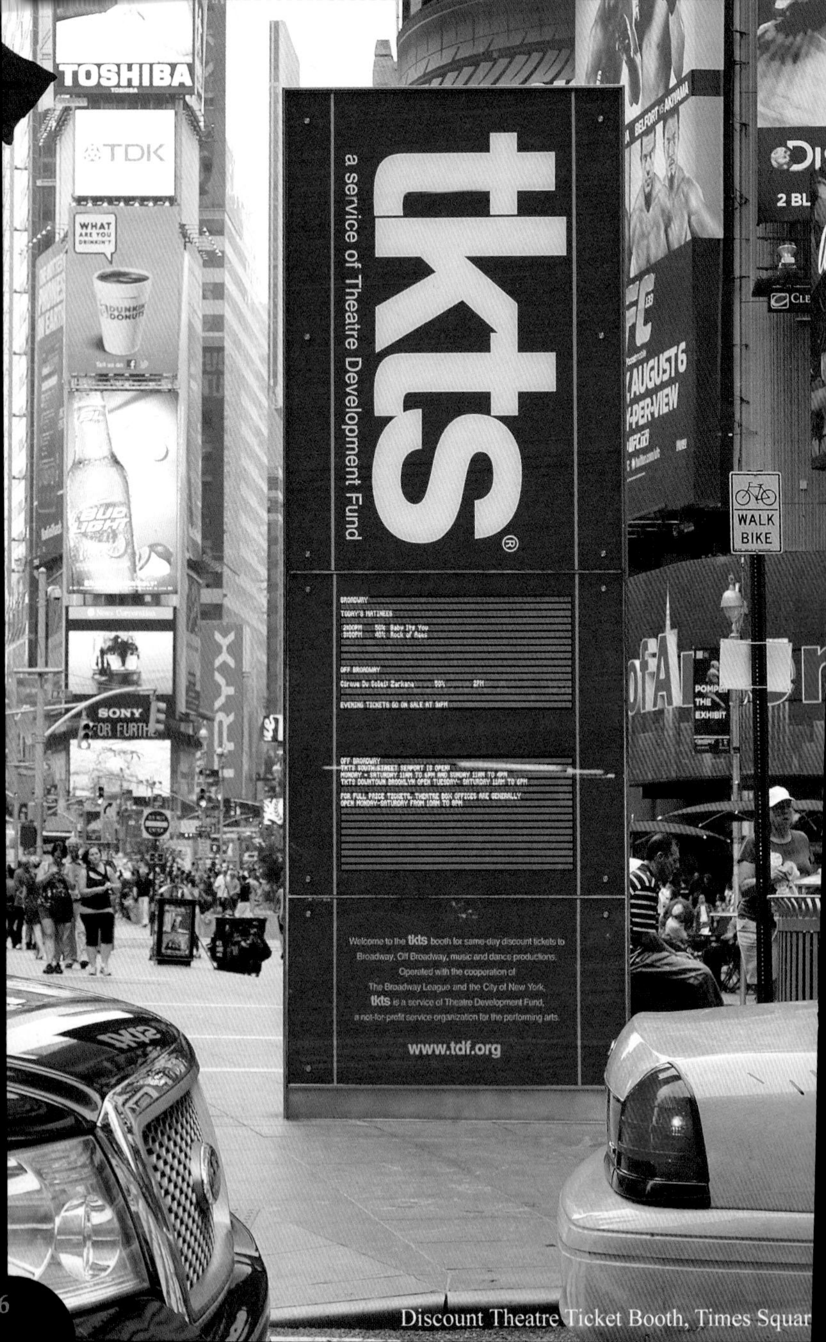

Discount Theatre Ticket Booth, Times Squar

FREEBIES AND CHEAPIES

INDEX

Central Park, 59th Street up to 110th Street and from 5th to 8th Avenues, UPTOWN
Telephone 212 360 3444 or 212 310 6600 www.centralpark.com

A swathe of greenery in the midst of Manhattan with 843 acres of parkland, millions of trees, several lakes, a zoo, gothic bridge, castle, an ice rink and a memorial to John Lennon (Imagine). It costs nothing to enter and holds various free events in the summer like open air films and Shakespearean plays. Look out for buskers as you move around the Park where you might see Jazz bands, violinists, harpists and guitarists.

Jazz Concerts, American Museum of Natural History, Central Park West (8th Avenue) at West 79th Street, Upper West Side, UPTOWN
Telephone 212 769 5100 www.amnh.com

This museum holds Jazz concerts during the year with dates, timings and general information on their website. As they are always popular it is worth keeping a look out for details and to book early.

Jazz Concerts, Guggenheim Museum, 5th Avenue at East 89th Street, Upper East Side, UPTOWN
Telephone 212 423 3500 www.guggenheim.com

At various times from January to December the Guggenheim holds Jazz concerts on site. Again the tickets are sought after so obtain yours in advance to avoid disappointment and look at their web pages for further information.

Lincoln Centre for the Performing Arts, Lincoln Centre Plaza, 9th Avenue at West 64th Street, Upper West Side, UPTOWN
Telephone 212 875 5000 or 212 875 5456 www.lincolncenter.org or www.newyorkphilharmonic.com or www.nyphil.org

With 12 resident performing arts housed in one 16.3 acre site, this establishment is home to the New York Ballet, Opera, Theatre, Film and Jazz Societies plus many more. Each year they run a series of free outdoor concerts featuring an array of music including Flamenco Guitar.

Ballroom Dancing at the Manhattan Ballroom Society, 8th Avenue at West 55th Street, MIDTOWN
Telephone 917 734 4778 www.manhattanballroom.net

With prices from just £16 per person, try the Manhattan Ballroom Society and their Friday Night Dance Party, where you can either take advanced classes, brush up on your existing skills or simply enjoy the social dancing.

Blues and Folk Concerts, Madison Square Park at 5th Avenue and East 23rd Street, Flatiron District, MIDTOWN
Telephone 212 538 1884 www.madisonsquarepark.org

A small park filled with trees and exquisite light, hugging 5th Avenue in the heart of MIDTOWN. Each autumn (Fall) it plays host to free Blues and Folk concerts. See their website for dates.

109

Film Festival, Bryant Park between West 40th and West 42nd Streets at 5th and 6th Avenues, MIDTOWN

Telephone 212 768 4242 www.bryantpark.com

From late June to mid August each year, Bryant Park hosts a free open air Summer Film Festival every Monday evening. A variety of classic movies are shown such as China Syndrome and French Connection on a first come first served basis. Go early as it is popular and people turn up in their droves.

Theatre Tickets at discount prices

TDF (Theatre Development Fund), West 47th Street at Times Square, MIDTOWN OR Corner of Front and John Streets, South Street Seaport, DOWNTOWN

Telephone 212 221 0013

Try this booth for discount theatre tickets which can only be purchased on the day of the performance. If you are flexible about what you want to see then this could be worthwhile.

Brooklyn Bridge near Chambers Street and Park Row, Lower Manhattan, DOWNTOWN

www.mybrooklynbridge.com

This iconic bridge offers stunning views of the New York skyline and is absolutely free. Walk across and look back at every opportunity or drop down to water level when you reach the other side and take in the enchanting vistas. For evening photo opportunities of the Bridge take a night tour (see Tours and Excursions).

Film Screenings, live Music and Dance nights at various locations in the DOWNTOWN Area

www.rivertorivernyc.com

Free admission to a variety of events in the DOWNTOWN area is provided by this "not for profit" organisation. These include film screenings, live music events and dance nights. You might like to join in the fun at South Street Seaport for one of their Latin Nights offering a lively, entertaining evening.

Highline Elevated Park (under the Standard Hotel) between Gansevoort Street and West 14th Street, Meatpacking District, DOWNTOWN

Telephone 212 500 6035 www.thehighline.org or www.aaa.org

Once a derelict railway, the Highline has undergone a transformation and is now an elevated park which still retains the old rail line and sleepers tucked away amongst the foliage. From here you have great views over the Hudson River to New Jersey and are only a short walk from the Meatpacking District.

Staten Island Ferry, Whitehall Terminal, South Ferry, DOWNTOWN

Telephone 718 815 BOAT (only from within New York) or 212 248 8097
www.siferry.com

On the Southern tip of Manhattan within walking distance of Wall Street
and the 9/11 Memorial, this ferry sails to Staten Island past the Statue of
Liberty. If you stay on the ferry when you reach Staten Island and don't
get off the ride is free and you can get some great photos on the way.

**Classical Concerts free of charge
in New York's Parks,** UPTOWN,
MIDTOWN and DOWNTOWN

Telephone 212 NEW-YORK
www.nycgovparks.org

There are several free classical
concerts in a variety of parks
throughout New York during
the summer. Visit the website
for more details and performance
schedules.

Eating out - UPTOWN,
MIDTOWN, DOWNTOWN

www.opentable.com

Many restaurants offer fixed price
menus if you eat an early dinner
and also at certain times of the
year during food festivals or New
York Restaurant Week. Look at
the Calendar of Events and always
check with individual restaurants as
you might just save some money.

Metro Card - UPTOWN,
MIDTOWN, DOWNTOWN

www.mta.info/metrocard.com

Metro Cards offer savings on buses
and the Metro with 1,7,14 or 30
day passes. Cards can be bought
at underground station vending
machines using cash, debit or credit
cards and are sometimes available
from hotels. Always check first to
see if they meet your needs.

**New York City Pass and the
New York Pass -** UPTOWN,
MIDTOWN, DOWNTOWN

www.newyorkcitypass.com or
www.newyorkpass.com

Both of these passes are discount
cards and offer savings on major
attractions if you plan on seeing
several. Individual websites will
give more details so you can
ensure they are worthwhile.

New York Philharmonic Orchestra, UPTOWN, MIDTOWN, DOWNTOWN

Telephone 212 875 5656
www.bewyorkphilharmonic.com

Every year there are free New York Philharmonic concerts in the five boroughs with Central Park as one of the venues. See website for dates.

Tourist Buses for Sightseeing - UPTOWN, MIDTOWN, DOWNTOWN

Telephone 212 445 0848
www.grayline.com or
www.newyorksightseeing.com

Look out for the "Hop on Hop off" buses, a good way of getting to know the City when you first arrive. They will drop you near the major attractions so you simply "Hop on and off" whenever you wish. Purchase either 2, 3 or 7 day passes.

Walking the Streets - UPTOWN, MIDTOWN, DOWNTOWN

New York is definitely a walking City even though Manhattan is around 13 miles long and 2.3 miles at its widest. Whilst the bus, Metro or a yellow cab will take you between each of the three main areas of UPTOWN, MIDTOWN and DOWNTOWN, once there resume walking and enjoy the scenery. Don't forget to look up at the architecture as you stroll around as there is much to see skyward with a real mix of styles and facades on the buildings.

Useful Website:
www.freenyc.com
Things which you can do
for free in New York.

Soho

If you are travelling with your man to New York, he may on occasion want some "Guy" stuff to occupy him while you do your own thing. There are lots of choices on offer from bike hire, sporting events, sports bars, sports shops, photography and technology centres, right through to a golf driving range, horse racing and tenpin bowling. See below for ideas.

BUILDINGS, LANDMARKS AND MUSEUMS

Brooklyn Bridge, Chrysler Building, Empire State Building, Hayden Planetarium, Intrepid Sea, Air and Space Museum, Museum Mile, New York Fire Department Museum, Skyscraper Museum, the Museum of New York, 9/11 Memorial and the Rockefeller Centre.

GOLF DRIVING RANGE, PACKAGE AND GOLF SHOP

Golf Driving Range at Chelsea Piers, Pier 59, West 23rd Street at Hudson River Park, MIDTOWN
Telephone 212 336 6400 or 212 336 6666 www.chelseapiers.com

This driving range looks out over the Hudson River, is multi tiered with automatic ball providers (yes you can tell I am a non golfer) and offers an inner City solution for those who cannot get enough of the game.

New York Golf Centre, West 35th Street between Broadway and 7th Avenue, MIDTOWN
Telephone 212 564 2255
www.nygolfcenter.com

Here you will find golf equipment, bags, shoes, wet weather gear and the latest styles in golf wear.

SPECTATOR SPORTING EVENTS AND TICKETS

Basketball - New York Knicks at Madison Square Garden, MIDTOWN Manhattan
www.nba.com/knicks

Hockey - New York Rangers at Madison Square Garden, MIDTOWN Manhattan
www.rangers.nhl.com

TENPIN BOWLING

Bowlmor Lanes, West 44th Street between 7th and 8th Avenues, Times Square, MIDTOWN
Telephone 212 680 0012 www.bowlmor.com/newyork

This is a fun way to spend some time if you are feeling in the mood for something energetic. There is a sports bar with television screens and a grill serving pizza, burgers and chicken wings.

Harley-Davidson Shop

OUTER BOROUGHS - SPECTATOR SPORTING EVENTS AND TICKETS

Baseball - New York "Yankees" at the Yankee Stadium, Bronx
www.newyork.yankees.mlb.com

Baseball - New York "Mets" at Citi Field, Queens
www.mets.com

US Open Tennis Championships at Flushing Meadow, Queens
www.usopen.org (Summer)

NEW JERSEY - SPECTATOR SPORTING EVENTS AND TICKETS

American Football New York "Giants" at the Giants Stadium, New Jersey
www.giants.com

American Football New York "Jets" ➔ at the Giants Stadium, New Jersey
www.newyorkjets.com

TOURS AND EXCURSIONS - VARIOUS LOCATIONS (SEE SEPARATE CHAPTER FOR MORE DETAILS)

There are a myriad of Tours to choose from which include the West Village Music Tour and Pub Crawl, Revolutionary New York Tour, Champagne, Beer or Wine Tasting Tours, Foods of New York Tour, Helicopter Scenic Flight, Harlem Soul Food, Hip Hop or Gospel Tours plus many more.

On these pages there are some suggestions for handy beauty products and gadgets which could prove useful on your travels. However if you want to take them with you in the aircraft cabin be sure to check the up-to-date information for hand luggage as some items may carry restrictions.

Bath Sachets - Thalgo Marine Algae Sachets - www.lookfantastic.com
Natural marine algae in a relaxing bath after a long journey could help to detoxify and ease the jet lag from your weary body.

Clothes/Garment Steamer
Telephone 0844 822 0099 www.garmentsteamer.org.uk
An upright travel steamer to banish wrinkles from your clothes and help them smell fresher after hours of being squashed in your case.

Deodorant Wipes - www.asda.co.uk
Deodorant wipes are useful to freshen up during your flight or when out and about in New York.

Eye Mask in Silk and Velvet - www.holisticsilk.com
This soft eye mask is infused with lavender and comes in a range of beautiful colours. It will block out the light as you drift off to sleep and lists Celebrity clients amongst its wearers.

Face Wipes - www.neutrogena.com
These refreshing facial cleansing wipes will remove all that travelling grime whilst in the air and on the ground.

Headphones by Bose - www.bose.co.uk
Push the budget for peace and quiet during the flight with the Bose Quiet Comfort sound cancelling headphones.

Headphones by Logitech - www.logitech.com
Noise reducing headphones. Just sit back and listen to your music.

iPOD Touch by Apple - Telephone 0800 048 0408 www.apple.com
A useful piece of kit with storage for 700 songs and 40 hours of video to keep you entertained whilst away.

HANDY TRAVEL GADGETS AND BEAUTY PRODUCTS

Journal for Travel Notes - www.papernation.co.uk
A travel journal to record your special memories with a pocket for storing receipts, tickets and mementos.

Lipstick by Yves St. Laurent - www.ysl.com or www.boots.com
Try the YSL Lip Twins range which is a lipstick, lip gloss, mirror and brush all in one neat little package.

Moisturiser (Luxury) - Crème de La Mer - www.cremedelamer.co.uk
This for me is the queen of face creams and perfect for plane journeys as it is long lasting, rich in texture and the ultimate in luxurious moisturisers.

Moisturising Face Cloths by Skin Vitals - www.skinvitals.com.au
Impregnated with moisturiser these face cloths help to soothe and revive dehydrated skin during the flight.

Pore Minimiser Oil Blotting Sheets by Bobbi Brown
www.bobbibrown.co.uk
To prevent facial shine and pore clogging these blotting sheets could prove useful in-flight or whilst in New York.

Sleep Pillow - Aroma Snoozer - www.sadler.co.uk/aromasnoozer
An inflatable neck cushion with in-built aromatherapy dispensers and lavender oil to soothe a weary mind and body.

General Sherman's Statue, West 59th Street at 5th Avenue, Midtown

INDEX

Party Bus

Going abroad for a "Hen" weekend has become a popular choice amongst Brides to be, so you might like to consider New York for your very own celebration. Two nights are possible if you take an early morning flight out and a late night one back although three nights or more would be a better option.

Here are some ideas to inspire you and include a Bachelorette Party, Belly, Lap or Pole Dancing classes and also Shopping and Nightclub Tours. If you want a day of pampering then a Beauty Spa is included here or see the Tours section for more alternatives.

Go Hen, The Old Brewery, Newtown, Bradford on Avon, Wiltshire, BA15 1NF
Telephone 0845 130 5225 or 0333 800 8020
Email: hen@gohen.com www.gohen.com

These people put together Hen weekends in New York and you can either book one of their laid down packages or ask them to tailor-make an itinerary. See their website for more ideas or contact them directly for a chat. Don't forget to mention Lipstick City Guides!

Uncle Sam's New York Tours
Telephone 888 491 9824 www.unclesamsnewyorktours.com

This tour lasts a full day and night including shopping, an outfit makeover, a spa and nightclub visit, whilst enjoying the ultimate Bachelorette Party. Prices from £285 ($430) per person.

Susan Ciminelli Day Spa, 2nd Floor 120 East 56th Street between Lexington and Park Avenues, MIDTOWN
Telephone 212 750 4441 www.susanciminelli.com

This spa will host your Hen Party to include a salt scrub, reflexology, make up application and facial. Champagne and strawberries will ease away those pre wedding nerves and their website will give you up to the minute details of packages available. Prices from £350 per person

Belly Dancing Classes, Serena Studios, 8th Avenue between West 55th and West 56th Streets, MIDTOWN
Telephone 212 245 9603 www.serenastudios.com

Have you ever wanted to try the seductive art of belly dancing? Then head to Serena's Studios for lessons in how to move with grace and style, plus a chance to tone your tummy at the same time.

Pole Dancing Classes, Exotic Dance Central, 4th Floor, 253 5th Avenue between East 28th and East 29th Streets, MIDTOWN
Telephone 212 679 2540 www.exoticdancecentral.com

This studio offers pole dancing classes as well as Bachelorette parties, birthday parties, private dance lessons and workshops.

Also try: Manhattan Ballroom Society for Ballroom lessons

EXCLUSIVE – "JUST FOR YOU" FASHION-ABLE SHOPPING TOUR OR NEW YORK PHOTO MEMENTO

Acclaimed New York Photographer and Writer Jill Lynne has put together two unique opportunities "Just for YOU" with either a portrait photograph taken at your favourite New York location or a tailor-made behind the scenes FASHION-able Shopping Tour. See the Tours Section for more details or email Jill directly for a tailor-made quote on jilllynne1@mac.com

PARTY RIDE

The Party Ride, MIDTOWN
Telephone 866 275 5466
www.thepartyride.com

A sugar pink bus will provide transportation for your group whether a Hen party, bar and club hopping or just a birthday bash. Contact these people for your tailor made quote.

Also try: www.newyorkhummerlimousine.com

DANCE CLASSES

The New York School of Burlesque Dancing, 167 Orchard Street at Stanton Street, Lower East Side, DOWNTOWN

Telephone 212 253 7246 www.schoolofburlesque.com

Based at the Slipper Room Variety Club, the New York School of Burlesque has dance classes showing you how to shimmy, grind, bump and chair dance. They also offer lap dancing lessons if that is your desire

Party Hummer

TOURS AND EXCURSIONS

Uncle Sam's New York Tours

www.unclesamsnewyorktours.com

Options here include SATC and Gossip Girl Tours, Spa packages and a Literary Pub Crawl. For the ultimate in evening tours take the Frank Sinatra Nightlife Limousine excursion and follow in his famous footsteps. Visit classic bars, lounges and the hottest nightclubs where he liked to drink and eat when in town.

HOMES NEW YORK STYLE

Midtown

Uptown

Midtown

Uptown

126

HOMES NEW YORK STYLE

HOMES NEW YORK STYLE

As with all Cities, there are a variety of home styles within New York
and here are just a few you might glimpse as you go about your day.
These include Brownstone houses in Greenwich Village and the Upper
West Side, historic mansions and luxury condominiums on the Upper
East Side, with loft apartments in converted warehouses throughout
Soho and Tribeca. There are also top of the range Penthouses scattered
around Central Park.

Some homes are functional, others decadent, while a selection have
gardens, roof terraces or balconies. All have their charm and uniqueness
from minimalist contemporary spaces to luxurious traditional homes
and featured are a just few external photographs to give you an idea of
the architectural styles and designs.

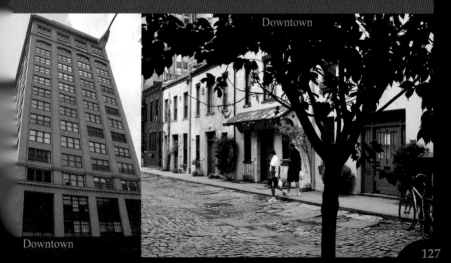

Downtown

Downtown

ONE WAY

5 AV

E 60 ST

Fairmont Plaza Hotel, Midtow

HOTELS AND APARTMENTS

INDEX

New York is filled with places to stay, from hip, contemporary, Art Deco and traditional, to budget, deluxe, quiet or bustling. A selection are shown here for your consideration offering variety in style and size.

Facilities within each hotel can vary with some offering a swimming pool, spa, coffee shop, restaurant or 24 hour reception. Most of these hotels have a bar of some description including piano lounges, cocktail bars, cabaret clubs and rooftop terraces, while some have nothing more than other travellers for company.

Hotels in Street locations may be quieter, those on Avenues could be noisier and generally the higher the floor the less street activity you will hear. However, you are in a City and it will be noisy! Individual websites will give you more information about each hotel.

CELEBRITY FAVOURITES

Carlyle Hotel 5*, East 76th Street at Madison Avenue, Upper East Side, UPTOWN
Telephone 212 744 1600 www.thecarlyle.com

This luxurious hotel plays host to "A" list Celebrities and is a quiet sanctuary of privacy and discretion. The 188 rooms are exquisitely decorated in traditional style with soft muted colours and dark wood furniture. Dining and entertaining options include the renowned Bemelman's Bar and Café Carlyle.

Photo Courtesy of The Carlyle Hotel

**Trump International Hotel 5*,
Central Park West (8th Avenue)
at West 61st Street, Upper West
Side, UPTOWN**
**Telephone 212 299 1000
www.trumpintl.com**

Classy and chic with service
to match, this "Forbes" rated,
five star hotel has a pool, spa
and health club. The 167 rooms
enjoy floor to ceiling windows
some with views over Central
Park, and for dinner you could
try the renowned Jean-Georges
restaurant.

HISTORIC HOTEL

**Mark Hotel 4 ½*, East 77th
Street at Madison Avenue,
Upper East Side, UPTOWN**
**Telephone 212 744 4300
www.themarkhotel.com**

Housed in a landmark 1924
building, this gem is steps from
Museum Mile and Central Park.
Contemporary in style, the
monochrome reception area is
striking, whilst traditional accents
are reflected in the 150 rooms
with their Italian linens, soft tone
colours and stylish bathrooms.
Try Mark's Bar for a pre-dinner
cocktail.

HOTELS AND APARTMENTS

ART DECO IN STYLE

Chatwal Hotel 5*, West 44th Street between 6th and 7th Avenues, MIDTOWN

**Telephone 212 764 6200
www.thechatwalny.com**

Transporting you back to the 1930s, the chic 88 roomed Chatwal Hotel is vintage in style with chrome, mirrors and wood, giving it a luxurious club-like feel. The rooms are in shades of cream and white with suede effect walls, while the popular Lambs Club Grill and Bar offer seafood, steaks and drinks. Try the soothing Spa when you crave an indulgent moment.

BOUTIQUE AND INTIMATE

Giraffe Hotel 4*, Park Avenue South at East 26th Street, MIDTOWN
Telephone 212 685 7700 www.giraffehotel.com

The warm muted colours and gentle African theme give this 72 roomed hotel a calm and welcoming feel. There are 24 hour refreshments, live piano music on week nights and breakfast included daily. The penthouse is where "Big" had his apartment in Sex and the City.

132

Library Hotel 4*, **Madison Avenue at East 41st Street,** MIDTOWN

Telephone 212 983 4500 or 1-800 480 9545 www.thelibraryhotel.com

A charming 60 roomed hotel tucked away off Madison Avenue, with a rooftop conservatory, wood and leather furnishings plus a library of over 6,000 books. The hotel includes a European style breakfast, a wine reception and 24 hour tea/coffee for all guests. Try the Love Suite for a romantic weekend away and find the Literary plaques on the pavement outside leading to the New York Public Library.

Also try: The Casablanca Hotel and The Elysee Hotel

BRIGHT AND BASIC

Gershwin Hotel 2*, **East 27th Street between 5th and Madison Avenues,** MIDTOWN

Telephone 212 545 8000 www.gershwinhotel.com

This quirky hotel has an arty interior and 150 rooms, ranging from basic "bunkers" with bunk beds and shared bathrooms, to the "essential" rooms which are tiny doubles. Located near the Empire State Building, there is a coffee shop, wireless internet access and 24 hour reception.

CELEBRITY FAVOURITES

Gramercy Park Hotel ★ ★, **Lexington Avenue between East 21st and East 22nd Streets,** MIDTOWN

Telephone 212 920 3300
www.grammercyparkhotel.com

Bohemian in style with a rich eclectic feel, the 185 rooms offer luxuriant touches, velvet furnishings and modern artwork. The Jade and Rose bars are delightful spaces, one in soft shades of pink the other in greens, blues and reds, whilst both require bookings after 9pm.

St. Regis Hotel ★ ★, **East 55th Street at 5th Avenue,** MIDTOWN

Telephone 212 753 4500
www.starwoodhotels.com/stregis

Refined and gracious this New York institution with 164 rooms and 65 suites, has antique furnishings, silk walls and marble baths giving it an elegant air. Go to the King Cole Bar for a pre-dinner cocktail or try the Alain Ducasse "Adour" Restaurant.

Waldorf Astoria Hotel and Towers
4★, Park Avenue between East 49th
and East 50th Streets, MIDTOWN
Telephone 212 355 3000 or 212 355 3100
www.waldorfastoria.com/newyork

This Grand Dame of New York society is historic and charming with protected status. It exudes old money in elegant surroundings, with 1,413 traditional rooms, modern touches and classic furnishings. If it is. Celebrities you want then check in to the Waldorf Towers.

FASHIONABLE AND TRENDY

Chambers Hotel 4★**, West 56th**
Street between 5th and 6th Avenues,
MIDTOWN
Telephone 212 974 5656
www.chambershotel.com

With David Rockwell interiors and only 77 rooms, this modern retreat has a subtle décor with soft wood tones, in sharp contrast to the many pieces of contemporary art. There is a restaurant and bar on site for guests and it is well situated in the heart of MIDTOWN.

Morgans Hotel 3 ½ ★**, Madison Avenue between East 37th and East**
38th Streets, MIDTOWN
Telephone 212 686 0300 www.morganshotel.com

A monochrome lobby is the first hint of what lies beyond in this small contemporary hotel. The 113 rooms mingle shades of caramel, honey and taupe for a modern yet comfortable feel, and an added bonus is the Asia de Cuba restaurant which featured in Sex and the City.

Also try: Bryant Park Hotel, Fashion 26 Hilton, Hudson Hotel , Indigo Hotel, Shoreham Hotel, Royalton Hotel, Strand Hotel and W Hotel.

Fairmont Plaza Hotel 5*, **5th Avenue at Central Park South (59th Street),** MIDTOWN

Telephone 212 759 3000 (PHOTO 13) www.fairmont.com/theplaza

Scene of the Michael Douglas/ Catherine Zeta Jones wedding and synonymous with old World style, this Landmark hotel is opposite Central Park with 282 rooms, crystal chandeliers and a traditional décor. Try afternoon tea in the Palm Court for a time honoured tradition or a meal in the famed Oak Room.

Roosevelt Hotel 3½*, **East 45th Street at Madison Avenue,** MIDTOWN

Telephone 212 661 9600
or 888-Teddy-NY
www.roosevelthotel.com

Opened in 1924, the Roosevelt is classic New York in style with beautifully restored architectural features, 1,015 rooms and every modern amenity. With its rooftop Bar (Mad46), Madison Club Lounge and Roosevelt Grill this hotel has much to offer the traditionalist and although large, it still has a personal feel.

Le Parker Meridien ★, **West 56th Street between 6th and 7th Avenues,** MIDTOWN

Telephone 212 245 5000
www.leparkermeridien.com/newyork

An indoor pool awaits guests of this 731 roomed hotel with its quiet décor, cherry and cedar wood touches, sleek lobby, popular breakfast restaurant (Norma's) and welcoming Spa.

Peninsula Hotel 5★, **5th Avenue at West 55th Street,** MIDTOWN

Telephone 212 956 2888
www.peninsula.com/ newyork

A classy Beaux-Arts hotel with 239 rooms, an indoor pool, rooftop bar with awesome views down 5th Avenue and five restaurants. Its style is contemporary with traditional twists, Art Deco touches and beautiful fresh flowers.

Also try: The Manhattan at Times Square Hotel

Night Hotel ⁴⁄⁵, **West 45ᵗʰ Street between 6ᵗʰ and 7ᵗʰ Avenues,** MIDTOWN

Telephone 212 835 9600
www.nighthotelny.com

This hotel has a sexy décor, dark and gothic in shades of black and white. The animal print furnishings, abundant mirrors and brass accents reflect its ambience while the Nightlife restaurant is a trendy place to meet.

Sanctuary Hotel ⁴¹⁄₂⁵, **West 47ᵗʰ Street between 6ᵗʰ and 7ᵗʰ Avenues,** MIDTOWN

Telephone 212 234 7000 www.timesquarenewyork.com/sanctuary

Aptly named and a visual delight, this peaceful hotel exudes calm with a décor in shades of pink and mauve. The feel is plush and exotic, the bar welcoming, while the bedrooms have leather headboards, sail cloth curtains and open plan bathrooms. A restaurant and bar completes the scene.

The Inn at Irving Place 3 ¹⁄₂⁵, **56 Irving Place between East 17ᵗʰ and East 18ᵗʰ Streets, Gramercy Park,** MIDTOWN

Telephone 212 533 4600
www.innatirving.com

Housed in three old Brownstone houses, this quaint hotel has only 5 rooms, 6 suites, fireplaces, four poster beds, embroidered linens, cherry wood floors and Lady Mendyl's tea salon. Enter its front door and step back in time.

Also try: Chelsea Pines Inn

CELEBRITY FAVOURITE

Greenwich Hotel 4 ½*, Greenwich Street at North Moore Street, Tribeca, DOWNTOWN

Telephone 212 941 8900 www.thegreenwichhotel.com

Owned by Robert De Niro and oozing old world charm, this enchanting hotel won my heart with its mix of pieces from around the globe. There are English leather settees, Swedish beds, Moroccan tiles and Tibetan rugs. With only 88 rooms, the hotel has a pool, gym, spa, drawing room and courtyard all for the exclusive use of guests. Try the Locande Verde restaurant or the Tribeca Grill, both De Niro interests.

EXCLUSIVE AND ELUSIVE

Soho House Hotel 4*, **9th Avenue between West 13th and West 14th Streets, Mcatpacking, DOWNTOWN**

Telephone 212 627 9800 www.sohohouseny.com

This tiny 24 roomed hotel is private in every way with a style which is both modern and antique. The trendy bar, heated rooftop pool, library, spa and restaurant are for the exclusive use of guests and members.

HOTELS WITH POOLS AND SPAS

Gansevoort Hotel 3 ½*, **9th Avenue at West 13th Street, Meatpacking District, DOWNTOWN**

Telephone 212 206 6700 www.hotelgansvoort.com

A modern hotel in the trendy Meatpacking District with 210 rooms, a heated outdoor pool and a rooftop lounge offering views over Manhattan. The basement G Spa transforms into a bar at night whilst Provocateur is a trendy place to be seen.

Trump Soho Hotel 5*, Spring Street between 6th Avenue and Varick Street, Soho, DOWNTOWN

Telephone 212 842 5500 or 877 538 7389 www.trumpsohohotel.com

As with anything bearing the "Donald's" name, this hotel is stunning and vibrant in equal measures. There are 391 rooms, an outdoor pool, cocktail lounge and Turkish hammam to pamper your every need.

Note: If you are looking for Hotel chains try Hilton, Holiday Inn and Comfort Inn.

APARTMENTS

There are numerous apartments and houses to rent within Manhattan, Brooklyn and Queens, from a duplex or Brownstone to a loft and studio. Check out the website below for details.

The Apartment Service, Telephone 0208 944 1444
www.apartmentservice.com

THE CITY QUILTER

THE CITY QUILTER®
133 West 25th Street

Learn to Quilt Here!

SPRINKLER
SIAMESE

PATCHWORK AND KNITTING CLASSES

**The City Quilter, West 25ᵗʰ Street
between 6ᵗʰ and 7ᵗʰ Avenues, Chelsea, MIDTOWN**

Telephone 212 807 0390 www.cityquilter.com

If quilting is your hobby then head here for "Big Apple" related fabrics
such as "Olde New York", "New York Subway" and "Times Square".
There are also Batiks and hand dyed fabrics on offer, with patchwork
and sewing classes sometimes available.

COOKERY CLASSES

**Camaje Bistro, MacDougal Street between West Houston and
Bleecker Streets, Greenwich Village, DOWNTOWN**

Telephone 212 673 8184 www.camaje.com

If you love to cook then try these classes run by Abigail Hitchcock,
Head Chef at the Camaje Bistro. First you head to a local market for
the ingredients before heading back to the restaurant for a lesson in
cooking. On other occasions you may just participate in preparation
and cooking, so check first.

KNITTING CLASSES

**Purl Soho, Broome Street between Greene and Mercer Streets,
Soho, DOWNTOWN**

Telephone 212 420 8796 www.purlsoho.com

Packed full of beautiful material, yarn, books, patterns, magazines
and craft supplies, this is not to be missed for all your patchwork and
knitting needs. Check out their website for details of classes as you
may like to go along for a taster.

Lower Manhattan from South Street Seaport, Downtown

Love Sculpture by Robert Indiana (6th Avenue at West 55th Street)

LOVE AND ROMANCE

INDEX

New York is considered to be one of the most romantic Cities in the World with a softer side that many people never experience. It is definitely worth seeking out, especially if you are visiting with a loved one. Here are a few of my favourite things to do with that special person!

Loeb Boathouse, Dinner and Gondola Ride, East 72nd Street at Park Drive North, Central Park, UPTOWN

Telephone 212 517 2233
www.thecentralparkboathouse.com

Go here for dinner at sunset or take a Venetian Gondola ride on the lake, as the sun disappears beyond the magical skyline of New York.

Horse and Carriage Rides, Central Park South (59th Street) between 5th and 6th Avenues, UPTOWN

Telephone 212 736 0680 or 646 399 7404 www.centralpark.com

Take a horse drawn carriage through Central Park and learn something about this swathe of nature along the way. Look out for the castle, fountains, statues and restaurants as you savour the peace and greenery. A great thing to do on a cold winters day when you will snuggle up under a warm fur throw.

Diamond District, along West 47th Street between 5th and 6th Avenues, MIDTOWN

Hub of the New York diamond industry this area is bling, bling, bling all the way, with many of the jewellery shops owned by Hasidic Jews. Drag your loved ones here when you need some serious spoiling!

Also try: Tiffany, Bulgari and Harry Winston

Dinner at Beekman Tower Hotel, Mitchell Place at East 49th Street and 1st Avenue, MIDTOWN

Telephone 212 355 7300 www.thebeekmanhotel.com

Situated on the 26th floor of the Beekman Tower Hotel, this intimate restaurant and piano bar offers rooftop views and classic American cuisine in a setting which is cosy and romantic.

Inn at Irving Place, Irving Place between East 17th and East 18th Streets, Gramercy Park, MIDTOWN

Telephone 212 533 4600
www.innatirving.com

Housed in three old brownstone buildings, this enchanting hotel is full of atmosphere with only 5 rooms, 6 suites, fireplaces, four poster beds, embroidered linens, cherry wood floors and the Lady Mendyl's tea salon.

La Petite Maison, West 54th Street between 5th and 6th Avenues, MIDTOWN

Telephone 212 616 9931 **photo 4** www.lapetitemaisonnyc.com

This tiny French restaurant tucked away beneath an attractive mansion has lots to offer in the way of food and atmosphere. With indoor and outdoor areas, you will need to book well in advance to enjoy a romantic night out with that special person.

Library Hotel, Madison Avenue at East 41ˢᵗ Street, MIDTOWN

Telephone 212 983 4500 or 800 480 9545
www.thelibraryhotel.com

For a romantic weekend away try the "Love Room", at this charming 60 roomed hotel. The daily rate includes breakfast, a wine reception and 24 hour tea/coffee, with a rooftop conservatory and outdoor terrace for guests to enjoy.

Love Sculpture by Robert Indiana, 6ᵗʰ Avenue at West 55ᵗʰ Street, MIDTOWN

Have your photograph taken in front of this huge, red, Robert Indiana pop art "Love" sculpture, the second most photographed icon in New York City. (See first photo of this chapter)

The House Restaurant, East 17ᵗʰ Street between Irving Place and Park Avenue South, MIDTOWN

Telephone 212 253 2121
www.thehousenyc.com

A restored 1854 carriage house is where you will find "The House" restaurant, filled with character. The food is traditional, the background music is swing or jazz, the skylights and windows afford views of the stars and the vibe is pure romance.

World Yacht Cruises, Pier 81, West 41st Street at the Hudson River, MIDTOWN

Telephone 212 630 8100 www.worldyacht.com

If a romantic dinner with live music appeals, try this yacht cruise and view the City from a different perspective. Drink in the dramatic night skyline whilst sailing around Manhattan.

Agent Provocateur, Mercer Street between Prince and Spring Streets, Soho, DOWNTOWN

Telephone 212 965 0229 www.agentprovocateur.com

Oozing glamour with luxurious lingerie, take a look at this Soho shop for thongs, suspenders corsettes and basques, in a sexy space made for fantasies.

Also try: La Perla

Brooklyn Bridge, Chambers Street Station at Park Row, Lower Manhattan, DOWNTOWN

Many tours of New York include a visit to Brooklyn Bridge for the spectacular views, but for the romantics amongst you, take a night tour with that special someone for a vista which is pure magic.

One if By Land Two if By Sea, Barrow Street at 7th Avenue and West 4th Street, Greenwich Village, DOWNTOWN

Telephone 212 255 8694
www.oneifbyland.com

One of the most charming restaurants in New York, with soft lighting, soothing music and traditional American food. Enjoy a cosy night in the heart of the "Village", or try Sunday brunch with live jazz.

Also try: River Café, One Water Street, Brooklyn, (across Brooklyn Bridge from Downtown).

Stargazing on the Highline, under the Standard Hotel between Gansevoort and 14th Streets, Meatpacking District, DOWNTOWN

Telephone 212 206 9922 www.thehighline.org or www.aaa.org

Once a derelict railway, the Highline is now an elevated park where every Tuesday (weather permitting) you can try your hand at stargazing. Amateur astronomers with telescopes will guide you through the celestial delights and show you stars and galaxies you never knew existed.

New Jersey

OL1914H

· LIMOUSINE ·

Broadway at West 51st Street, Midtown

LUXURIES AND LIMOUSINES

INDEX

If you really want to push the budget and enjoy a bit of unashamed luxury then there are lots of treats to choose from in New York. Perhaps you would like to splash out on tickets to the Opera or persuade the man in your life to buy you a $10,000 "Proposal Martini"? You choose and whatever it is - enjoy.

Metropolitan Opera House Tickets, Lincoln Centre, 9th Avenue at West 64th Street, Upper West Side, UPTOWN

Telephone 212 362 6000
www.metoperafamily.org

With prices as high as £280 ($420) per person for the best seats in the house, a night at the Opera would be a great occasion to treat yourself to a bit of culture. A glance at their website will give you details.

Oscar de la Renta, Madison Avenue at East 66th Street, Upper East Side, UPTOWN
Telephone 212 288 5810 www.oscardelarenta.com/newyork

Oscar de la Renta entered the world of fashion in the Fifties when he worked for Balenciaga. Today he lays claim to one of the top fashion design houses in the World. His bridal collection is embellished with the finest embroidery so go here for high end couture at its very best.

Afternoon Tea at the Fairmont Plaza Hotel, 5th Avenue at Central Park South (West 59th Street), MIDTOWN
Telephone 212 759 3000 www.fairmont.com/theplaza

Enjoy a sumptuous afternoon tea at the famed Plaza Hotel with prices from £33 ($50) per person for the Classic afternoon tea, and from £47 ($72) per person if you want the Champagne version.

Bulgari Jewellers, 5th Avenue at West 57th Street, MIDTOWN

Telephone 212 315 9000 www.bulgari.com/newyork

Filled with glamorous Italian style, gaze at the stunning jewellery and watches when you enter this dream shop.

Cocktail - The World's Most Expensive Martini (allegedly), The Algonquin Hotel, West 44th Street between 5th and 6th Avenues, MIDTOWN

Telephone 212 840 6800 www.algonquinhotel.com

A "sparkling" Martini costing a whopping £6,700 ($10,000) includes a diamond ring nestling at the bottom of the glass! Drop this into the conversation as a hint to your loved one if he really wants to make a lasting impression!

Harry Winston Jewellers, 5th Avenue at West 56th Street, MIDTOWN

Telephone 212 245 2000
www.harrywinston.com

Exquisite jewels are the trademark of this top establishment in a shop that would warm any girls heart (just in case your other half happens to be taking notes). It was a Harry Winston wreath necklace that Jennifer Lopez wore to the "Met" in the film Maid in Manhattan.

Lalique Crystal, Madison Avenue at East 58th Street, MIDTOWN

Telephone 212 355 6550
www.lalique.com/newyork

This iconic French crystal maker has been creating designs for more than a Century and is once more back in fashion. Lalique carries on its tradition of fine crystal carvings using 50 craftsmen, and some of the rarer pieces can fetch upwards of £200,000 pounds at auction.

Dinner (or Lunch) at the Chef's Table, Gordon Ramsey's Maze Restaurant, London NYC Hotel, West 54th Street, between 6th and 7th Avenues, MIDTOWN

Telephone 212 468 8888 www.gordonramsay.com

For the ultimate dining experience book a seat at the Chef's Table in the heart of the kitchen where you will watch in awe as your meal unfolds. Prices from around £720 ($1100) lunch and £1400 ($2100) for dinner per person. Check with the hotel before booking, as to who will be your Chef on the night.

Night Limousine Tour, MIDTOWN

Telephone 888 491 9824 www.unclesamsnewyorktours.com

For a night tour with a difference, this takes you to classic bars, lounges and the hottest nightclubs on the Frank Sinatra Nightlife Limousine Tour. Prices from £220 ($330)to £450 ($680) per person

Sunday Brunch at the Waldorf Astoria Hotel, Park Avenue, between East 49th and East 50th Streets, MIDTOWN

**Telephone 212 355 3000
www.waldorfastoria.com**

This Park Avenue landmark hosts a sumptuous Sunday brunch in Peacock Alley every week. There are

12 themed food displays and over 180 gourmet dishes from which to choose. Dress the part as this is a time honoured New York tradition. Prices start from £68 ($105).

Ty Warner Suite, Four Seasons Hotel, East 57th Street between Park and Madison Avenues, MIDTOWN

Telephone 212 759 5700 www.fourseasons.com/newyork

A stunning penthouse suite consisting of nine rooms on the 52nd floor of the Four Seasons Hotel. There are 360 degree views over the City, a waterfall, Zen room, grand piano, library, hot tub and walls of gold in-laid fabric. Prices from around £25,000 ($35,000) per night.

Helicopter scenic flight over New York, Heliport, Pier 6 at the East River, DOWNTOWN

Telephone 212 967 6464 or whilst in New York 1-800 542 9933
www.libertyhelicopters.com

Several companies feature scenic helicopter flights over New York with variations in price and content so check for details before booking. Prices from £100 ($150) per person

OTHER LUXURIES AND LIMOUSINES

Helicopter Airport Transfer from JFK or Newark to either MIDTOWN OR DOWNTOWN

Telephone 212 335 0801 wwwheliny.com

For a real treat, take a helicopter from the airport to Manhattan with a transfer time of around 15 minutes. Prices from £1,400 ($1850) per helicopter for up to six people.

Private Jet Charter from London to New York, Diamond Air, Suite 10, 2B High Street, Loddon, Norwich, England NR14 6AH

Telephone 01508 528 880 www.diamondair.com

Chartering a private jet to fly the Atlantic gives you the freedom to travel when and from where you choose, with none of the hassle normally encountered on scheduled flights. At upwards of £60,000 one way from most UK airports, this has to be the pinnacle of air travel.

Stretch Limousine Airport Transfer from either JFK or Newark Airports

Telephone 212 465 2277 www.gothamlimo.com or www.nyclimousine.com

Limousine transfers are available both to and from either JFK or Newark Airports. What better way to arrive at your destination if you want to make an impression or just for that pure "wow" factor. Prices from around £200 (USD$300) each way for 6 people in a Stretch 6 limousine.

Stretch Limo Reflections

MAPS AND ORIENTATION

The New York City map provided here is divided into three main areas, namely UPTOWN, **MIDTOWN** and DOWNTOWN, each colour coded for easy orientation.

UPTOWN - 60th Street up to 119th Street
Approximately 3.5 miles long x 2 miles wide

(Leafy area around Central Park, Museum Mile, Upper West Side, Upper East Side and Harlem)

MIDTOWN - 59th Street down to 14th Street
Approximately 2 miles long x 2.3 miles wide

(Heart of the City including 5th Avenue Shopping, Times Square and the Theatre District)

DOWNTOWN - 13th Street down to Battery Park
Approximately 3 miles long x 2.3 miles wide

(Bohemian areas including Greenwich Village, Soho, Tribeca and the Financial District)

UPTOWN AND MIDTOWN - GRID ROAD SYSTEM

The Areas of UPTOWN and **MIDTOWN** are mainly based on a grid road system with Avenues (numbered, named or both) running roughly North to South, and Streets (named or numbered) running roughly East to West. Broadway crosses these diagonally from an approximate North to South perspective.

LOCATING AN ADDRESS IN UPTOWN OR MIDTOWN (GRID SYSTEM)

For addresses on Avenues check the cross Streets, for example:
5th Avenue between West 47th and West 48th Streets

For addresses on Streets check the cross Avenues, for example:
West 57th Street between 5th and 6th Avenues

MAPS AND ORIENTATION
Pages 160-167

TIMINGS TO WALK A BLOCK IN UPTOWN OR MIDTOWN (GRID SYSTEM)

Avenues (walking North or South) - approximately 5 minutes per block

Streets (walking East or West) - approximately 10 minutes per block

DOWNTOWN - RANDOM ROAD SYSTEM

By way of contrast the Downtown area has a slightly more random layout with mostly named Streets, although there are still some numbered Streets and Avenues.

LOCATING AN ADDRESS IN DOWNTOWN

For addresses in Downtown check the cross Streets, for example: Hudson Street between West 12th and West 13th Streets

WEST SIDE AND EAST SIDE - UPTOWN/MIDTOWN/DOWNTOWN

"West Side" is everything "West" of 5th Avenue and "East Side" is everything "East" of 5th Avenue.

Pleasant Ave

F D R Dr

East River

East River Dr

East En

York

E 119th St
E 117th St
E 115th St

1st Ave

E 111th St
E 110th St
E 109th St

2nd Ave

3rd Ave

E 103rd St
E 101st St
E 99th St

Metropolitan Hospital

E 97th St

1st Ave

E 95th St
E 93rd St
E 91st St
E 89th St
E 87th St

Lexington Ave

E 107th St
E 105th St

UPTOWN

Lexington Ave

Park Ave

Park Ave

Madison Ave

Madison Ave

5th Ave

5th Ave

MUSEUM MILE

UPPER EAST SIDE

HARLEM

Lenox Ave

Central Park N

Museum of the City of New York

97th St Transverse

Guggenheim

85th St Transverse

St Nicholas Ave

8th Ave

Central Park W

Manhattan Ave

W 118th St
W 116th St

Columbus Ave

W 94th St
W 92nd St
W 90th St
W 88th St
W 86th St

W 114th St
W 113th St
W 112th St

Cathedral Pky

W 108th St
W 106th St
W 104th St

Amsterdam Ave

Broadway

Broadway

W 102nd St
W 100th St
W 98th St
W 96th St

W End Ave

Broadway

Riverside Dr

UPPER WEST SIDE

Henry Hudson Pky

Hudson River

UPTOWN LENGTH

East River

FDR Dr

st End Ave

York Ave

York Ave

1st Ave

1st Ave

2nd Ave

2nd Ave

3rd Ave

3rd Ave

E 85th St
E 83rd St
E 81st St
E 79th St
E 77th St
E 75th St
E 73rd St
E 71st St
E 69th St
E 67th St
E 65th St
E 63rd St
E 61st St
E 60th St
E 59th St
E 58th St
E 57th St
E 56th St
E 55th St

UPPER EAST SIDE

Lexington Ave

Park Ave

Madison Ave

5th Ave

Lex

Pa

Ma

5th

Designer Shopping

• Bloomingdale's

• Metropolitan Museum of Art

• Loeb Boathouse Restaurant

CENTRAL PARK

85th St Transverse

72nd St Transverse

65th St Transverse

• American Museum of Natural History/ Hayden Planetarium

• Dakota Building

Central Park S

Columbus Circle

Trump Tower •

Rockef

6th

7th

8th

9th

Central Park W

• Time Warner

Columbus Ave

• Lincoln Centre

Amsterdam Ave

Broadway

10th Ave

W 86th St
W 84th St
W 82nd St
W 80th St
W 78th St
W 76th St
W 74th St
W 72nd St
W 70th St
W 68th St
W 66th St
W 64th St
W 62nd St
W 61st St
W 60th St
W 59th St
W 58th St
W 57th St
W 56th St
W 54th St

UPPER WEST SIDE

11th Ave

Miller Hwy

3.5 MILES

Hudson River

East River

F D R Dr

United Nations

MIDTOWN

EAST SIDE

York Ave

1st Ave   1st Ave

2nd Ave   2nd Ave

3rd Ave   3rd Ave

• Lipstick Building

Lexington Ave

Park Ave

Madison Ave   Vanderbilt Ave

5th Ave (Shopping)

Rockefeller Centre •

6th Ave (Av of the Americas)

MIDTOWN

7th Ave

Broadway

8th Ave

• Time Warner Centre

9th Ave

10th Ave   10th Ave

11th Ave   11th Ave

DIAMOND DISTRICT

• New York Public Library

Bryant park •

Fashion Ave

8th Ave

FASHION DISTRICT

9th Ave

Grand Central

Chrysler Building

TIMES SQ

THEATRE DISTRICT

Trump Tower •

Radio City

Central Park S

Columbus Cierle

Designer Shopping

Bloomingdale's

Lincoln Centre •

65th St Transverse

Central Park W

Broadway

Hudson River

Lincoln Tunnel

E 67th St, E 65th St, E 63rd St, E 61st St, E 60th St, E 59th St, E 58th St, E 57th St, E 56th St, E 55th St, E 53rd St, E 51st St, E 49th St, E 47th St, E 45th St, E 43rd St, E 41st St, E 39th St, E 37th St, E 35th St

W 68th St, W 66th St, W 64th St, W 62nd St, W 61st St, W 60th St, W 59th St, W 57th St, W 56th St, W 54th St, W 52nd St, W 50th St, W 48th St, W 46th St, W 44th St, W 42nd St, W 40th St, W 38th St, W 36th St

er Hwy

MIDTOWN LENGTH

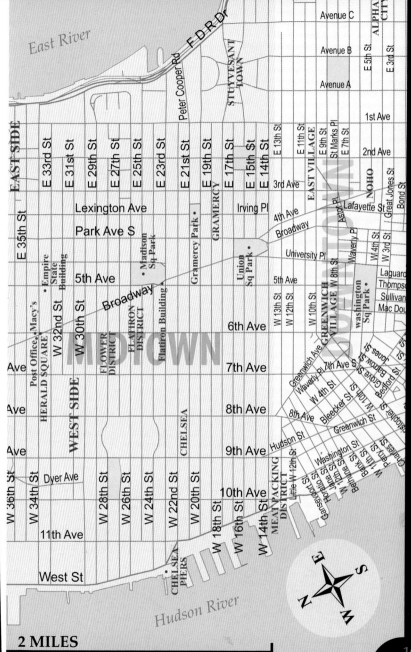

East River

F D R Dr

Avenue C

ALPHA CITY

Avenue B

E 5th St

E 3rd St

Peter Cooper Rd

STUYVESANT TOWN

Avenue A

1st Ave

EAST SIDE

E 33rd St
E 31st St
E 29th St
E 27th St
E 25th St
E 23rd St
E 21st St
E 19th St
E 17th St
E 15th St
E 14th St

E 13th St
E 11th St
St Marks Pl
E 9th St
E 7th St

2nd Ave

EAST VILLAGE

3rd Ave

NOHO

Great Jones St

Bond St

E 35th St

Lexington Ave

GRAMERCY

Irving Pl

Lafayette St

Astor Pl

Park Ave S

4th Ave

Broadway

MIDTOWN

Gramercy Park

Waverly Pl

W 4th St

W 3rd St

Madison Sq Park

University Pl

Empire State Building

5th Ave

Union Sq Park

5th Ave

Laguard

Thompson

Macy's

Broadway

Flatiron Building

W 13th St

W 12th St

W 10th St

washington Sq Park

Sullivan

Mac Dou

Post Office

FLOWER DISTRICT

FLATIRON DISTRICT

6th Ave

W 32nd St

W 30th St

HERALD SQUARE

MIDTOWN

GREENWICH VILLAGE

W 8th St

DOWNTOWN

Greenwich Ave

7th Ave

Waverly Pl

7th Ave S

Jones St

Barrow St

Bedford St

Ave

WEST SIDE

8th Ave

W 4th St

Bleecker St

8th Ave

Greenwich St

Christopher St

W 10th St

Ave

9th Ave

CHELSEA

Hudson St

Greenwich St

W 36th St

W 34th St

Dyer Ave

W 28th St

W 26th St

W 24th St

W 22nd St

W 20th St

W 18th St

W 16th St

W 14th St

10th Ave

MEATPACKING DISTRICT

Gansevoort St

Little W 12th St

Horatio St

Jane St

Washington St

Bank St

Bethune St

Perry St

W 12th St

W 11th St

Charles St

11th Ave

West St

CHELSEA PIERS

Hudson River

N E S W

2 MILES

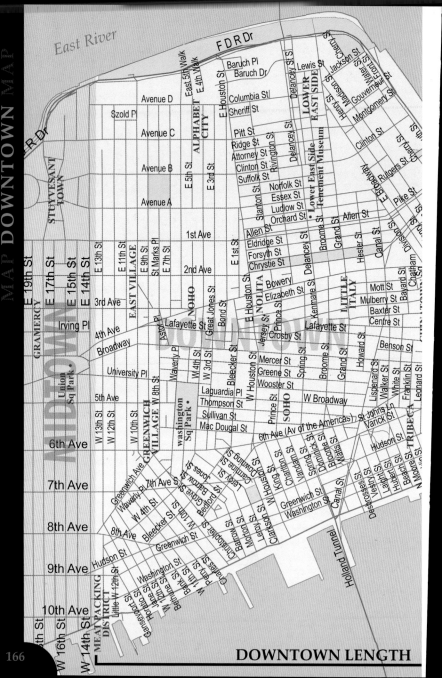

East River

FDR Dr

ER Dr

East 5th Walk
E 4th Walk

Baruch Pl
Baruch Dr

Columbia St

Delancey St S

Lewis St

LOWER
EAST SIDE

Jackson St

Water St
Cherry St
Front St

Avenue D

Szold Pl

E Houston St

Sheriff St

Henry St
Madison St

Gouverneur St
Montgomery St

Avenue C

Pitt St

Ridge St

Attorney St

Clinton St

Delancey St

Clinton St

E Broadway
Rutgers St

ALPHABET
CITY

E 5th St

E 3rd St

Avenue B

Suffolk St

Rivington St

Pike St

Avenue A

Norfolk St
Essex St
Ludlow St
Orchard St

Lower East Side
Tenement Museum

1st Ave

Stanton St

Allen St

Allen St

Hester St

Canal St

Division St

E 19th St
E 17th St
E 15th St
E 14th St

E 13th St
E 11th St

E 9th St
St Marks Pl
E 7th St

1st Ave

Eldridge St
Forsyth St
Chrystie St

E 1st St

Grand St

GRAMERCY

EAST VILLAGE

2nd Ave

Bowery

Broome St

LITTLE
ITALY

Mott St
Mulberry St
Baxter St
Centre St

Bayard St
Chatham Sq

3rd Ave

Irving Pl

NOHO

Great Jones St

Bond St

Elizabeth St
Prince St

Kenmare St

Delancey St

Howard St

Benson St

MIDTOWN

4th Ave

Broadway

Astor Pl

Lafayette St

E Houston St

NOLITA

Jersey St

Lafayette St

Grand St

Crosby St

Union
Sq Park

University Pl

Waverly Pl

W 4th St
W 3rd St

Bleecker St

Mercer St
Greene St
Wooster St

Spring St

Broome St

Grand St

Lispenard St
Walker St
White St
Franklin St
Leonard St

5th Ave

W 13th St
W 12th St

W 10th St

Laguardia Pl
Thompson St
Sullivan St
Mac Dougal St

W Houston St

Prince St

SOHO

W Broadway

6th Ave

GREENWICH
VILLAGE

W 8th St

washington
Sq Park

6th Ave (Av of the Americas)

St Johns Ln
Varick St

Hudson St

TRIBECA

7th Ave

Greenwich Ave

7th Ave S

Waverly Pl

W 4th St

Bleecker St

Bedford St

Grove St

Cornelia St
Downing St

Leroy St

Charlton St

Vandam St

Spring St

Dominick St
Broome St
Watts St

Beach St
Hubert St
Laight St
Vestry St
Desbrosses St

8th Ave

8th Ave

Bleecker St

Greenwich St

Christopher St
Barrow St

Morton St

Leroy St

W Houston St

King St

Clarkson St

Greenwich St
Washington St

Canal St

Hudson St

N Moore St

9th Ave

Hudson St

Gansevoort St
Horatio St
Jane St
W 12th St
Bethune St
Bank St

Little W 12th St

Washington St
Greenwich St

Barrow St
W 11th St
Perry St
Charles St

10th Ave

W 16th St
W 14th St

MEATPACKING
DISTRICT

Holland Tunnel

DOWNTOWN LENGTH

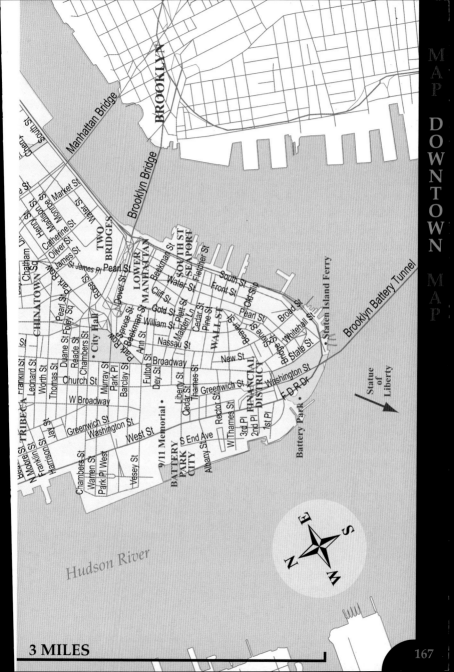

BROOKLYN

Manhattan Bridge

Brooklyn Bridge

TWO BRIDGES

CHINATOWN

South St

Cherry St

Madison St

Monroe St

Water St

Market St

Henry St

Catherine St

Oliver St

James St

St James Pl

Pearl St

Chatham Sq

Pearl St

Park Row

Rose St

Dover St

LOWER MANHATTAN

Beekman St

SOUTH ST SEAPORT

Fletcher St

South St

Front St

Old Slip

Water St

Cliff St

Gold St

Pearl St

Beaver St

Broad St

Foley Sq

Duane St

Reade St

Chambers St

City Hall

Ann St

Spruce St

Beekman St

William St

Maiden Ln

Platt St

Cedar St

Pine St

WALL ST

Stone St

Bridge St

Whitehall St

State St

Staten Island Ferry

Franklin St

Leonard St

Worth St

Thomas St

Nassau St

New St

FINANCIAL DISTRICT

Washington St

TRIBECA

Hudson St

Moore St

Franklin St

Harrison St

Jay St

Church St

W Broadway

Murray St

Park Pl

Barclay St

Vesey St

Fulton St

Dey St

Broadway

Liberty St

Cedar St

Thames St

Greenwich St

Rector St

W Thames St

3rd Pl

2nd Pl

1st Pl

Battery Park

Brooklyn Battery Tunnel

9/11 Memorial

BATTERY PARK CITY

S End Ave

Albany St

Chambers St

Warren St

Park Pl West

Greenwich St

Washington St

West St

Vesey St

F D R Dr

Statue of Liberty

N E S W

Hudson River

MODELLING
AND ACTING
AGENCIES

Many Women dream of being a model or actress and New York abounds with modelling and acting agencies. Just a couple are included below to get you started, however it is always essential that you personally check the background of any Agency you contact or deal with to ensure they will be suitable for you.

MODELLING AGENCIES

Ford Models, Flat 9, 111 5th Avenue between West 18th and West 19th Streets, MIDTOWN
Telephone 212 219 6500
www.fordmodels.com

IMG, 304 Park Avenue South, Penthouse North, at East 23rd Street, MIDTOWN
Telephone 212 253 8884
www.imgmodels.com

Rockport Fashion Shoot

ACTING AGENCY

William Morris Endeavour, 1325 6th Avenue between West 53rd and West 54th Streets, MIDTOWN
Telephone 212 903 1100 www.wma.com

MONEY, ATMS, BANKS, TAXES, TIPPING

Banks will change currency or travellers cheques as will Hotels, although a passport is required for identification. Chase Manhattan Bank has more than 75 foreign exchange outlets in the City (www.chasemanhattan.com). Check with your own bank in England as they may well have a branch in New York.

Cash points (ATMs) are located all over New York and it is rare to walk more than a couple of blocks without finding one. In some hotels you may find a machine in the lobby, however always be aware when using an ATM and be on the lookout for anything or anyone suspicious.

Chip and Pin - Always protect your pin number, be aware of who is around you and don't let your card disappear out of sight. Chip and Pin is not available everywhere so be prepared to sign a slip if asked.

Credit/Debit Cards - Always check with your card provider before you leave the UK that your particular card type is accepted when in America and for any additional charges or precautions you may need to take.

Currency and Exchange Rate - the exchange rate floats somewhere around $1.50 to the pound although it can fluctuate considerably so always check before buying dollars. They come in $1, $2, $5, $10, $20, $50, $100, $500 and $1,000 dollar notes.

Money Cards are available from any Post Office in England but check they are suitable for your needs.

Tax will be added to most things you purchase in New York (i.e. meals, clothes, food, drinks etc) so always check prior to buying any goods, services, meals or purchases as to the exact price you will pay.

Tipping is a way of life in New York and very much part of their culture. Add between 15% and 20% to your bill (if of course you are happy with the service). If tipping a porter then give one or two dollars per bag.

Metropolitan Museum of Art

MUSEUMS, LIBRARIES AND ART GALLERIES

INDEX

Museums in New York abound and offer a diverse choice for all tastes. Some are situated on "Museum Mile" (Guggenheim, Museum of New York, Metropolitan Museum of Art to name just few) which is on the Upper East Side of Central Park. On the Upper West Side you will see the American Museum of Natural History which also incorporates the Hayden Planetarium. The remainder are scattered throughout the City with just a selection featured here for you to consider.

Check individual websites for detailed information on opening times, eateries and content as some only open on certain days and times during the week.

American Folk Art Museum, Lincoln Square, 9th Avenue at West 66th Street, Upper West Side, UPTOWN
Telephone 212 595 9533 www.folkartmuseum.org

For anyone with a particular interest in sewing and quilts, this museum hosts exhibitions on American quilting, sculptures and paintings from the 18th and 19th Centuries, delving into America's folk art heritage.

American Museum of Natural History, Central Park West (8TH Avenue) at West 79th Street, Upper West Side, UPTOWN
Telephone 212 769 5100
www.amnh.org

With displays such as Dinosaurs, Fossils, Reptiles, Antarctic Exploration, Human Origins, Egyptology and a two feet long iridescent ammolite, this is all about the history of Earth and its many inhabitants.

Cooper-Hewitt National Design Museum, East 91st Street at 5th Avenue, Upper East Side, UPTOWN

Telephone 212 849 8400 www.cooperhewitt.org

Van Arpel's Jewellery, Lobmeyer Glass, Doodle 4 Google and Fashion by Sonia Delaunay are just some of the varied items on show at this design Museum.

Gagosian Art Gallery, Madison Avenue at East 76th Street, Upper East Side, UPTOWN

Telephone 212 744 2313
www.gagosian.com

A well known art gallery whose exhibits have included the likes of Damien Hurst, however expect to pay top prices for quality well known artists.

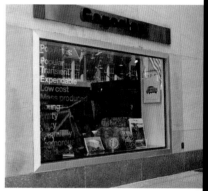

Also try: Goethe Institute

Guggenheim Museum, 5th Avenue between East 89th and East 90th Streets, Upper East Side, UPTOWN

Telephone 212 423 3500 www.guggenheim.org

This striking Frank Lloyd Wright building is a tribute to his distinct

architectural skills, in a space which exhibits Picasso and Kandinsky. A visual delight in its own right, the Guggenheim has featured in many films including The International with Clive Owen.

Hayden Planetarium, Central Park West (8th Avenue) at West 79th Street, Upper West Side, UPTOWN

Telephone 212 769 5100 www.haydenplanetarium.org

Part of the Rose Centre for Earth and Space, this is a dream for anyone interested in astronomy. Take a tour through the Milky Way and Solar System in the Imax theatre, with their virtual and digital universes.

Metropolitan Museum of Art, 5th Avenue at East 82nd Street, Upper East Side, UPTOWN

Telephone 212 535 7710 or 212 788 8770 **photo 5** www.metmuseum.org

Situated on the edge of Central Park, the "Met" as it is more commonly known, houses artwork covering 5000 years and is one of the Worlds largest art Museums. If you have time, go up to the Roof Garden Café for lovely views out over Central Park and the New York skyline.

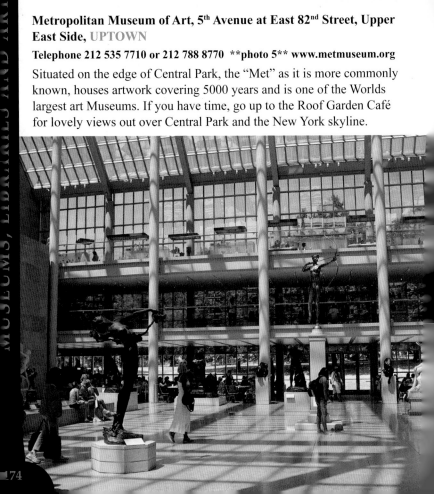

Museum of New York, 5th Avenue at East 103rd Street, Upper East Side, UPTOWN

Telephone 212 534 1672 www.mcny.org

A tribute to the history of New York itself, this Museum hosts various exhibitions including "New York Interiors" (1690 to 1906), "Cars, Culture and the City" plus many more.

New York Public Library for the Performing Arts, Lincoln Centre Plaza at Amsterdam Avenue, Upper West Side, UPTOWN

Telephone 917 275 6975 or 212 875 5000 www.lincolncenter.org

With a collection of reference material relating to the arts, there are stage designs, manuscripts, posters and autographs on show. Ongoing events include Dixieland Jazz, Chopin and Dance on Film.

Chelsea Art Galleries, West 14th to West 29th Streets around 9th, 10th and 11th Avenues, MIDTOWN

The biggest concentration of Art Galleries in New York is in the district of Chelsea, where you will come across more that 100 art studios, centres and galleries. If art is your thing then head here for the day.

Fashion Institute of Technology Museum, 7th Avenue at West 27th Street, MIDTOWN

Telephone 212 217 4558 (recorded 24 hour exhibition line) www.fashionmuseum.fitnyc.edu

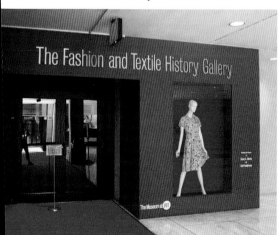

This Institute chronicles the many faces of fashion from the 18th Century to modern day, housing over 50,000 items and accessories within its archives. See the website for details of Tours.

Lladro Museum, West 57th Street between 5th and 6th Avenues, MIDTOWN

Telephone 212 838 9352
www.lladro.com

For anyone who loves porcelain figurines then this is the place for you. Dedicated to all things Lladro you can learn about their history, see how they are made and marvel at their exquisiteness.

Museum of Art and Design (MAD), Columbus Circle at Central Park South (59th Street), MIDTOWN

Telephone 212 299 7777 www.madmuseum.org

Explore art and design using clay, metal, glass, wood and many other materials, with displays of jewellery, nature and ceramics using every technique imaginable. Try the Robert restaurant with views to Central Park.

Museum of Modern Art (MOMA), West 53rd Street between 5th and 6th Avenues, MIDTOWN

Telephone 212 708 9400
www.moma.org

Filled with modern art in every form including sculpture, paintings, architecture, design, film, media, prints, books and drawings, this comprehensive Museum is a definite "must" for lovers of all things arty.

Museum of Sex, 5th Avenue at East 27th Street, Flatiron District, MIDTOWN
Telephone 212 689 6337 www.museumofsex.com

Located in an area of New York once famous for its bordellos, this museum explores all aspects of sexuality and its use in comics, the movies, magazines, dance, advertising and politics. There is a shop on site selling a variety of "goodies" and an Aphrodisiac Café called Oralfix!

New York Public Library and Shop, Main Branch, 5th Avenue between West 40th and West 42nd Streets, MIDTOWN
Telephone 917 275 6975 www.nypl.org

Flanked by two stone lions "Patience & Fortitude", this famous library has featured in many films, books and TV programmes such as Seinfeld, Gossip Girl, The Day After Tomorrow, as well as Sex and the City. It was built in 1911 and is a stunning Beaux-Arts masterpiece. Remember to visit the shop before you leave and check out the McGraw Rotunda room upstairs where Carrie should have married "Big".

Italian American Museum, Mulberry Street at Grand Street, Little Italy, DOWNTOWN

Telephone 212 965 9000 www.italianamericanmuseum.org

Housed in what was once a bank for Italian immigrants, and a vital link to home. This Museum tells the story of their culture, history, achievements, struggles, hopes and fears, when starting a new life in America.

Louis K. Meissel Art Gallery, Prince Street between West Broadway and Wooster Street, Soho, DOWNTOWN

Telephone 212 667 1340 www.meisselgallery.com

Louis K. Meissel is attributed with having coined the phrase "photo realism" in the 60s (where a painting is copied from a photograph) and it is also where Charlotte worked in Sex and the City.

Also try: Ellis Island Museum, Lower East Side Tenement Museum, Merchants House Museum, Morrison Hotel Art Gallery, New York Fire Department Museum and the Skyscraper Museum.

Pastiches of Venus de Milo by Jim Dine, 6th Avenue, Midtown

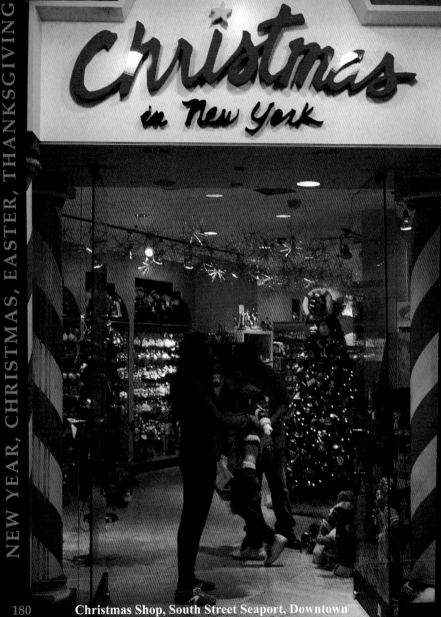

Christmas Shop, South Street Seaport, Downtown

Christmas

Christmas is a magical time of year in New York when hotels, shops and restaurants decorate with traditional trimmings.

Many hotels do special Christmas packages which include a festive lunch. Look out for the beautifully decorated Department store windows, the Cartier giant red ribbon, Tiffany's stunning jewellery displays and the enormous Rockefeller Christmas Tree.

Department store musical snow globes are a great gift to take back home but be prepared for the real thing at this time of year.

Easter

Easter would not be Easter without a parade complete with bonnets, and New York does it with style. 5th Avenue is closed to traffic and New Yorkers turn out in their droves dressed up for the occasion.

New Year

New Year in New York is the ultimate ring out the old, ring in the new experience. Enter Times Square by 9pm or miss out on seeing the awesome sight of the Waterford Crystal ball descend at midnight, bringing with it renewed hopes and dreams for the coming year.

Many bars, pubs, clubs and restaurants put on special New Year celebrations or as an alternative you could take the World Yacht Cruise and float around Manhattan, whilst you watch the spectacular fireworks.

Thanksgiving

Thanksgiving in New York is a huge event attracting thousands of people, and is the official start of the festive season. Christmas decorations are in place and stores like Saks, Barneys, Bloomingdale's and Macy's adorn their windows with Christmas style. The "Streets" and "Avenues" do their bit, whilst traditional meals are eaten of turkey, stuffing, mashed potatoes, cranberry relish and butternut squash, with pumpkin pie for dessert.

With around 28,000 acres of parkland and just under half still in their natural form, New York has several lush, green, wide open spaces. The trees and wildflowers soften the skyscrapers, oxygenate the air and give birds and wildlife an inner City place to live. These parks offer a chance to escape the Metropolitan madness, and in Winter have areas which transform into ice skating rinks. Please be aware that all parks are now non-smoking.

Central Park, 59th Street to 110th Streets between 5th and 8th Avenues, UPTOWN

www.centralpark.com

Covering 843 acres with 57 miles of pathways, 48 structures and buildings, 31 sculptures and 14 lakes, you can lose yourself in the vastness of Central Park. There are American Elms, an overgrown forest, waterfalls, tennis courts, lakes and a Wildlife Conservation Centre. Here you will also find the Conservatory Garden (5th Avenue at 105th Street), with its English, French and Italian areas, a place many people choose as a Wedding venue.

Riverside Park, West 72nd to West 158th Streets at Riverside Drive, Upper West Side, UPTOWN

Telephone 212 870 3070 www.riversideparkfund.org

A beautiful park hugging the Hudson River which is long, narrow and winding, with lawns, flowers and trees. Recognisable by the closing scene of the film "You've Got Mail" where Meg Ryan finally discovers the real identity of Tom Hanks, her cyber lover.

PARKS, GARDENS, ICE SKATING, ROLLER BLADING

Trump Wolman Ice Rink, Central Park, Central Park South entrance (59th Street), UPTOWN

Telephone 212 439 6900 www.wolmanskatingrink.com

Situated within Central Park, this Winter ice rink can be quite magical at night looking out over the surrounding skylines. In Spring, Summer and Autumn it offers inline roller blading and once you feel competent, they will let you go out and explore on your own in the Park.

Bryant Park, West 42nd Street between 5th and 6th Avenues, MIDTOWN

Telephone 212 768 4242 www.bryantpark.org

Nestling behind the New York Public Library, this small park with tall trees, shady areas and cafes, shows free movies every Monday night from late June to mid August. The park accommodates ice skating in Winter, filled with a feel good atmosphere of people having fun. Try the Bryant Park Café and Grill overlooking the rink for a warming bowl of soup.

**Madison Square Park,
East 23rd Street between
5th and Madison Avenues,
MIDTOWN**

Telephone 212 538 1884
www.madisonsquarepark.org

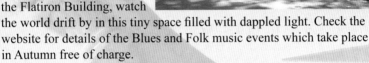

Situated just across from
the Flatiron Building, watch
the world drift by in this tiny space filled with dappled light. Check the
website for details of the Blues and Folk music events which take place
in Autumn free of charge.

**Rockefeller Centre Ice Rink, West 49th Street between 5th and 6th
Avenues, MIDTOWN**

Telephone 212 332 7654 www.rockefellercenter.com

Imagine ice skating
in the middle of New
York surrounded
by urban City life,
towering skyscrapers
and the statue of
←Prometheus. Twirl
the night away, show
off your skating skills
or just shimmy across
the ice for a moment
of pure magic.

**Battery Park, Battery Place at State and Whitehall Streets,
DOWNTOWN**

Telephone 212 344 3491 www.thebattery.org

This park is where Noel Coward spent many a day alone and penniless
yearning to sail home to England. It was also the site of the first Dutch
trading post in New York. Today you will see a collection of statues
and sculptures, including the battered Sphere which previously stood
between the World Trade Centre Towers.

Highline Elevated Park, between Gansevoort and West 14th Streets, Meatpacking District, DOWNTOWN

Telephone 212 206 9922 www.thehighline.org or www.aaa.org

Once a derelict railway, the Highline is now an elevated park which still retains the old rail line and sleepers tucked away amongst the foliage. From here you can see over the Hudson River to New Jersey and are just steps from the fashionable Meatpacking District.

OUTER BOROUGHS

The New York Botanical Gardens, 2900 Southern Boulevard, Bronx, New York 10458

Telephone 718 817 8700 www.nybg.org

This area is made up of 50 gardens in 250 acres with over 30,000 trees, a home gardening centre, native forest, rock garden and a scientific research organisation.

Also try: Brooklyn Botanical Gardens

Useful website - www.nygovparks.org

This section is for you to share a few of your own New York gems. Your suggestion may be featured in the future, with an acknowledgement to yourself, so please try to give as much detail as possible. For this edition I have included those from my Mum, nieces (Kate and Amy) plus two of my closest friends Terri and Sheila.

MUM'S RECOMMENDATIONS

Mum and I went to New York in November 2008 when she was 77, and these are her favourite things: "I especially liked the sights, sounds and aromas when walking the streets or on public transport, watching ordinary New Yorkers go about their lives. I liked the ethnic varieties, the street food stalls, the decorated shop windows at Christmas, plus the horse and carriage ride we took through Central Park, wrapped up in thick black fur. Particularly delightful was the Staten Island Ferry with views of the New York skyline and Statue of Liberty. These are a few of my "Big Apple" memories".

My nieces Kate and Amy who are in their twenties, came with us to New York as a family in 2000 and these are their thoughts:

KATE'S RECOMMENDATION

"I was fifteen when I went to New York. I'd seen so much of Brooklyn Bridge in books and films, but I don't think any description can come close to how I felt, walking on to one of the most iconic pieces of architecture in the City. Even now over 10 years later, the smallest glimpse of its enchanting gothic structure can transport me right back to that day, standing on that bridge. If you go nowhere else during your visit, be sure to take a walk across Brooklyn Bridge. Fall in love, as I did, with the greatest views and greatest City in the world".

AMY'S RECOMMENDATION

"I was looking forward to exploring the vast beautiful City of New York, but what sticks in my mind is always Central Park, a great way to relax and lay back after a busy day".

RECOMMENDATIONS FROM READERS

SHEILA'S RECOMMENDATION

My close friend Sheila has visited New York several times and recommends "The Lounge at New York Central, a cocktail bar situated within the Grand Hyatt Hotel. It's all glass and modern with a good atmosphere, overlooking the street opposite Cipriani's". She also mentioned Mercers Kitchen in Soho "which is great for a lazy Sunday brunch. There were some interesting choices on the menu and you can amble around the quirky art and fashion shops afterwards".

TERRI'S RECOMMENDATION

And finally my friend Terri who now lives in Perth - when I asked for her suggestion, she simply said "SHOP, SHOP, SHOP" - but then she is an out and out shopaholic!

Email: lipstickcityguides@hotmail.co.uk

Mum, Amy, Kate, Lin, Adam, Nic and Colin on the Staten Island Ferry

HOMESTEAD
STEAK
HOUSE
NEW YORK'S
OLDEST
Est 1868

We're The
King of Beef

No Stoppi

Chelsea, Midtown

RESTAURANTS, DINERS AND DELIS

INDEX

Eating out has become an essential part of British culture, and in New York it is often the highlight of any day. With a mind boggling array of places to eat, the restaurants offered here give variety in both food and price. Some even have spectacular views and music. It is also worth trying bars and pubs for traditional home cooked food.

Look out for festivals during your stay like "New York Restaurant Week (January, February, July), "A Taste of Times Square" (June) and the Italian Food Festival of San Gennaro (September). There are often special fixed price menus at these times, or alternatively just wander the streets until you find something to tease your taste buds.

DINE WITH A VIEW

Loeb Boathouse, Central Park, East 72nd Street and Park Side North, UPTOWN

Telephone 212 744 3949 www.thecentralparkboathouse.com

Overlooking a lake in Central Park, the Loeb Boathouse offers casual, formal or light dining with the Lakeside Restaurant, outside Grill and Express Café. Watch the ducks and rowboats as day slips into night.

STEAKS AND SEAFOOD

P. J. Clarke's, West 63rd Street at Broadway, Upper West Side, UPTOWN

Telephone 212 957 9700 www.pjclarkes.com

Opposite the Lincoln Centre and a favourite haunt of Frank Sinatra, this restaurant serves steaks, seafood and shepherd's pie, with Angus beef hamburgers, New England Clam Chowder and traditional desserts.

AMERICAN DINERS

Brooklyn Diner, West 57th Street between Broadway and 7th Avenue, MIDTOWN

Telephone 212 581 8900
www.brooklyndiner.com

Authentic American diners are in demand within New York by tourists and locals alike. This one is sought after for its ethnic Jewish, Italian and Irish dishes, Sunday brunch and huge desserts.

Ellen's Stardust Diner, Broadway at West 51st Street, MIDTOWN

Telephone 212 956 5151
www.ellensstardustdiner.com

With its 1950s memorabilia, variety shows and indoor train, this is a true American institution and very much a diner with a difference. Always popular so you may have to queue.

BURGERS AND BUNS

Dave and Busters, West 42nd Street between 7th and 8th Avenues near Times Square, MIDTOWN

Telephone 646 495 2015 www.daveandbusters.com

A casual dining experience with burgers, seafood, steaks and games galore. There are machines for trivia, ride simulators, dance pads and bowling, plus you may just see a Celebrity or two.

Also try: Five Napkin Burger in Hell's Kitchen and the Burger Joint at Le Parker Meridien Hotel.

191

CASUAL DINING

Chop't Creative Salads, West 51ˢᵗ Street between 6ᵗʰ and 7ᵗʰ Avenues, MIDTOWN

Telephone 212 974 8140
www.choptsalad.com

This slick operation is mesmerising to watch as they skilfully prepare your salad or wrap. There is a delicious and varied menu, making this a great vegetarian option. Dine in or take out, the choice is yours.

Also try: Au Bon Pain

CELEBRITY SPOTTING

Buddakan, 9ᵗʰ Avenue between West 15ᵗʰ and West 16ᵗʰ Streets, Chelsea, MIDTOWN

Telephone 212 989 6699
www.buddakannyc.com

Where Carrie and "Big" held their rehearsal dinner in the first Sex and the City film, this Asian fusion restaurant has ornate chandeliers, a sweeping staircase and framed Buddha's. Sit at the bar where Carrie tells "Big" this will be her "last single girl kiss", or take the SATC tour which includes a stop at Buddakan.

Michael Jordan's The Steakhouse, North and West Balconies, Grand Central Terminal, East 42nd Street at Park Avenue, MIDTOWN

Telephone 212 655 2300
www.michaeljordansnyc.com

Housed in Grand Central Terminal with views over the balcony to the concourse below, means this is an experience not to be missed. Sit at the oval bar and enjoy a cocktail, whilst you soak up the atmosphere.

Sardi's, West 44th Street, between 7th and 8th Avenues, MIDTOWN
Telephone 212 221 8440 www.sardis.com

Famous for its French and Italian food, every wall in this popular restaurant is covered with Celebrity caricatures. Steeped in Theatre District history, Sardi's has featured in many films including "Radio Days", "Frost/Nixon" and "The Producers".

Tao Restaurant, East 58th Street between Park and Madison Avenues, MIDTOWN

Telephone 212 888 2288 www.taorestaurant.com

Favoured by Celebrities, this Asian restaurant with speciality dishes from Thailand, Japan and Hong Kong, has a temple-like ambience with a huge Buddha as its focal point. Try the fixed price lunch menu.

Also try: 21 Club

RESTAURANTS DINERS AND DELIS

193

DINE WITH A VIEW

R Lounge, Renaissance Hotel, Times Square, 7ᵗʰ Avenue at West 48ᵗʰ Street, MIDTOWN

Telephone 212 261 5200 or 212 765 7676 www.rlounge

Stunning views await you at the R Lounge as it gazes out over Times Square. This is a "light bite" affair with grilled fish, soups, steaks and club sandwiches, or try the Blue Ribbon menu of pork sliders, chicken wings, hummus and shrimps.

World Yacht Cruises, Pier 81, West 41st Street at the Hudson River, MIDTOWN

Telephone 212 630 8100 www.worldyacht.com

For a romantic dinner with live music, sail around New York on a World Yacht, drink in the dramatic skyline and watch the City drift past in a blaze of evening light.

Also try: Rare View Lounge Affinia Shelburne, Classic Harbour Line Sailing, The View at the Marriott Marquis (revolving) and the Water Club Restaurant.

Useful website: www.rooftoprestaurants.com/newyork

EXCLUSIVE AND EXPENSIVE

Gordon Ramsay's Maze Restaurant, The London NYC Hotel, West 54th Street between 6th and 7th Avenues, MIDTOWN

Telephone 212 468 8856
www.gordonramsay.com

Dinner at the "Chef's Table" in the heart of the kitchen will see little change from £1,300 ($1,900) per person, at Gordon Ramsey's Maze restaurant. If French inspired cuisine in an intimate, exclusive setting is what you desire, then here is the place to splash the cash.

The Oak Room and Bar, The Plaza Hotel, 5th Avenue at Central Park South (West 59th Street), MIDTOWN

Telephone 212 758 7777 www.oakroomny.com

For the ultimate in dining experiences book a seat at the "Chef's Table" in the Oak Room which is part of the Plaza Hotel. Accessible only by private entrance, you must expect to pay top dollar for the privilege.

Also try: Per Se

FOOD COURT

Grand Central Terminal Food Court, Lower Level, East 42nd Street at Park Avenue, MIDTOWN

Telephone 212 340 2583 www.grandcentralterminal.com/diningconcourse

There is a dining concourse hidden away beneath the station offering an array of food, including pizzas, pasta, soups, burgers, curries, salads, sandwiches and steaks. Don't forget to look at the stunning architecture and ceiling as you make your way through this Landmark building.

RESTAURANTS, DINERS AND DELIS

INTERNATIONAL CUISINE

Asia de Cuba Restaurant, Morgans Hotel, Madison Avenue between East 37th and East 38th Streets, MIDTOWN

Telephone 212 686 0300 or 212 726 7755
www.morganshotel.com/asiadecuba

Serving Latin and Asian food, this Phillipe Starck designed restaurant has a large communal table which gives you a great opportunity to get to know the locals and maybe the odd Celebrity. This has also featured in Sex and the City.

Russian Tea Room, West 57th Street between 6th and 7th Avenues, MIDTOWN

Telephone 212 581 7100
www.russiantearoomnyc.com

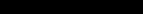

Founded by members of the Russian Imperial Ballet in 1927, Actors, Politicians and Writers have been past patrons. The feel is opulent with a rich gold, green and red décor. Choose from high tea, brunch or dinner.

Also try: La Grenouille

MUSIC AND FOOD

Caffe Taci at the Papillon Bistro, East 54th Street between 5th and Madison Avenues, MIDTOWN

Telephone 212 866 0111 www.caffetaci.com

Dinner upstairs at the Italian Caffe Taci is a haven for Opera lovers. You never know who might be performing as it often attracts budding professionals and international artists. Go here for a lively operatic experience.

Also try: BB Kings Blues Club

ROMANTIC RENDEZVOUS

The House Restaurant, East 17th Street between Irving Place and Park Avenue South, MIDTOWN

Telephone 212 253 2121 www.thehousenyc.com

A restored 1850s carriage house is home to this lovely restaurant. The food is traditional American, the background music swing or jazz, the skylights and windows afford views of the stars, and the atmosphere is pure romance.

La Petite Maison, West 54th Street between 5th and 6th Avenues, MIDTOWN

Telephone 212 616 9931 www.lapetitemaisonnyc.com

This tiny French restaurant has lots to offer in the way of food and ambience, tucked away beneath an attractive mansion. With indoor and outdoor areas, go here to enjoy a romantic night out with that special someone.

Also try: Top of the Tower at the Beekman Hotel.

STEAKS AND SEAFOOD

Bobby Van's, West 50th Street between 6th and 7th Avenues, MIDTOWN

Telephone 212 957 5050 www.bobbyvans.com

This is a popular steak house just steps from Times Square and the Theatre District. Mum and I ate here when we visited New York in 2008 and loved every minute. From the wood panelling and Italian lights, to the etched glass and lively atmosphere, it was a real treat and a night we will always remember.

Oyster Bar, Grand Central Terminal, East 42nd Street at Park Avenue MIDTOWN

Telephone 212 490 6650
www.oysterbarny.com

The Oyster Bar at Grand Central is as famous as the station itself, and renowned for its Maine oysters, clam chowder and chilled champagne. What better way to spend a lazy New York afternoon.

Smith and Wollensky, 3rd Avenue at East 49th Street, MIDTOWN

Telephone 212 753 1530
www.smithandwollensky.com

New York steak at its best, with enormous portions at reasonable prices. Featured in "The Devil Wears Prada", try the late night Wollensky Grill which is open until 2am, for any night owls amongst you.

Also try: The Old Homestead Steakhouse.

SUNDAY BRUNCH

Peacock Alley, Waldorf Astoria Hotel, Park Avenue at East 49th Street, MIDTOWN

Telephone 212 355 3000 or 212 872 1275 www.waldorfastoria.com/newyork

Sunday brunch in New York is an age old tradition and nowhere will you find a more sumptuous offering, with a wide array of delicious food, than at Peacock Alley in the Waldorf Astoria. Dress the part and enjoy the experience, in one of my hotels of choice.

Also try: B B Kings and Bryant Park Grill

THEMED RESTAURANT

Hard Rock Café, Broadway at West 44th Street, Times Square, MIDTOWN

Telephone 212 343 3355 www.hardrock.com/newyork

Serving sandwiches, salads and burgers, the walls are covered in historic rock memorabilia with items from Madonna, Gwen Stefani, The Beatles and Elvis.

Also try: TGI Friday's and Planet Hollywood

CELEBRITY SPOTTING

Minetta Tavern, MacDougal Street at Minetta Lane, Greenwich Village, DOWNTOWN

Telephone 212 475 3850 or 212 475 5000 www.minettatavernny.com

An enchanting Parisian steakhouse and bar in the heart of the "Village", where Celebrities have been known to dine. Ernest Hemingway, Dylan Thomas and Eugene O'Neill were once frequent visitors, so you will follow in famous footsteps.

Nobu Restaurant, Hudson Street at Franklyn Street, Tribeca, DOWNTOWN

Telephone 212 219 0500 www.noburestaurant.com/tribeca

Nobu restaurants have long had a Celebrity following, with many living in the Tribeca area. The menu is Japanese with a modern twist, while the restaurant is filled with natural elements and textures like birch trees and wooden floors.

Standard Grill, Washington Street at West 13th Street, Meatpacking District, DOWNTOWN

Telephone 212 645 4100 www.thestandardgrill.com

A Grill room serving hearty American food, with tables either on the pavement (sidewalk) overlooking cobblestone streets, or alternatively choose one in the bar or dining room. Celebrities have been spotted here so eyes peeled.

Tribeca Grill, Greenwich Street at Franklin Street, Tribeca, DOWNTOWN

Telephone 212 941 3900 www.myriadrestaurantgroup.com/tribecagrill

Housed in a converted warehouse with attractive Tiffany style lights, tiled floors and an oak bar, this friendly restaurant is part owned by Robert De Niro. Try the fixed price Sunday brunch at around $20.00 per person and be on the prowl for famous diners.

Also try: B Bar and Grill, Balthazar, Lucky Strike, Market Table, Odeon Restaurant, and Pastis.

DELI

Katz Deli, East Houston Street at Ludlow Street, Lower East Side, DOWNTOWN

Telephone 212 254 2246 www.katzdeli.com

Around since 1888 and famed for its hot pastrami on rye, this popular deli is where Meg Ryan faked an orgasm in the film "When Harry Met Sally".

DINE WITH A VIEW

River Café, Water Street next to Brooklyn Bridge, Brooklyn, (across the river from DOWNTOWN)

Telephone 718 522 5200 www. rivercafe.com

This American restaurant opened in 1977 and nestles beneath Brooklyn Bridge, across the East River. Overlooking one of the most photographed views in New York, from the outside it is just an East River barge, but step inside at night and the transformation is staggering. Awarded many accolades, go here for fine dining and romance in an unforgettable setting.

Also try: Cabana Nuevo Latino and Harbour Lights at South Street Seaport.

ENGLISH STYLE FOOD

Tea and Sympathy, Greenwich Avenue between West 12th and West 13th Streets, Greenwich Village, DOWNTOWN

Telephone 212 989 9735 www. teaandsympathynewyork.com

Serving all your favourite English dishes of Roast Beef and Yorkshire pudding, treacle tart or rhubarb and custard. Nip next door to buy English tea and groceries or go to "A Salt and Battery" (next door again) for fish and chips.

201

INTERNATIONAL CUISINE

Fig and Olive, West 13ᵗʰ Street between 9ᵗʰ Avenue and Washington Street, Meatpacking District, DOWNTOWN

Telephone 212 924 1200 www.figandolive.com/meatpackingdistrict

This restaurant has a Mediterranean feel in both décor and food, using quality extra virgin olive oils from Spain, Italy and France. The menu includes fish, chops, salads and sorbets to tempt your palate.

Spice Market, West 13ᵗʰ Street at 9ᵗʰ Avenue, Meatpacking District, DOWNTOWN

Telephone 212 675 2322
www.spicemarket.com

World renowned Head Chef, Jean-Georges took inspiration from his travels in the Far East for this authentic Asian restaurant, with oriental food to match the surroundings.

Also try: Sofia's and Tortilla Flats

ROMANTIC RENDEZVOUS

One if By Land, Barrow Street at 7th Avenue and West 4th Street, Greenwich Village, DOWNTOWN

Telephone 212 228 0822 or 212 255 8649 www.oneifbyland.com

One of the most romantic restaurants in New York, it was named after an early warning system for an attack on America (one signal if the attack was by land and two if by sea). Try the American Sunday brunch with live jazz or go here for an intimate dinner with your loved one.

Also try: Barrow Street Ale House next door for a pre or post dinner drink.

STEAKS AND SEAFOOD

Delmonico's, Beaver Street at William Street, Financial District, DOWNTOWN

Telephone 212 509 1144
www.delmonicosny.com

Birthplace of Eggs Benedict and Baked Alaska, Delmonico's first opened in 1837 and is in the heart of the financial district. As an alternative try their Grill Room next door for a more casual dining experience.

Also try: Strip House Steak House and the Gotham Bar and Grill

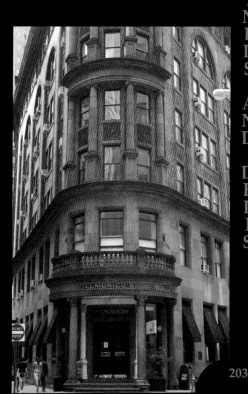

INDEX

SHOPS AND MARKETS

A trip to the shops in New York is a given as many things are cheaper than in the UK. There are even Fashion and Shopping tours on offer (see Tours section) which will give you the insiders nod on where to shop, bargains to be had as well as lots of hints and tips. New York has it all including Designer Wedding dress shops, Boutiques, Department stores, Jewellers, Lingerie shops and Markets.

This chapter gives you choices of shop type (Department stores, Boutiques etc) as well as areas where certain retailers are grouped together (Bridal). There is even an out of town discount shopping outlet (Woodbury Common) around one hour by bus from New York.

Always remember to add any State or City taxes to the cost of goods bought as these may not be shown on the label but will be added at the till. They can vary depending on the goods so check before you buy.

New York is a City forever changing so what once existed may well have disappeared, but there is often another little gem in its place.

UPTOWN/MIDTOWN/DOWNTOWN

"Fashion's Night Out" - www.fashionsnightout.com

"Fashion's Night Out" is held every September for just one night when stores re-open from 6pm to 11pm with designers, Celebrities, models and editors participating in the event. There is a real party atmosphere on 5th Avenue and the "Fashion's Night Out" clothing collection donates 40% of takings to the New York City Aids Charity. Join in the fun and you may also grab a bargain along the way.

Other Useful Websites: **www.fashionista.com**

www.celebrityclothingline.com

www.whatcelebswear.com

www.clothingline.com

www.racked.com/ny

BOOK STORE

Kitchen Arts and Letters, Lexington Avenue at East 94th Street, Upper East Side, UPTOWN

Telephone 212 876 5550 www.kitchenartsandletters.com

A book store devoted entirely to food and wine which stocks over 7,000 titles on the subject so you have lots to choose from if this is your interest.

BRIDAL SHOPS AND ACCESSORIES

The area around Madison Avenue from East 65th Street and above is where you will find a selection of shops and boutiques catering to the Wedding market and just some are detailed below.

Vera Wang, Madison Avenue ➔ between East 76th and East 77th Streets, Upper East Side, UPTOWN

Telephone 212 628 3400 or 212 628 9898 www.verawang.com/newyork

Designer bridal gowns with style and class from the inimitable Vera Wang. Visit her showrooms and be prepared to fall in love with the wedding dress of your every dream.

Also try: J. Crew Bridal, Clea Colett, Oscar de la Renta and Reem Accra for wedding dresses, Miriam Rigler for Mother of the Bride outfits, Suzanne Rigler a Couture Milliner and L'Olivier a Floral Artist.

DEPARTMENT STORE

Barneys, Madison Avenue at East 61ˢᵗ Street, Upper East Side, UPTOWN

Telephone 212 826 8900
www.barneys.com

This high end department store attracts wealthy clients with over fifty featured designers including Balenciaga, Carven, Christian Louboutin, Helmut Lang, L'Wren Scott and Nina Ricci. Quality shoes, clothes and handbags could spoil you for choice as you mix with the swanky upper echelons of New York society.

DESIGNER BOUTIQUES

Around Madison Avenue in the UPTOWN area (60ᵗʰ Street and above) there are end to end Designer boutiques filled with temptation. Look out for ←DKNY, Donna Karan, Oscar de la Renta, Jimmy Choo, Calvin Klein and Ralph Lauren amongst others.

DESIGNER SECOND HAND SHOP (CONSIGNMENT STORE)

Michaels, The Consignment Shop for Women, Madison Avenue between East 79ᵗʰ and East 80ᵗʰ Streets, Upper East Side, UPTOWN

Telephone 212 737 7273
www.michaelsconsignment.com

For over 45 years this is where ladies of the Upper East Side have deposited their pre-worn designer clothes. This shop specialises in their resale, some barely worn. Rummage with gusto!

MARKETS

Green and Flea Markets, Columbus Avenue between West 76th and West 77th Streets, UPTOWN

Telephone 212 788 7476
www.grownyc.org

Open only on Sunday from 10am to 6pm, these markets are huge with both outdoor and indoor stalls selling everything from handmade crafts, antiques and books. Fresh produce is also available from the Farmers market stalls.

5TH - 7TH AVENUES, MADISON, PARK, LEXINGTON AVENUES AND 3RD AVENUE FROM EAST 59TH TO EAST 39TH STREETS - MIDTOWN

One of the main shopping districts in New York and home to Department stores, Designer boutiques, High Street chains, Sports wear outlets, Jean shops, Jewellers, Photography shops and Technology stores. A selection of retailers follows.

AMERICAN CRAFTS

An American Craftsman, West 52nd Street at 7th Avenue, MIDTOWN

Telephone 212 399 2555
www.anamericancraftsman.com/newyork

This delightful shop sells a range of authentic American gifts for you to take home, with glassware, jewellery and carved wooden boxes for sale, bringing together American artists and showcasing their work.

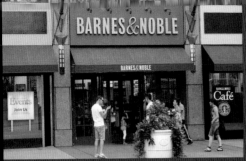

BOOK STORE

Barnes and Noble, 5th Avenue between West 45th and West 46th Streets, MIDTOWN
Telephone 212 697 3048
www.barnesandnoble.com

This well known book store sometimes holds author book signing events for the likes of Harry Belafonte, William Shatner and Bill Cosby. The dates are normally posted on their website so you can see if any coincide with your trip to New York.

CHEMIST (PHARMACY)

Duane Reade Pharmacy
Telephone 212 541 9708
www.duanereade.com

This pharmacy opens 7 days a week 24 hours a day with several locations throughout MIDTOWN, selling snacks, sandwiches, soft drinks, cakes and chocolate plus all the usual things you would expect in a chemist.

Also try: CVS Chemists

DEPARTMENT STORES

Bloomingdale's, Lexington Avenue at East 59th Street, MIDTOWN
Telephone 212 705 2000 www.bloomingdales.com

"Bloomies" is a New York landmark loved by most and covering an entire block that brims with mini boutiques, from DKNY to Calvin Klein. It also sells reasonably priced clothing and shoes with cafés and toilets on site.

Saks, 5th Avenue between East 49th and East 50th Streets, MIDTOWN

Telephone 212 753 4000
www.saksfifthavenue.com

A 5th Avenue institution with 8 floors of Designer collections from around the World. Shoe and beauty departments also reside here with a choice of restaurants, cafes and those all important toilets. Look out for the Christmas musical snow globes showing views of New York, as they make great souvenirs or presents.

Also try: Bergdorf Goodman, Henri Bendel and Macy's

DESIGNER BOUTIQUES

The shops around 5th and Madison Avenues from East 59th to East 39th Streets feature many Designer boutiques to keep you enthralled for hours, some of which are detailed below as a taster.

Dior, East 57th Street at Madison Avenue, MIDTOWN

Telephone 212 931 2950 or 212 207 9245 www.dior.com/newyork

With a luminescent exterior that resembles Mother of Pearl, it only hints at what lies within this flagship store. Selling haute couture and ready to wear items, expect your purse to be seriously challenged.

Louis Vuitton, East 57ᵗʰ Street on the Corner of 5ᵗʰ Avenue, MIDTOWN
Telephone 212 758 8877 www.louisvuitton.com/newyork

Iconic handbag and luggage retailer revered by Carrie Bradshaw and friends in Sex and the City, this store stocks leather goods, shoes, watches and clothes. Look out for the eye catching window displays.

Also try: Armani, BCBG Max Zria, Chanel, Gucci, Prada, Ralph Lauren and Miu Miu.

DESIGNER SHOES

Jimmy Choo, 5th Avenue at East 51ˢᵗ Street, MIDTOWN
Telephone 212 593 0800 www.jimmychoo.com

Jimmy Choo is a name synonymous with footwear offering Bridal

shoes as part of his collection. Styles include his classic range right up to exquisite jewel encrusted shoes, some almost too precious to wear. Step inside and drool.

Also try: Manolo Blahnik

DISCOUNT DESIGNER STORE

Barney's Warehouse Sale, (back entrance) West 17th Street between 7th and 8th Avenues, Chelsea, MIDTOWN

Telephone 212 593 7800 www.barneys.com

In August and September each year New York holds its breath for the much awaited Barney's Warehouse sale. Chaotic - yes. Insane - definitely. But usually perfect for picking up those Designer bargains.

Also try: Filene's Basement and Loehmann's Discount Department Store

FUN SHOP

Disney Store, Times Square at Broadway between West 45th and West 46th Streets, MIDTOWN

Telephone 212 626 2910
www.disneystore.com/newyork

A visual display of all things Disney much as you would expect from this fantasy shop, which attracts adults and children in equal measures.

GARMENT (FASHION) MANUFACTURING DISTRICT - WEST 34TH TO WEST 42ND STREETS AND 5TH TO 9TH AVENUES, MIDTOWN

Filled with fashion wholesalers and shops selling sewing thread, buttons, embroidery and embellishments, this is where "Showroom New York" (www.showroomny.com) a group of local designers work together to promote the New York fashion industry. Keep an eye open for sample sales and see the Exclusive Jill Lynne "Just for You" Fashionable Tour (Tours and Excursions).

HIGH STREET CHAINS

Anthropologie, Rockefeller Plaza, West 50th Street between 5th and 6th Avenues, MIDTOWN

Telephone 212 246 0386
www.anthropolgie.com

A stylish store which sells everything from fashionable clothes, home ware, shoes, boots, jewellery and accessories, their aim being to offer a beautiful shopping experience in attractive surroundings

H & M, 5th Avenue at East 51st Street, MIDTOWN
Telephone 212 489 0390 www.hm.com/newyork

All you know and love from the H & M brand is Stateside in New York. There are several locations in MIDTOWN and DOWNTOWN to choose from including 5th Avenue and Soho. Go here if familiarity calls.

Also try: Quicksilver and Zara

INTERIORS AND HOME FURNISHINGS

The area around West 18th Street between 6th and 7th Avenues is where you will find a concentration of furniture and interior stores such as Bed, Bath & Beyond as well as Lazzoni. These are great to explore and give you a real insight into the style choices of resident New Yorkers.

JEANS AND DENIM

As with much of America there are a variety of stores selling denim and jeans from designer to vintage and everything in between. Mostly they are cheaper than in the UK so take advantage and shop, shop, shop!

AX (Armani Exchange), 5th Avenue at East 51st Street, MIDTOWN
Telephone 212 980 3037 www.armaniexchange.com/newyork

Armani Exchange offers you designer denim with a choice of looks, from boot cut and flared to skinny and straight legged. See their website for the fit and style guide.

Also try: Diesel and Levi Jeans

JEWELLERS

Cartier Jewellers, Cartier Place, 5th Avenue at East 52nd Street, MIDTOWN

Telephone 212 446 3400
www.cartier.com/newyork

The respected French jewellers Cartier are so highly thought of in New York they have a Street named after them, meaning you should expect to pay top prices for the honour of shopping here! If it is fine watches and jewellery you want then this is your place.

Swarovski, Madison Avenue at East 58th Street, MIDTOWN

Telephone 212 308 1710
www.swarovski.com/newyork

Crystals, crystals and more crystals are the name of this game and whether adorning watches or set in bracelets, things that glitter here are not always gold. This shop will seduce you with its clever displays and appealing colours not to mention the attractive jewellery, charms, fashion gadgets and bejewelled boxes.

Also try: The Diamond District, Harry Winston plus Tiffany and Co.

MALLS

Time Warner Centre, Columbus Circle at West 59th Street and Broadway, MIDTOWN

Telephone 212 823 6300 or
212 484 8000
www.shopsatcolumbuscircle.com/
timewarnercenter

A classy mall for upmarket shopping, eating and entertainment. The Time Warner Centre has an organic food market, fitness centre, restaurants, cafes, bars and even jazz, so a great place for a few hours wandering.

Also try: Rockefeller Centre (Lower Level) and the Manhattan Mall

MOVIE NEWS

Movie Star News, West 18th Street between 6th and 7th Avenues, Chelsea, MIDTOWN

Telephone 212 620 8160
www.moviestarnews.com/newyork

For real movie buffs who yearn for reproduction posters and photographs of their favourite films or stars of the screen, head to West 18th Street and browse their extensive stock.

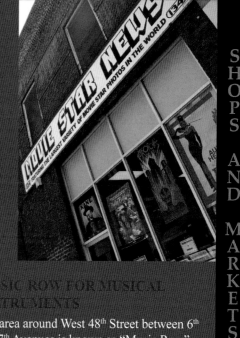

MUSIC ROW FOR MUSICAL INSTRUMENTS

The area around West 48th Street between 6th and 7th Avenues is known as "Music Row" with a collection of shops selling guitars, pianos, drums and percussion instruments. Most are part of the Sam Ash brand which has been around for more than 80 years and all are welcome to have a play.

PHOTOGRAPHY

International Photography Centre, 6th Avenue at West 43rd Street, MIDTOWN

Telephone 212 857 9725 or 212 857 0000
www.icp.org

Housing a shop, museum, research facility, school and café, this is well worth a visit to see the various exhibitions on show and to compare them with your own efforts.

Note: For photographic equipment, go to Best Buy on 5th Avenue at East 44th Street.

SUPERMARKETS

Whole Foods Market, Time Warner Centre, Lower Ground Floor, Columbus Circle at West 59th Street and Broadway, MIDTOWN
Telephone 212 823 6300 www.wholefoodsmarket.com/newyork

This supermarket sells quality organic food in a well thought out space, below the Time Warner Centre. Their displays are eye catching, the food inviting and the service excellent. With meat, fruit, vegetables, New York style cheesecake, cheeses and much more on offer, stop here if you are heading into Central Park for the day as this is the perfect place to shop for your picnic.

Also try: Morton Williams and The Food Emporium

VINTAGE CLOTHING

Cheap Jack's Vintage Clothing, 5th Avenue at East 31st Street, MIDTOWN
Telephone 212 777 9564
www.cheapjacks.com

Around since 1975, this store offers a vast selection of all things vintage and is often frequented by stars of the stage, as well as film production companies.

Also try: New York Vintage (MIDTOWN), Screaming Mimi's and Star Struck Vintage (DOWNTOWN)

DESIGNER BOUTIQUES AND INDIVIDUAL SHOPS

Greenwich Village, Soho, Noho, Tribeca and the Meatpacking District host a concentration of individual boutiques and designer stores housed in renovated warehouses, wrought ironwork buildings or converted terraces. Shops include Agnes B, Aphrodesia, Bookmarc, Emporio Armani, Juicy Couture, Karen Millen, Lulu Guinness, Miu Miu, Phat Farm, Prada and many more. Here are a few temptations to get you excited!

Dash Boutique, Spring Street at Greene Street, Soho, DOWNTOWN

Telephone 212 226 2646
www.kimkardashian.celebuzz.com
www.khloekardashian.celebuzz.com
www.kourtneyk.celebuzz.com

A Soho boutique owned by the Kardashian sisters and made famous by their reality TV programme. With a mix of fashion items from boho woven bracelets to figure hugging stretchy dresses, there will be times when you may have to queue just to get in the door. If you are a fan you will at least get a glimpse of their domain and style in clothes.

Diane Von Furstenberg, Washington Street at West 14th Street, Meatpacking District, DOWNTOWN

Telephone 646 486 4800 www.dvf.com

This is where Carrie Bradshaw rings Samantha to tell her she is marrying "Big" in the film Sex and the City. It is a high end boutique that stocks Diane's famous wrap dresses, vintage inspired pieces and her latest collections.

Also try: Patricia Field (Designer for Sex and the City)

DESIGNER SECOND HAND STORE (RESALE)

A Second Chance, Prince Street between Thompson Street and West Broadway, Soho, DOWNTOWN

Telephone 212 673 6155 www. asecondchanceresale.com

Here you may find pre-worn Chanel, Prada, Pucci, Gucci and Hermes at a fraction of the retail cost as this is a Designer resale boutique carrying all the top names. Time may be needed however to seek out that special item.

DISCOUNT DESIGNER STORE

Century 21, Cortlandt Street between Broadway and Greenwich Streets, DOWNTOWN

Telephone 212 227 9092 www.century21.com

This is for discount Designer shopper's, where shoes, clothes and accessories are on sale at below normal prices. Be prepared to jostle with fellow hunters in your quest for a bargain. Also popular with Celebrities.

FAKE DESIGNER GOODS - CANAL STREET AND BELOW, AROUND LAFAYETTE AND ALLEN STREETS, CHINATOWN

For cheap, fake designer goods head to Chinatown where you will find copies of everything at bargain prices. The shops and markets are bursting with choice but expect to be hassled in this lively, vibrant area.

FOOD LOVERS - CANAL STREET AND ABOVE, AROUND MULBERRY AND MOTT STREETS, LITTLE ITALY

If you are a fan of all things edible take a look here for an abundance of shops and markets all devoted to food. Alternatively, take a Food Lovers tour that will guide you through this area. (see Tours and Excursions).

HIGH STREET CHAINS - SOHO

Look out for H & M, Quicksilver and Top Shop in Soho if you want recognisable High Street Chains, selling all your favourite and familiar items. Of course there are also an abundance of Designer stores to keep you busy.

LINGERIE

Agent Provocateur, Mercer Street between Prince and Spring Streets, Soho, DOWNTOWN

Telephone 212 965 0229
www.agentprovocateur.com

Oozing glamour with luxurious lingerie, nightwear, accessories and gifts, take a look at this Soho shop for thongs, suspenders corsettes, basques and bras in a sexy space made for fantasies.

Also try: La Perla, Meatpacking District Victoria's Secret, 6th Avenue at West 32nd Street

221

RECORD SHOPS

The heart of New York's music scene is around Greenwich Village, the East Village, Lower East Side and Noho with stores selling both new and used records, plus musical instruments. This area is where you will also find the Bowery Ballroom, a live music venue.

Bleecker Records, Bleecker Street between Carmine and Leroy Streets, Greenwich Village, DOWNTOWN

Telephone 212 255 7899 www.bleeckerstreetrecordsnyc.com

For vintage records, head to this record store in the midst of the "Village". You will find walls of vinyl, used CDs, DVDs, tee shirts and a selection of music posters.

Also try: Tower Records

PEDESTRIANISED SHOPPING

South Street Seaport, Pier 17 at South and Fulton Streets, Lower Manhattan, DOWNTOWN

Telephone 212 732 7678 or 212 732 8257
www.southstreetseaport.com

Similar to Covent Garden in London with cobblestone streets and converted warehouses, parts of this area look out over the East River and Brooklyn Bridge. There are quaint shops, bars and restaurants far removed from the retail gods of 5th Avenue. Take a water taxi to see the Statue of Liberty.

PET SHOP

Zoomies, Hudson Street at Morton Street, West Village, DOWNTOWN

Telephone 212 462 4480 www.zoomiesnyc.com

If you own a pampered pooch or feline friend then this is the place to visit. Filled with delightful items from collars and blankets to toys and the cutest doggy jackets, it will seduce you with colourful displays. Don't forget that all important "I bone NY" hoodie dog tee!

SHOES

Shoegasm, 8th Avenue between West 13th and West 14th Streets, Meatpacking District, DOWNTOWN

Telephone 212 691 2091
www.shoegasm.com

There are three of these shops in New York selling up to the minute shoes at reasonable prices, all in stylish surroundings with exposed brick walls and antique furniture. The name, of course, says it all.

STATIONERY SHOP

Kate's Paperie, Broome Street between Crosby Street and Broadway, Soho, DOWNTOWN

Telephone 1-800 809 9880 or 212 941 9816
www.katespaperie.com

If paper is your thing then slip in here and see what they have to offer. Paper of every colour and type awaits together with pens, calendars, greetings cards, journals and notebooks. It is a visual delight with items from around the World.

OUT OF TOWN - DISCOUNT DESIGNER SHOPPING OUTLET

Woodbury Common Discount Village, 498 Red Apple Court, Central Valley, New York State 10917

Telephone 845 928 4000 www.premiumoutlets.com

Take the Grayline bus from the Port Authority bus station with return tickets from £25 ($38). Open every day from 10 am to 9pm this discount designer "Village" has over 200 outlets such as Nike, Dior, Gucci, Chloe and Ralph Lauren all in one place.

Travelling "solo" to New York can feel challenging, even for the most seasoned wanderer, so here are a few suggestions to ease you into Big Apple life.

Useful website: www.thelmaandlouise.com

BROADWAY SHOWS (Page 229)

Watching a show on Broadway can be a good way of meeting people and gives you a starting point to strike up a conversation with those sat nearby. There are lots of shows on offer including Phantom of the Opera, Wicked, Jersey Boys, Mamma Mia and many more. There is a "same day" discount ticket booth in Times Square if you are flexible, or you could look at **www.broadway.com** for full price tickets.

COFFEE SHOPS, TEA ROOMS AND CHOCOLATE CAFES (Page 28)

Tea and Coffee shops are great places to stop for a break and give you an opportunity to mix with others. Some of the larger Starbucks even have communal tables, offering a chance to chat with locals and other tourists alike.

HOTELS (Page 128)

Smaller boutique hotels often include little extras like breakfast, tea, coffee, wine and cheeses, giving you a chance to meet and mingle with other guests. Here are just a few you might like to consider or see the separate Hotel section.

Casablanca Hotel www.casablancahotel.com MIDTOWN

Elysee Hotel www.elysseehotel.com MIDTOWN

Giraffe Hotel www.hotelgiraffe.com MIDTOWN

Library Hotel www.libraryhotel.com MIDTOWN

Alternatively you could stay somewhere like the Inn at Irving Place, a friendly, welcoming 12 roomed hotel which is beautifully furnished in a traditional way. There are four poster beds, open fires and antique furniture. **www.innatirvingplace.com/newyork MIDTOWN**

SINGLE OR TRAVELLING ALONE

Some people on the other hand, prefer hotels with more facilities, like swimming pools, gyms and spas where you may get to chat to others. Try those shown here.

Le Parker Meridien, www.leparkermeridien.com/newyork MIDTOWN
Peninsula Hotel, www.peninsula.com/newyork MIDTOWN
Greenwich Hotel, www.greenwichhotel.com/newyork DOWNTOWN

TOURS AND EXCURSIONS (Page 236)

This is a great way to meet fellow tourists with a good choice on offer, from fashion and shopping right through to food, wine and Night Tours.

TRANSFERS (Page 234)

You might want to pre book your arrival transfer in advance so there is someone waiting to collect you at the airport in New York. Alternatively you may feel confident enough to take a taxi (cab). Most airports have someone outside the terminal in charge of yellow cabs, but always check first how much it will cost.

Inn at Irving Place   Library Hotel

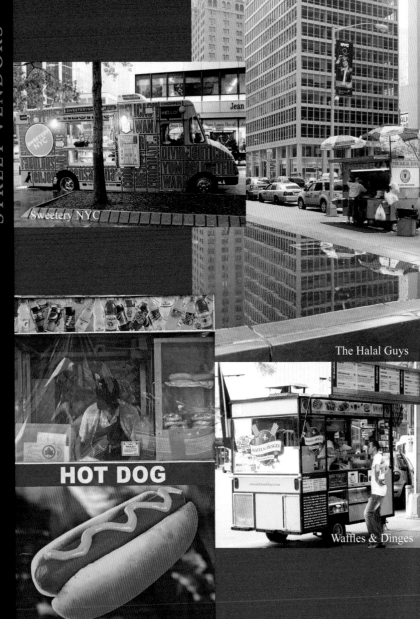

Sweetery NYC

The Halal Guys

HOT DOG

Waffles & Dinges

Cake & Shake

Fruit n Juice

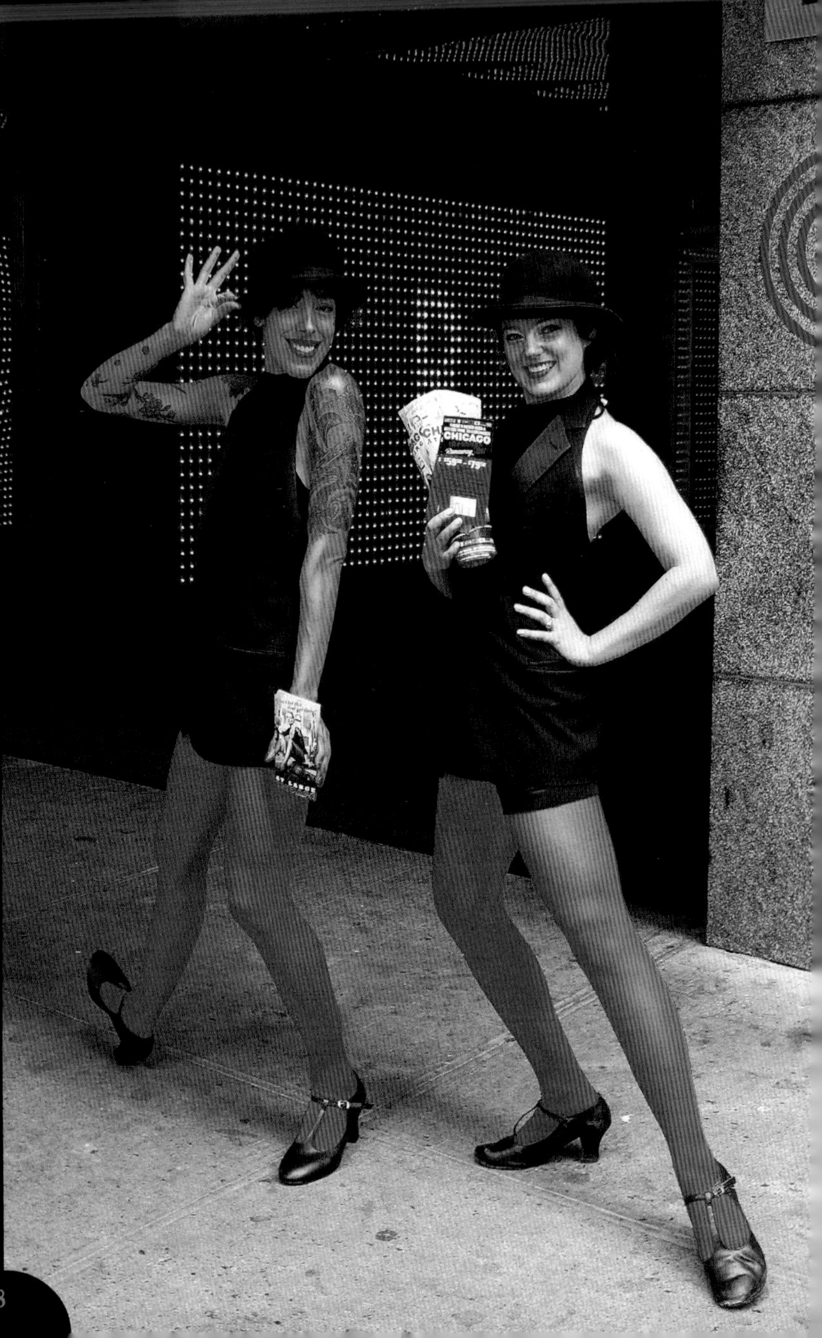
CHICAGO

THEATRE, BALLET, CINEMA, CONCERTS, OPERA

INDEX

There is much on offer when it comes to entertainment in New York, and featured are just a selection for your consideration. These include theatres, cinemas, ballet and opera, or if you are interested in attending a concert or gig, there is everything from Classical and Jazz through to Rock and Recital. As the programmes change constantly, I have given the individual websites for you to access.

BALLET, CONCERTS, OPERA

Lincoln Centre, 9th Avenue at West 64th Street, Upper West Side, UPTOWN

**Telephone 212 870 5570 www.nycballet.com
www.nyphil.org   www.metoperafamily.org**

The Lincoln Centre for the performing arts is home to the Metropolitan Opera House, New York City Ballet and the New York Philharmonic, amongst others, offering quality choices for your entertainment. The "Met", as the Opera House is fondly known, hosts world class operatic performances or you may prefer a classical concert by the Philharmonic Orchestra. If Ballet is your interest, then this dance company presents a range of productions throughout the year, solely training their own dancers. Head here for a night of refined culture where you will also find a Film Society, Library for the Performing Arts and Chamber Music Society.

CINEMA/THEATRE

Central Park, 59th to 110th Street and 5th to 8th Avenues, UPTOWN

Telephone 212 360 3444 www.centralpark.com

Central Park is the green hub of New York City and holds a variety of free events throughout the Summer, such as film nights and Shakespearean performances, details of which can be found on their website.

BROADWAY SHOWS

Theatres, around West 42nd to West 53rd Streets, from 6th to 8th Avenues around Broadway, MIDTOWN

www.broadway.com

There are many shows to choose from in and around the Theatre District, including Phantom of the Opera, Rock of Ages, Chicago, Memphis, Jersey Boys, Mamma Mia, West Side Story and Wicked. Look at the website for details of ticket prices or if you are flexible try the discount ticket booth in Times Square for same day performances.

Also try: Late Show with David Letterman

Clearview Ziegfeld Theatre, West 54th Street between 6th and 7th Avenues, MIDTOWN

Telephone 212 307 1862 www.clearviewcinemas.com/ziegfeldnewyork

This historic picture house was once a Broadway Theatre and home to the Ziegfeld Follies, who took their inspiration from the Paris based Folies Bergeres. Memorabilia relating to this era is located on the lower level. In more recent times it played host to the Harry Potter 2011 Premiere.

Also try: AMC Empire

CONCERTS AND GIGS

Radio City Music Hall, 6th Avenue at West 50th Street, MIDTOWN

Telephone 212 247 4777 www.radiocity.com

Stars like Willie Nelson, Cheryl Crow and the Rockettes feature at this world renowned music hall, built by J.D. Rockefeller Junior in 1929. A "Palace for the People" was his vision, and today it hosts stage shows, musicals and concerts. Take a back stage tour and meet a Rockette.

Also try: Carnegie Hall ➜ and Madison Square Garden

CONCERTS AND GIGS

←**The Bowery Ballroom,
6 Delancey Street at Chrystie
and Bowery Streets, Lower
East Side,** DOWNTOWN

**Telephone 212 533 2111
www.boweryballroom.com**

A concert venue since 1998,
the Bowery Ballroom offers a
wide choice of live music, with
rock and roll, pop, soul and
much more lined up for your
entertainment. Check the website
for performances

FILM FESTIVALS

Every year New York holds a
"River to River" series of film
festivals in several locations around the DOWNTOWN region. These
include South Street Seaport, Battery Park Esplanade, Castle Clinton
and the World Financial Centre. www.nycgo.com/free

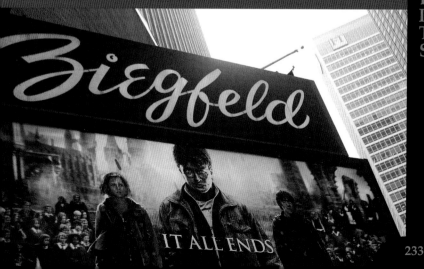

TOURIST INFORMATION, TOILETS, TRANSPORT

TOURIST INFORMATION AND VISITORS CENTRE

Times Square, 7th Avenue at Broadway between West 46th and West 47th Streets, MIDTOWN

Telephone 800 692 8474 (24 hours a day) www.timessquarenyc.org

Tourist Information Centre

9am to 6pm Monday to Friday, 10am to 6pm Saturday and Sunday. Go here for City, Bus and Metro Maps plus to book Tours. Useful websites: www.nycvisit.com and www.nycgo.com

TOILETS

Unlike the UK, there are not many "public" toilets in New York, so you may like to try those in cafes, department stores, museums, hotels, bars and restaurants. They are often hidden away, so ask staff for directions. Here are just a few establishments which have toilets within their premises:

Uptown

American Folk Art Museum, American Museum of Natural History, Apple Store, Crate & Barrel, Hayden Planetarium, Lincoln Centre (Avery Fisher Hall), Central Park Zoo, Loeb Boathouse (Central Park) and the Museums around "Museum Mile" on the Upper East Side.

Midtown

Argo Cafes, Barnes & Noble, Barneys, Bergdorf Goodman, Bloomingdale's, Bryant Park, Grand Central Terminal, Lord and Taylor, Macy's, Manhattan Mall, McDonald's, Museum of Art and Design (MAD), Museum of Modern Art (MOMA), New York Public Library, Penn Street Station, Rockefeller Centre, Saks 5th Avenue, Starbucks, Time Warner Centre, Trump Tower, Whole Foods Chain (Chelsea and Union Square).

Downtown

Argo Cafes, McDonald's, Starbucks and Whole Foods Chain (Tribeca), plus there are public toilets at Washington Square.

www.nyrestroom.com OR www.sitorsquat.com/newyork

TOURIST INFORMATION CENTRE, TOILETS, TRANSPORT

TRANSPORT AND TRANSFERS

AIRPORT - John F. Kennedy New York - JFK - 15 Miles
Telephone Number 001 718 244 4444
www.panynj.gov/airports/jfk or www.worldairportguides.com

AIRPORT - Newark Airport, New Jersey - EWR - 16 Miles
Telephone Number 001 973 961 6000
www.newarkairport.com or www.worldairportguides.com

Airport Transfer Options - www.ny.com/transportation/airports

Air Train - www.panynj.com

Coach - www.nyairportservices.com

Limousine - www.gothamlimo.com or www.nyclimousine.com

Yellow Cab - Go to the taxi rank.

Metropolitan Transport Authority - www.mta.com

BUSES - UPTOWN/MIDTOWN - These run mainly North and South on Avenues and Broadway, plus East and West on Streets. DOWNTOWN buses are more random as it is not part of the grid layout. **www.mta.com**

METRO (UNDERGROUND) TRAINS - These trains run roughly North to South or East to West, though some do both. **www.mta.com**

METRO CARDS FOR TRAINS AND BUSES - Buy at most Metro Stations with 1, 7, 14 or 30 day passes. Each time this card is used the amount left is displayed. **www.mtainfo/metrocard.com**

STATEN ISLAND FERRY, Whitehall Terminal, DOWNTOWN Manhattan to Staten Island sailing past the Statue of Liberty. Free if you don't get off. **www.siferry.com**

TAXIS (YELLOW CABS) - Hail in the street or at a taxi rank. Fares are regulated plus peak/night surcharges apply. Tip 15% and get a receipt.

WATER TAXIS - Water taxis are "Hop on Hop off", stopping at West 48th Street, South Street Seaport and Battery Park. **www.nywatertaxis.com**

TOURS AND EXCURSIONS

INDEX

Brimming with life at every turn, New York is bursting with things to do and see with not enough time to cover everything. A tour or excursion can be the perfect way to scratch the surface and to learn about the City that really, never sleeps.

Mix with fellow travellers and chat to locals, on tours ranging from music, shopping, Celebrities, fashion and food, to history, culture, literature, wine tasting and architecture. The choice is yours entirely. Many of the companies featured here have a wide variety of options so look at their websites for alternatives.

Bike Tours (Central Park and beyond), located at West 58th Street at 7th Avenue, MIDTOWN

Telephone 212 541 8759 www.centralparkbiketour.com

With tours that cover Central Park, Greenwich Village, Times Square, Little Italy and the Hudson River Parkway, you have lots of itineraries to choose from or you could just hire a bike and explore on your own.

Also try: Bike the Big Apple, www.bikethebigapple.com

Celebrity/Rich and Famous Tour of New York - bus or walking tour, UPTOWN/MIDTOWN

Telephone 212 462 9250 www.richandfamoustours.com

This tour gives insider knowledge on where the rich and famous dine and party, film location sites, where to get autographs and how to secure audience tickets for your favourite TV shows.

Chocolate Lovers Luxury Tour, Upper East Side, UPTOWN

Telephone 917 292 0680 www.sweetwalks.com

For the ultimate chocoholics experience, take this chocolate tour, find out how its made and try loads of delicious samples, in this very posh area of New York.

Historic Harlem or Upper West Side Walking Tours, UPTOWN

Telephone 212 606 9255 www.bigonionwalkingtours.com

Harlem is often described as the Black capital of the World, so experience its vibrant, colourful culture first hand. Or take the Upper West Side Walking Tour including the Lincoln Centre and Dakota Building.

Also try: Harlem Spirituals Soul Food, Gospel or Hip Hop Tours.

Horse and Carriage Tour, Central Park South (59th Street) between 5th and 6th Avenues, UPTOWN

Telephone 212 736 0680 www.centralpark.com

If you would like a tour with a difference then try a Horse and Carriage ride through Central Park lasting anything from 20 minutes upwards. Chat to the driver beforehand to decide on a suitable itinerary.

Bachelorette Party, MIDTOWN

Telephone 888 374 0658 www.unclesamsnewyorktours.com

A full day and night tour which includes shopping, an outfit makeover, spa and nightclubbing. Meet other "Girlies'" for the ultimate Bachelorette Party.

EXCLUSIVE "Just for You" Customized FASHION-able SHOPPING Tour of New York's BEST-in-Design

www.jilllynne.com or Email on jilllynne1@mac.com

For decades Ms Lynne has written about and photographed New York's Fashion Scene. With an intimate knowledge of The Designers, their Private Studios, Industry Showrooms and Secret Boutiques, Ms Lynne will develop an Individualized Tour just for You or with Your Best Friends and Associates. Jill Lynne's Fashion Editorials are archived on **www.newyorksocialdiary.com** and on her Website **www.jilllynne.com**

FASHION
WALK of FAME

Fashion Walk of Fame celebrates excellence in American design by honoring the New York designers who have had a significant and lasting impact on the way the world dresses.

New York has been the undisputed center of American fashion since the mid-19th Century when the development of mass production led to the growth of the apparel trades. The birth of the Fashion District, also known as the Garment Center, occurred in the 1920s, when a large group of garment manufacturers relocated to Seventh Avenue. New loft space was developed especially to accommodate "modern" manufacturing and to satisfy labor's demands for safer working conditions. By 1931 this District had the largest concentration of apparel manufacturers in the world and since then has been home to the greatest names in American design.

A project of The Fashion Center
Business Improvement District.

Established 1999

EXCLUSIVE "Just For You" Photo Opportunity by acclaimed New York Photographer and Writer, Jill Lynne.....

www.jilllynne.com or Email on jilllynne1@mac.com

A New York photo-memento of you with Family and Friends or Solo at your favourite NYC Place. With over 40 solo exhibitions, and published internationally, multi-generational New Yorker, Jill Lynne, will document your special visit to her city with a memorable Portrait at your favourite NYC site - from a horse-drawn carriage in Central Park, a Boat on the Hudson River, or atop the Empire State Building.

Note: Ms Lynne is recommended by the prestigious Mandarin Hotel, as well as additional celebrated Hotels and Restaurants.

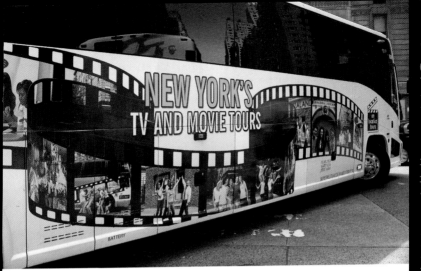

Movie and Television Location Tours, MIDTOWN

Telephone 212 683 2027 (General) or 212 209 3370 (Tickets - Zerve)
www.screentours.com or www.onlocationtours.com

Visit Movie and TV location sites such as The Devil Wears Prada, Friends, When Harry Met Sally and The Sopranos. Guides often include local actors and actresses giving a fun dramatic edge to this tour.

Also try: NBC, CBS or CNN Television Studio Tours

Night Coach Tour of New York, MIDTOWN

Telephone 212 445 0848 or 0808 189 0474 (Toll free from the UK)
www.grayline.com

This two hour night tour takes you by coach through the City, past some of the main attractions such as the Empire State Building, Greenwich Village and Soho.

"See it All" New York Tour

Telephone 212 852 4821 www.onboardnewyorktours.com

Take this 5 hour tour by coach, boat and walking, visiting many of the major sights, to include sailing past the Statue of Liberty and Brooklyn Bridge, walking through South Street Seaport and Wall Street, as well as stops at the Rockefeller Centre and Madison Square Park.

Sex and the City Tour, MIDTOWN/DOWNTOWN

Telephone 212 683 2027 (General) or 212 209 3370 (Tickets - Zerve)
www.screentours.com or www.onlocationtours.com

Visit some of the many places Carrie Bradshaw and friends frequent, like "Scout" bar owned by Aidan and Steve (Onieal's), the gallery where Charlotte worked (Louis Meissel), the bakery where Carrie and Miranda enjoy cupcakes (Magnolia Bakery) and the shop where Charlotte buys her "rabbit" (Pleasure Chest).

Also try: Gossip Girl Tour

Theatre District Walking Tour including Times Square and Broadway, MIDTOWN

Telephone 888 374 0658 www.unclesamsnewyorktours.com

Hear how Times Square began its days as horse stables, and then take a walk through one of the most globally recognisable Theatre Districts, learning about the shows, theatres and actors.

Foods of New York Tour, DOWNTOWN

Telephone 212 209 3370 www.foodsofny.com

Several food walking tours are on offer including one in Greenwich Village, where you learn the history and culture of the area and get a taste of foods relevant to this district.

Also try: Walking Tours Manhattan

Ghosts, Murders and Mayhem Walking Tour of Greenwich Village, DOWNTOWN

Telephone 212 252 2625 www.ghostsandmurders.com

Join this spooky lantern lit walk around Greenwich Village, with haunting tales of ghosts and mayhem. Fun to do around Halloween if you're not faint of heart.

Literary Pub Crawl, Greenwich Village, DOWNTOWN
Telephone 212 613 5796 www.bakerloo.org/pubcrawl

See pubs where Dylan Thomas, Ernest Hemmingway, Jack Kerouac, Jackson Pollock plus many more artists, poets and writers used to frequent, on this fun literary pub tour.

Music Tour/Pub Crawl, West Village, ➔ DOWNTOWN
Telephone 888 491 9824
www.unclesamsnewyorktours.com

Relive some of New York's rock music history where Bruce Springsteen, amongst others, launched his career, as you enjoy a pub crawl through the West Village.

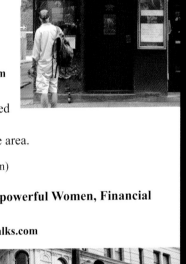

Revolutionary New York, DOWNTOWN
Telephone 212 439 1090 www.bigonion.com

This walking tour of Lower Manhattan gives details of the part New York played in America's battle for Independence, whilst visiting many historic sites in the area.

Also try: Greenwich Village Tour (Big Onion)

Wall Street Walks including its most powerful Women, Financial District, DOWNTOWN
Telephone 212 209 3370 www.wallstreetwalks.com

Learn about America's financial industry, Women of Wall Street, Stock Market History, Wall Street Crashes and the Federal Gold Reserve, on tours lead by industry insiders.

Wine Tasting at TriBeCa Grill, Greenwich Street at Franklyn Street, TriBcCa, DOWNTOWN

Telephone 212 941 3900
www.myriadrestaurantgroup.com

Every year this restaurant, part owned by Robert de Niro, holds a "Wine Walk Around" where their wine Director talks you through 25 different varieties. Book early and try the Grill afterwards for dinner.

Also try: Champagne, Beer or Wine Tasting Cruises (www.sail-ny.com)

OTHER TOURS - VARIOUS AREAS

Big Apple Greeters

Telephone 212 669 8159 www.bigapplegreeter.org

This free public service was founded in 1992 and allows visitors to have a resident New Yorker act as an "unofficial" tour guide. Whilst it is non-profit making, they will accept "donations" on their website.

Big Onion Walking Tours, UPTOWN, MIDTOWN, DOWNTOWN

Telephone 212 439 1090 www.bigonion.com

Historical and cultural tours with a "pay as you go" facility. Just turn up at the relevant meeting point for tours of Chinatown, Immigrant New York, Ellis Island and many more.

Hop-on Hop-off Bus Ticket, UPTOWN/MIDTOWN/DOWNTOWN →

Telephone 212 812 2700 www.citysightsny.org or www.grayline.com

The "All Around Town" 48 hour "Hop on Hop off" bus ticket takes you to within close proximity of most major sights, allowing you to then explore each area on your own. Admissions are not included.

OUTER BOROUGH TOURS

Bronx - Discover the Bronx Tour
Telephone 305 395 4958 www.trustedtours.com

Brooklyn Bridge and Brooklyn Heights Tour
Telephone 212 439 1090 www.bigonionwalkingtours.com

Brooklyn - Hassidic Jewish Walking Tour
Telephone 718 953 5244 or 212 209 3370 (Tickets from Zerve)
www.jewishtours.com

Staten Island - Pizza Tour
Telephone 347 273 1257 www.sinewyork.org

Useful Website: www.newyorksightseeing.com/www.sceneontv.com

ESSEX
HOUSE

View towards Midtown from Central Park, Uptown

Chrysler Building from Lexington Avenue,

Times Square, Midtown

View from the Rockefeller Centre, Midtown

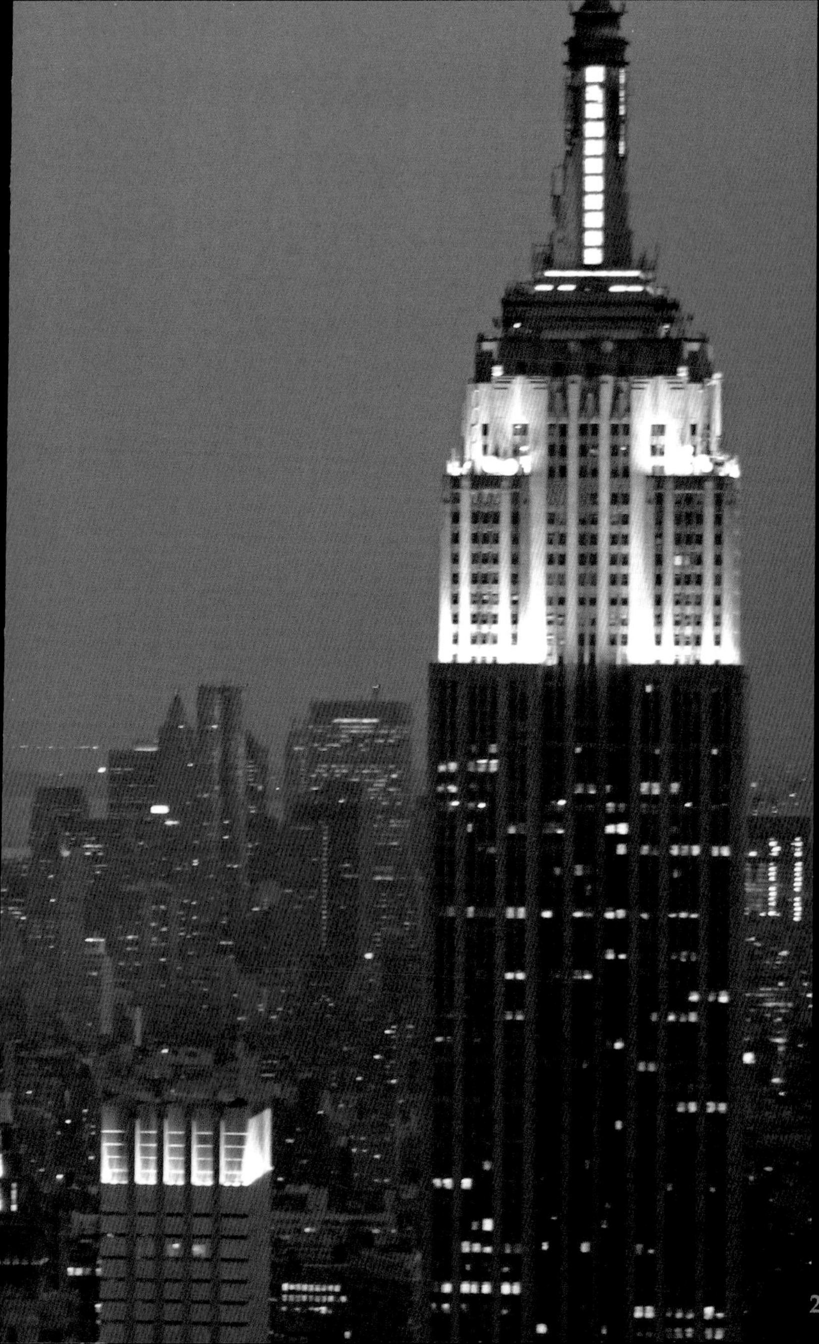

VIEWS AND PANORAMAS

View from Salon de Ning, Peninsula Hotel, Midtown

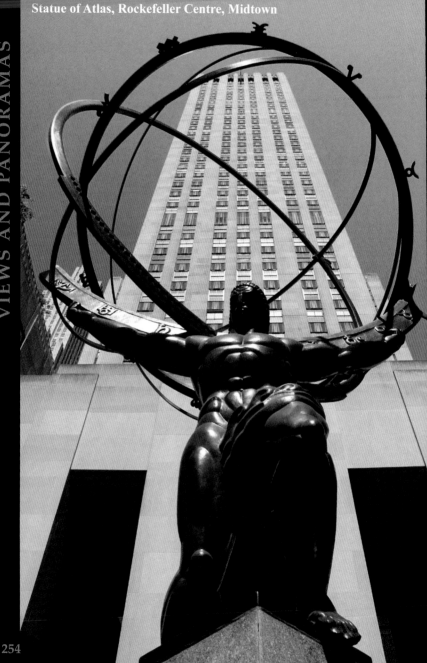

VIEWS AND PANORAMAS

View from the New York Public Library, Midtown

WEATHER:

New York is a City of seasons, being warm and pleasant in Spring, hot and humid in Summer, mild with a sprinkling of sunny days in Autumn and cold with some snow in Winter.

Rain falls year round with January, March and July the wettest, whilst September, October and November are slightly drier. However there is not much variation at anytime during the year. Rainfall averages from 9cm to 12cm per month so it is always wise to pack something for rain just in case.

September, October and November are considered to be the best months weather wise to visit, although some hotels offer reduced rates from January to mid-March when it is much colder.

Month	Lowest	Highest
	(Degrees Centigrade)	
January	-3	4
February	-3	5
March	1	8
April	6	16
May	11	21
June	17	27
July	18	29
August	19	28
September	16	25
October	10	19
November	5	12
December	-1	5

WEATHER AND
WHAT TO WEAR

WHAT TO WEAR:

Layers are appropriate year round, with comfort the most important thing especially when it comes to day wear, as you may be doing lots of walking. In the evening it will depend on what you intend to do as some upmarket restaurants have a dress code and will require smart attire, whilst for some, casual or smart casual will be acceptable.

SPRING, SUMMER AND AUTUMN

It is advisable to take layers including a cardigan, light rainproof jacket, scarf and comfortable shoes. In Summer, New York is generally very hot outside and cold inside due to the air conditioning. Many Streets and Avenues are cast in shadows from the skyscrapers, so this can make them feel slightly cooler.

WINTER

Again take layers but to include a warm coat, scarf, gloves, hat, thermals and safe, warm, comfortable shoes. New York generally freezes at some point during Winter so pack wisely as you may end up trudging through snow and ice!

Vera Wang, Madison Avenue at East 77th Street, Uptown

WEDDINGS AND ANNIVERSARIES

INDEX

Have you ever dreamed of getting married in New York? Many before you have fulfilled that fantasy and chosen the "Big Apple" for their special day. The City is enchanting with a variety of alluring venues, including Central Park, the New York Public Library, Empire State Building and Brooklyn Bridge, to name just some of the endless possibilities.

Getting married abroad needs careful planning, so included are contact details for a Wedding Planner and a couple of Hotels who could organise everything on your behalf. Before making any decisions it is always advisable to do your own research as there are many options and styles available to make your day unique. Below are just a few to get you started and remember the old cliché "the devil is in the detail" so check and double check everything! **www.theknot.com**

LEGAL FORMALITIES FOR A WEDDING IN NEW YORK

As with all weddings, there are certain legal formalities that have to be carried out when getting married in New York. It is important to check before you leave the UK what documentation is required by the US State Department, so go to their website for further information at **www.health.state.ny.us/weddings** or contact Ultimate USA Weddings at **www.ultimateusaweddings.com**

WEDDING DRESSES (Page 207)

New York is often called the shopping capital of the World for wedding dresses and in particular the area around Madison and 5th Avenues on the Upper East Side (UPTOWN). Here you will find Designer bridal shops with anything from Oscar de la Renta and Vera Wang, to J. Crew Bridal and Clea Colet.

If you are not averse to a quality second hand gown, then head to Michael's Consignment Store on the Upper East Side (UPTOWN) which sells high end, previously worn dresses.

Alternatively you may prefer to check out some of the MIDTOWN Department Stores like Bergdorf Goodman, Saks or Bloomingdale's. Then there is Filenes Basement where each February they have a sale of discount designer wedding dresses. Be prepared to rummage hard as it has been branded "The Running of the Brides" and can end up a bit of a scrum. Other stores you might like to try are Kleinfeld Bridal or the Gabriella Bridal Salon both in MIDTOWN.

WEDDINGS AND RECEPTIONS (HOTELS Page 129)

Four Seasons Hotel 5*, 57 East 57th Street between Park and Madison Avenues, MIDTOWN

Telephone 212 758 5700 www.fourseasons.com

If you decide to get married in New York then you might want to consider this Hotel as it will organise everything (at a cost of course) from the reception, entertainment and ceremony, to your wedding night accommodation. However, it is a 5* establishment and weddings do not come cheap.

Waldorf Astoria Hotel 4*, Park Avenue between East 49th and East 50th Streets, MIDTOWN

Telephone 212 872 4700
www.waldorfastoria.com/
newyorkweddings

This iconic, historic, hotel offers guests a full wedding service, whereby they will take care of the details for your special day, with their dedicated wedding planners.

Also try: Fairmont Plaza, Giraffe Hotel, Library Hotel, New York Palace Hotel

WEDDING PLANNER

Ultimate USA Weddings, Suite 5520, Empire State Building, 5th Avenue, MIDTOWN

Telephone 212 563 3525 www.ultimateusaweddings.com

Ultimate USA Weddings are a specialist Company who will help organise your wedding day, from the marriage venue, legal requirements and license, to the flowers and limousine. Look out for them on Sky Wedding TV, and provided it exists, they should be able to help with the arrangements. Don't forget to mention Lipstick City Guides.

WEDDING VENUES UPTOWN/MIDTOWN/DOWNTOWN

When it comes to getting married in New York you have a grand selection of venues to choose from, with just some shown here for your consideration.

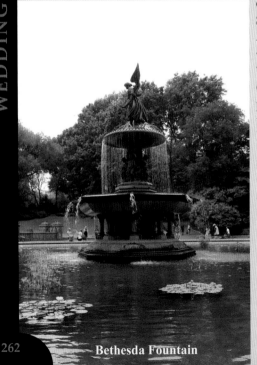

Central Park, 59th to 110th Streets between 5th and 8th Avenues, UPTOWN

www.centralpark.com/weddings

One of the most photographed places in the world, Central Park has many Wedding venues including the Conservatory Garden (with its English, French and Italian areas), the Ladies Pavillion and Bethesda Fountain. With 843 acres of lush, green parkland, it is easy to see why this is a popular choice.

Bethesda Fountain

Empire State Building, 5th Avenue at West 34th Street, MIDTOWN
www.ultimateusaweddings.com/www.esbnyc.com

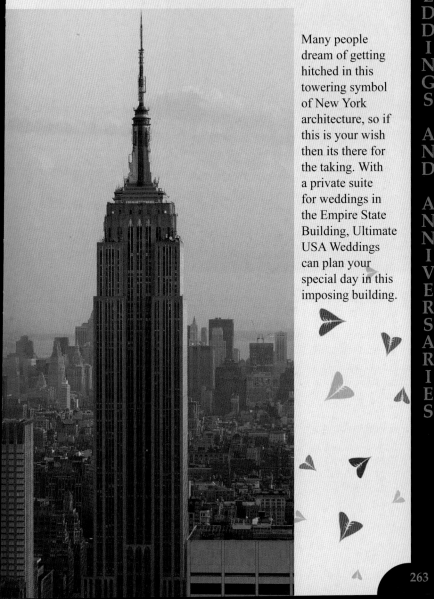

Many people dream of getting hitched in this towering symbol of New York architecture, so if this is your wish then its there for the taking. With a private suite for weddings in the Empire State Building, Ultimate USA Weddings can plan your special day in this imposing building.

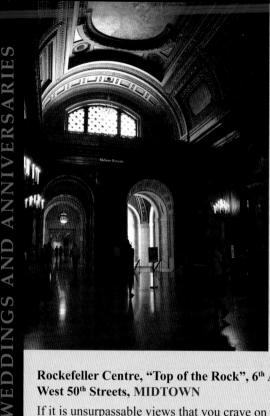

New York Public Library, 5th Avenue at West 42nd Street, MIDTOWN

www.nypl.com

Where "Big" should have married Carrie in the film Sex and the City 1, ←the McGraw Rotunda room in the landmark New York Public Library is a popular place to tie the knot, with its medieval murals and Corinthian architecture. The wood panelling gives it warmth, whilst the lighting is soft and welcoming.

Rockefeller Centre, "Top of the Rock", 6th Avenue at West 48th to West 50th Streets, MIDTOWN

If it is unsurpassable views that you crave on your Wedding day, then get hitched at the "Top of the Rock", with its 360 degree vistas out over New York. Tie the knot with iconic views of the Chrysler Building, Central Park and Empire State Building as your backdrop.

Russian Tea Room, West 57th Street between 6th and 7th Avenues, MIDTOWN

www.russiantearoom.com

The Russian Tea Room is an opulent restaurant with a rich red, gold and green décor. This would be a Wedding with a difference, full of Russian charm, heritage, caviar and vodka, if you so desire.

World Yacht Cruise, Pier 81, West 41st Street at 12th Avenue, MIDTOWN

www.worldyacht.com

If getting married whilst taking a cruise around New York appeals, then this could be the option for you. Drift around Manhattan and enjoy your nuptials riverside.

Brooklyn Bridge, Chambers Street Station at Park Row, DOWNTOWN

This striking bridge which connects Manhattan to Brooklyn, is always a popular request for New York Weddings, with views that will stun you, out over the East River. There are several restaurants where you could have lunch afterwards like the renowned River Café tucked away beneath the bridge on the Brooklyn side, or you could head to the

Water Club, a taxi ride away. Alternatively there are several options at South Street Seaport like Harbour Lights, which has terraces overlooking Brooklyn Bridge.

City Hall, Broadway at Chambers Street, Lower Manhattan, DOWNTOWN

Telephone 212 788 3000
www.cityhallnewyork.com
www.cityclerk.nyc.gov/html/ marriage

New York's equivalent of a registry office wedding with a "hitch and go" ceremony lasting five minutes. That said, there are beautiful gardens outside for your photographs and Brooklyn Bridge is only a few minutes away. Again South Street Seaport is close by with a choice of restaurants for your reception, or you could organise something at the Tribeca Grill, a taxi ride away.

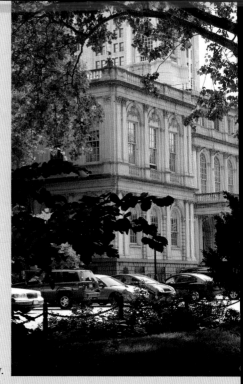

Also try: Queen Mary 2 or Queen Victoria for a Transatlantic Wedding en Route to New York. **www.cunard.com** Telephone 0843 374 2224

ANNIVERSARIES

If you have a special Anniversary to celebrate or indeed have previously married in New York, you might like to consider the Big Apple in your plans. Check out the chapters on Love and Romance, Luxuries and Limousines plus Tours and Excursions for some ideas of where to go and what to do for that memorable celebratory experience.

ABOUT THE AUTHOR

For as long as I can remember I have been mesmerised by travel and loved nothing more when organising a trip abroad, than to pour over guide books with a thirst for knowledge.

As a child my father was in the Navy so we moved frequently. When not at home he was off to faraway places on board ship, sending postcards from pastures new, stirring my imagination, entrancing my every thought. Some of those cards I still have today as a poignant reminder of him, of the many distant lands he visited, and of a desire that has never left me, to travel the World.

We settled in Somerset when I was 7 years old having lived in England, Ireland, Scotland and Malta. At eighteen I moved to Australia, lived in New Zealand, spent ten years in London before returning to the West Country.

My working career has covered both the hotel and travel industries, with my passion for travel steady throughout. During that time I made a dozen trips to New York and from my first glimpse I was smitten.

With each journey I did my research, and after many years of travelling the World, working in travel and living abroad, I yearned for something more from a guide book. One which explored the softer side of a City and held my interest. A journal which captured a gentler, more feminine image of a place and its people.

So for Female travellers everywhere, I offer you the Lipstick City Guide to New York.

ABOUT THE AUTHOR AND ACKNOWLEDGEMENTS

ACKNOWLEDGEMENTS

The writing, photography and design vision for this book were created by the author. However, thanks go to Matt Swann of 21st Book Design, for his interpretation of that vision and for making it a reality.

I would like to thank Jill Lynne, renowned New York Photographer and Writer who provided me with two "Exclusives" to include in this book, after a chance meeting on a New York bus.

Thank you to Gomer Press Ltd of Llandysul, Wales for their advice and guidance.

And finally, I want to express my love and gratitude to the following people without whom I would never have made it to the end - Colin, Mum, Dad, Chris, Kate, Amy and Kitty.

In memory of Dad, where it all began

CONTENTS

Lipstick Building

LIPSTICK CITY GUIDES

Lipstick Building

271

Brooklyn Bridge, Lower Manhattan, Downtown